# ALLISON ASHLEY

# the Roommate Pact

mira

Recycling programs
for this product may
not exist in your area.

ISBN-13: 978-0-7783-3424-8

The Roommate Pact

For questions and comments about the quality of this book, please contact us at
CustomerService@Harlequin.com.

Mira
22 Adelaide St. West, 41st Floor
Toronto, Ontario M5H 4E3, Canada
BookClubbish.com

Printed in U.S.A.

# Praise for *The Roommate Pact*

"Allison Ashley's signature wit and charm shine through every page of *The Roommate Pact*. Graham and Claire's journey had me laughing, crying, and literally hand-on-heart swooning."
—Ava Wilder, author of *How to Fake It in Hollywood*

"*The Roommate Pact* gives us two leads who discover that love doesn't always follow the rules, and when something feels so right in so many ways—that's because it is. Nobody hits the delicious balance between playful and sexy quite like Allison Ashley."
—Jen Devon, author of *Bend Toward the Sun*

"Deliciously sexy with undeniable heart, *The Roommate Pact* is a friends-to-lovers story you can't help but fall for."
—B.K. Borison, author of *Lovelight Farms*

"Allison Ashley masterfully blends the heartfelt tenderness of friends-turned-lovers with delicious sexual tension, resulting in an all-consuming story about two people who are so perfectly unaware of how perfect they are for each other."
—Jenny L. Howe, author of *The Make-Up Test*

"With on-point banter, and off the charts sexual tension, *The Roommate Pact* gave me all the feels! A fabulous friends-to-lovers rom-com!"
—Farah Heron, author of *Kamila Knows Best* and *Accidentally Engaged*

"Allison Ashley crafts a heart-melting and swoony story in *The Roommate Pact*. This frenemies-to-lovers romance is filled with first-rate banter and yummy tension. It will make your heart sing."
—Sarah Smith, author of *Faker* and *Simmer Down*

"*The Roommate Pact* gave me a literal heartache and this book secures Allison's title of Writer of All the Best Kisses. Anyone who wants to swoon needs to read this book!"
—Falon Ballard, author of *Just My Type*

"*The Roommate Pact* is a hilarious, steamy, and breezy read that I couldn't put down. The banter is like watching a great Nora Ephron–style romcom unfold, and I absolutely adored Claire and Graham's journey from roommates to lovers."
—Erin La Rosa, author of *For Butter or Worse*

**Also by Allison Ashley**

*Would You Rather*

For additional books by Allison Ashley,
visit her website, AuthorAllisonAshley.WordPress.com.

To my first responder and all the spouses, partners
and children of first responders.

# 1

Claire Harper was holding a penis when the commotion started.

Nothing to get excited about—the appendage belonged to an eighty-six-year-old man and she was a nurse inserting a much-needed catheter so the poor guy could pee.

Still, not where one wanted to be when all hell broke loose.

A loud screech and a crash sounded just outside the pulled curtain.

Then, all went quiet.

As Claire struggled to remain focused on her task, because at this point she couldn't just stop, her mind scrolled through possible scenarios. Some stemmed from real-life experience after six years as a critical care and emergency room nurse, while others came from decades of watching *Grey's Anatomy* and *ER* reruns.

The funny thing was, some of the wildest ones weren't from the TV shows.

Was it someone with a gun? A bomb?

A heinous injury? It was an emergency room, sure—but

even the most seasoned workers could experience a brief moment of shock depending on what they encountered.

Maybe it was simply something unexpected—like the time a drunk guy in a clown suit stumbled through the doors, bypassing the check-in desk and getting halfway to the med room, where narcotics were stored, before security took him down.

She heard nothing but silence for several seconds. Relative silence, rather—an emergency room was never completely quiet. Pumps beeped, swiped badges clicked open secure access doors, and the phone rang with incessant regularity. But if something happened that was truly an emergency, Ruthie would have been shouting directions to every person in her path by now.

What was going on?

Her patient's eyes had widened a little, and Claire finished up and covered him with a sheet. "All done. I'll be right back."

She slowly peeked out toward the central nursing station. Several people in scrubs congregated near one of the curtained areas opposite her, but she didn't see a crash cart and the code alert wasn't flashing.

Fairly certain it was safe to come out, she crossed the linoleum and stopped next to Ruthie, the charge nurse.

"What's going on?" Claire whispered.

Ruthie's eyes were glassy and she covered her mouth with her hand, sniffling. She didn't reply, as if she hadn't even realized Claire had spoken.

Claire went up on her tip-toes to get a better look. A woman wearing a hospital gown lay on the bed, crying, but on closer inspection, they weren't tears of pain or sadness.

Not entirely, at least.

A man knelt on one knee beside her, reaching forward to hold one of her hands in both of his. The moment was so tender, Claire barely harbored a passing thought about how nasty the hospital floor must be.

The man spoke quietly, his voice thick and raspy. The woman kept shaking her head in disbelief, her hand visibly trembling in his.

The woman had several lacerations across her face and arms, and the guy didn't look so great, either. By the looks of it, they'd been brought to the ER from a car accident.

Dr. Hansen, one of the surgeons, gingerly stepped forward, put his hand on the man's back and leaned forward to speak to him. The man nodded and straightened his back a little, as if realizing he needed to hurry.

"Is she okay?" This time Claire nudged Ruthie with her elbow.

"They're about to take her back for surgery. They came in from an MVA, and were in the pods beside each other. When the guy got word she was about to be taken away he leaped up and lunged to her side. Tore his IV out and everything. Nearly took out the admissions rep and knocked a cart over."

*Wow.*

"Are they in a relationship?"

"Don't know." Ruthie sighed wistfully. "With the way they look at each other, I'm guessing so."

Their conversation halted when the woman nodded her head, the tears coming in earnest, and the man stood, leaning over to kiss her.

The crowd clapped and whistled, and within minutes the surgery team wheeled her away. The man stood in the middle of the vacated room, palm cupping the back of his neck, a mixture of love and worry on his face. He stumbled backward and fell into a chair, burying his face in his hands. Ted, the nurse covering that side and likely the one taking care of both the man and his new fiancée, approached him.

"Wow," Claire breathed, following Ruthie back to the nursing station as everyone dispersed. "What a story that's gonna be, huh?"

"Right? Proposal in the ER after a near-death experience."

"Was the accident that bad?"

"I don't think so. But it sounds more dramatic that way."

"True." Claire sat beside Ruthie. "I was inserting a catheter when I heard her shriek."

Ruthie winced.

"Don't worry." Claire held up her hands, fingers splayed. "Steady as a rock."

"Believe me, I know. If I ever need stitches I won't let anyone else near me with a needle."

"I'm not allowed to do that, yet." Wouldn't stop her, of course, but technically it wasn't in the scope of practice for a nurse to suture. She'd learned the skill during her recent training to become a nurse practitioner—and had even passed the licensing exam, hell to the yes—but had to wait on the slow-as-molasses hospital credentialing office to finish up all the paperwork before making the transition.

"It would be under the table, obviously. Or, I could just hold off on obtaining open wounds until you're official. How much longer?"

"Are you asking because you want me on speed dial for cleaning you up or because you'll need to fill my nursing shifts?"

"Both."

"The NP from ortho said it took two months to get his through." Claire had only found out she'd passed her exam last week, so it might be a while.

"I won't hold my breath, then."

One of the medical assistants called for Ruthie, and she leaped to her feet.

Claire roused the computer screen and while she waited for the program to load, sneaked a glance behind her at the man who had just proposed. Still in the chair, his expression remained a little dazed, but something in his eyes seemed... exhilarated. Happy, even—an emotion not so common in the emergency room.

She could only assume it was a rash, spur-of-the-moment decision, but even in the few moments she'd watched, the connection between the two had been palpable. Thick with emotion and a slight sense of urgency.

Turning back to the screen, she frowned. When had she ever felt such desperation? She'd never even told a man she loved him, let alone felt that burn in her heart that if she didn't do it right that second—make sure he knew just how lost she was over him—that she'd break through any barrier to get it done.

And at thirty-one and single as the day she was born, she was starting to lose hope she ever would.

* * *

"I need a drink."

Claire made the announcement the second she walked into the condo she shared with two roommates. Her standard shift was 7:00 a.m. to 7:00 p.m., and by the time she'd passed off to the incoming nurse and driven home, daylight was fading. Her stomach growled, making a fair argument that dinner was more important than alcohol.

*Noted and ignored.*

Graham regarded her over the back of the couch with a raised eyebrow. He wore his standard lounging uniform of gray joggers and a T-shirt, legs extending the length of the couch and one tanned, muscled arm draped along the back. His expression was curious but not surprised. Ever since she'd moved from ICU to the ER, she'd come home frazzled and in search of alcohol on a semiregular basis. Taking classes for the NP program on the side hadn't helped matters, either.

Down the hall, Reagan's head popped out of her room. "I'm in."

Graham stood and stretched his arms above his head. "I'll see what we've got while you change."

Claire didn't slow in the trajectory to her room, but as she went her eyes dipped briefly to the ridged abs he'd revealed. Her and Graham's relationship was purely platonic—always had been—but she could appreciate her roommate was damn fine.

"You two are the best roommates a girl could ask for," she called over her shoulder before kicking the door shut. She made quick work of her scrubs and slipped into yoga pants and a gray Broncos sweatshirt she'd commandeered from an old boyfriend.

In fact, she had an entire drawer full of men's clothing she'd collected over the last decade of failed relationships. T-shirts, sweatshirts, a ball cap. All but one had broken up with her, and she'd figured they didn't deserve their shit back.

They were just clothes, after all.

Tiny nails click-clacked against the aged hardwood floor in the hallway. Claire opened her bedroom door and looked down.

"Gertrude."

The six-pound Yorkshire terrier, aka Graham's beloved pet, sat in the doorway and stared, her beady brown eyes calculating.

Most people adored Gertrude. On the rare occasion Claire accompanied Graham when he took her on a walk or tucked her under his jacket while roaming the aisles at Target, everyone who passed cooed and raved in ridiculous, high-pitched voices about how cute she was.

And when Graham was around, Gertrude did indeed act the perfect pet. Tiny, cute, and cuddly...and with a face like that, she had to be sweet and affectionate, right?

Wrong.

Less than twenty-four hours after Graham had moved into the condo with Claire and Reagan—which, at first, seemed like the perfect solution to fill the vacant roommate spot— Gertrude had made her true personality known.

She was a possessive, high maintenance, domineering little bitch.

The first time Claire had touched Graham in Gertrude's presence—a friendly but well-deserved slug to the shoulder after he'd said something sarcastic—Gertrude had gone batshit. As if Graham, over six feet and as athletic as they came, needed a miniature, maniac dog to defend him.

Somehow, with time, Reagan had gotten past the little terror's defenses. But not Claire.

Gertrude hated her, and the feeling was mutual.

Keeping one eye on the dog, Claire pulled her hair back into a ponytail and secured it with a band from around her wrist. She took one step closer to the threshold and put her hands on her hips, tipping her chin up a notch as if performing a stare-down ritual with an opponent in a boxing ring.

"I see what you're doing, G."

Gertrude didn't even blink. The nameplate on her bright pink collar reflected the light from the hallway. An attempt to blind Claire before she went in for the attack, probably.

"I'm not afraid of you." Claire scooted to the side and went around the dog, who rumbled a growl as she passed. "If you so much as touch another pillow with your teeth, I'm evicting Graham."

"Are you threatening the dog again?" Reagan asked as

Claire entered the kitchen. Graham must have already gone to the porch, where they usually congregated.

"Indirectly." They made their way to the front door. "Do you see the way she looks at me?"

"You're not so nice to her, you know."

"She started it."

Claire opened the door and followed Reagan outside. Graham was in the rocking chair, leaving them to take the porch swing he'd finally installed after several weeks of Claire's whining.

Could she have done it herself? Yes.

Well, possibly.

Was it easier to badger Graham into doing it for her? Also yes.

She wasn't a helpless woman by any means, but it was still nice to have a man around every now and again.

The trio had been roommates for almost a year now. Claire had lived in the condo with her best friend, Mia, for several years, and a little over a year ago they'd decided to add a third person to share a piece of the exorbitant Denver rent. They met Reagan, a grad student looking for a place to live, and it had worked out great for the first month.

Then Mia had up and gotten married and moved out, sending Claire and Reagan into a search for a replacement. Even though Claire had been friends with Graham for years, she hadn't considered asking a guy to move in until he brought up needing a new place. Sure, she'd had a few drinks when she agreed to the arrangement, but it had actually turned out well.

Other than a constant battle over the thermostat and his hellion terrier, he was a damn good roommate.

Case in point—he handed over the bottle of wine he'd brought outside along with two sticks of string cheese.

"I heard your stomach growling when you passed me," he said quietly. "And I'm not sure how bad your day was."

Read: *I don't know how much you'll drink tonight.*

Graham popped the cap off a beer as Reagan took the wine bottle and poured two healthy glasses. She handed one to Claire. "Okay. I'm armed and read to listen. What happened at work?"

Claire took a deep breath and a long sip of wine before she spoke. "I witnessed a marriage proposal."

Graham sucked in a breath. "Shit, are you okay?"

She glared at him. "Shut up."

"I'm serious." He looked it, too. "That's traumatic."

Reagan leaned down to set the wine bottle on the porch, keeping her glass in her hand. "A proposal in the emergency room? Was it an employee or something?"

"No. Two patients. They'd just come in from an accident and were pretty beat-up. She was about to go to surgery and he did this like…incredible, spur-of-the-moment, emotional proposal. Like he thought she might not come out of it and he didn't want to waste another second without telling her how he felt."

Reagan's eyes went wide. "If this story ends with you telling me she died, I swear—"

"She's fine."

Reagan exhaled, a palm to her heart. "Good. Then what happened?"

"That's it."

Graham took a deep pull from his beer, apparently too shaken over the prospect of anything related to marriage or engagements to comment.

Reagan regarded Claire over her glass and twisted her lips to the side. "I mean, I'm always down for wine on the porch and it's perfect weather tonight. But that really warranted all this?"

Claire sighed. "You don't get it. You're still young."

"I'm twenty-five," she defended.

Claire (thirty-one) glared, and Graham (thirty-six) made a choking noise.

"You're a baby," Claire said. "I'm thirty-one, single, and without prospects. Everywhere I turn, people are getting engaged or married. It just… I don't know. Reminded me I'm not even close to that."

"Good thing we have a pact," Graham said.

"What?" Claire said, at the same time Reagan asked, "Pact?"

He blinked, as if unsure whether Claire was joking. "The whole 'backup' thing. Remember? We marry each other if we're still single at forty?"

Claire laughed. "We're not really doing that."

He straightened. "What?"

She squinted at him. "Are you being serious? I'm not actually marrying you."

"I'm completely serious," he said. "I've been banking on our deal. Made plans and everything."

"What plans?"

"I'm planning to avoid serious relationships until I'm forty and we get married."

A mocking laugh bubbled up. "You've been avoiding serious relationships your entire life."

"How is that relevant?"

Reagan waved her arm in the air. "Will someone tell me what's going on here?"

Claire dragged her eyes from Graham's face—which harbored a mixture of surprise and his signature playfulness—and cast Reagan an impatient glance. "Last year we were out with friends and I proposed we act as each other's backups and all marry each other if we were still single at forty. I got stuck with Graham."

He leaned forward and cleared his throat. "You mean you *picked* me."

Claire continued as if he hadn't spoken. "I only brought it up in hopes Mia and Noah would get their heads out of their asses and realize how badly they wanted each other. And it worked. They were married a few weeks later. In keeping up with the ruse, though, at the time I ended up with Graham as my backup." She used air quotes as she said "backup," because it hadn't been real.

At least, not in her mind. Had Graham actually believed it all this time?

Graham crossed one ankle over the opposite knee. "You say 'ended up with,' I say 'will be blessed with.'"

"There's no way you actually want to marry me."

"I'd marry the hell out of you. Have you seen you?"

Claire snorted at the same time Reagan said, "Aww."

Useless flattery would get him nowhere. "It's not happening, Graham."

He pursed his lips and frowned as he looked at her for a long moment. He seemed to be gauging how serious she was, then dropped his shoulders in surrender. "Fine."

"Why do you even want to hold up the pact, anyway? You don't want to get married."

"This is different. We both know it's just a convenience thing, no pressure for more. I'm not opposed to a guaranteed date for work functions, the tax benefits, splitting chores with someone. I hang the porch swings, you wash the cars. Seems like a win-win."

Those things did sound nice, but that wasn't all she wanted out of a marriage.

Before Claire could say as much, Reagan spoke again, her voice strangely thoughtful. "You know, it's not such a bad idea."

Claire shot her the side-eye. "What isn't?"

"You and Graham. You've been friends for years. And you're actually really similar, now that I think about it."

Intrigue settled across Graham's features as he sat back, apparently intent on spurring on the ridiculous conversation. "How so?"

"You're both fun, of course," Reagan said. "But more than that, you're outgoing and opinionated. Hardworking and strong-willed. You both have jobs where you help people, but are also stressful and that have weird hours. I would actually think you're pretty compatible. You'd understand each other, at the very least."

"Opinionated, strong-willed, stressful job, and weird hours? You just listed all the things men end up leaving me for," Claire muttered into her glass.

"The men you date are fools," Graham said. "Those are my favorite things about you."

Her eyes flew to his face. "Really?"

"Absolutely. I mean, I don't like that your job stresses you out, but I admire what you do."

She smiled, feeling a little better. "Well. Thank you."

"Now will you marry me?"

"Definitely no."

"Why not?"

Reagan nudged her ribs. "He's nice to look at."

Graham preened.

They had a point. He was ridiculously attractive. Tall and muscular without being oversize. Thick, wavy dark hair that he kept just a smidge too long, a look that somehow came off dashing and playful. His kind, dark eyes were the type that spoke of trustworthiness but held a spark of endearing mischief. But most of all, it was his smile that made him stand out. When he smiled—really smiled—it was almost as if she could feel warmth blooming deep inside her. He was impossible to look away from in those moments, like trying to tear her gaze from a shooting star bursting across the sky.

But physical attraction was only one point of consideration when it came to husband potential. Among many others, another important element was the man's interest and willingness to commit.

It was probably a cheap shot, but she didn't see another way out of this. "Have you ever been in a serious relationship, Graham?"

He glanced at her and crossed one ankle over the opposite knee. "You know the answer to that."

"You're the one insisting we go down this road, and Reagan doesn't know you like I do. Answer the question."

"No."

"And why not?"

"Because I'm not the marrying kind. Their words, not mine. But they're not wrong, and I've always been on the same page so it doesn't bother me." His voice was light but the spark in his eyes dimmed a fraction. "But I don't know, I thought you and I got along pretty well. Didn't think you'd choose being completely alone over hanging out with me when we're old."

He looked away and directed his gaze to the street, and Claire was struck by a slow swirl of discomfort in her belly. She'd wanted to prove he wasn't the marrying kind and had always assumed *he* was the one who bowed out of relationships when things got too serious. She hadn't meant to imply he was inherently lacking—as a friend, roommate, or as someone's future spouse.

Reagan kept silent, staring into her wineglass.

Shifting in the swing, Claire scrambled to find something

to ease the sudden discomfort. Marriage was a big deal to her, and she couldn't imagine going about it so casually.

But...

"Maybe we could have some other arrangement," she blurted out, and immediately wanted to slap her hand over her mouth.

Graham's head snapped around. "What?"

*Shit.* She knew better than to word-vomit into awkward silences, which never failed to land her in some kind of trouble.

She darted wide eyes in Reagan's direction, but her roommate offered no help. Reagan simply looked back at her with big eyes and a raised eyebrow that said, *Where are you going with this?*

Valid question. Where *was* she going with this?

Obviously, the unfiltered version of herself had meant sex. And, strangely, her buttoned-up counterpart wasn't completely appalled by the idea, either.

"Tell us," Graham drawled, the glimpse of insecurity from seconds ago nowhere to be found. Maybe she'd imagined it. "What kind of arrangement, Claire?"

Claire scrunched her nose and rubbed the back of her neck. *No need to be embarrassed. You're a grown woman, and he's an attractive man.* "Well, I was just thinking...pact or not, you're not the marrying type. And I could give several reasons why you're not right for me. But I'd be open to discussing the benefits of, um..."

"Sex?" Graham supplied.

Reagan's voice floated over Claire's shoulder. "Should I leave?"

"No," Graham said at once. "I think I need a witness for this."

Reagan stayed put and Graham cocked a brow at Claire in expectation.

"Yes. Um, sex." Claire wanted to keep her voice strong in the hopes of hiding her awkwardness, but it just came out loud and high-pitched. "If we're forty and still single…I'd be okay with hooking up every once in a while. You know, to scratch the itch. By that point I doubt I'll be as successful picking up men at the bar."

"I would argue because you'll still be smoking hot at forty, but I benefit from that assumption. So I won't."

"You're up for it, then?" At Graham's smirk, she pursed her lips, the familiar competitive discord between them putting her on more steady ground. "Pun not intended."

Graham's eyes were shining. "Sure. Why wait, though?" He set his bottle down, clapped once, and stood. "Reagan, if you'll excuse us—"

"Sit down," Claire ordered. "The terms of the pact still stand. Forty."

He pouted and sat. "When I turn forty, or when you do?"

He was only four years away from the target age. But if she still hadn't found the love of her life when she'd reached thirty-five…she'd probably be down for the occasional night with Graham. "You."

A muscle in his jaw twitched, and he just looked at her for a second. Reagan's gaze burned into the back of her neck.

"Reagan, are you getting this?" He extended his right hand. "Is a handshake good, or should we put it in writing?"

Claire rolled her eyes and reached forward to grip his strong hand in hers. When she went to withdraw, he tightened his grip.

"Reagan! Photo evidence," he shouted even though they were all right there, then added, "please."

Phone in hand, Reagan stood, put her glass on the porch railing, and positioned herself to aim the camera at Graham and Claire's clasped hands.

"I'll take a few," she said, looking at the screen and dropping her arm when she'd taken satisfactory shots. "Wow. I can't wait to see how this turns out."

Claire released Graham's hand. "Don't be so sure it will. I could meet my future husband tomorrow, which would void the agreement."

"Or you'll never meet him," Graham said. "Maybe we'll grow old together. Come to think of it, this is way better than the original idea. Fuck buddies for life."

Claire groaned. "Oh, no." What had she done? "Can I take it back?"

Graham and Reagan spoke simultaneously.

"Nope."

# 2

Graham Scott made a point of risking his life at least once a month.

Nothing completely overboard. He wasn't out BASE jumping or highlining every weekend. Rock climbing, mountain biking, and skiing were more his style—he was always up for the toughest routes and rarely let extreme weather keep him down.

He'd started chasing the thrill of adventure the summer after eighth grade and never stopped. That rush of adrenaline never got old, and the few times he'd taken things too far and injured himself did nothing to cool his ardor. If anything, it made him want to up the ante even more.

His love for action wasn't the reason he became a firefighter, but it sure as hell kept him interested. Before the prospect had come to mind he'd been worried he'd never find a career he'd truly enjoy short of becoming a climbing or white water rafting guide for some mountain adventure company.

And dealing with amateur tourists would have gotten old pretty damn quick.

He loved nothing more than pushing his body and doing things only an elite few ever would. Even if Eldorado Canyon was often full of other climbers—like today—they still made up a small percent of the population. This was Colorado and housed arguably one of the most active populations in the United States.

Here, he was with his people.

Pulling himself over the final edge of Vertigo, one of his favorite routes in the canyon, Graham was met by the smiling face of his best friend, Noah.

"Nice climbing, man."

"You, too." Graham shook out his arms, muscle fatigue telling him he'd used them more than usual. Footwork was most important, and he knew better than to rely on upper body. But with the overhang on the fourth pitch he'd had no choice. He pressed his back to the wall and looked out at the red-and-yellow rock formations jutting out in the canyon beyond, dotted with the green trees. "I'll never get tired of this view."

Noah pressed a chalked palm against the ledge. "I wonder how many people have stood right here in this exact spot."

Graham unhooked his water from his harness and took a swig, shaking his head. "Dunno. I'm just glad I get to be one of them."

Noah didn't respond, which wasn't unusual. He was the quietest, most introspective person Graham had ever met.

As he often did at the top, Graham thought about Nathan, Noah's late brother and the brother he'd met first, and wished he was here. Nathan and Graham had been the same age, and after meeting at orientation their first year at CU and bonding over a love of rock climbing, they'd become fast friends. Graham had quickly been introduced to Nathan's younger brother, Noah, and the three often embarked on mountain expeditions together. After a car accident that took Nathan's life, Noah and Graham's friendship had remained a welcome constant in an otherwise tumultuous few years that followed.

He wouldn't ask, but Graham would bet good money Noah was thinking about his brother, too.

Graham wasn't one to dwell, so after a moment of remembrance he cleared his mind, but wanted to give Noah the time he needed. They stood in silence, listening to the sounds of nature, letting their bodies breathe before rappelling back down to solid ground. After a few more minutes, Graham tipped his head at Noah, his helmet sliding forward. "What do you say we head down, clean up, and grab a beer?"

"Can Mia come?"

If his friend had married anyone else, Graham would have groaned and tried to push for a guys' night out. But he adored Mia, and if he said no, Noah wouldn't come. "You know she's always welcome, man."

Noah gathered handfuls of rope and nodded. "Let's do it."

★ ★ ★

"Need a wingman?" Noah asked, elbowing Graham in the ribs.

Graham took a swig of beer and grunted. "Please. I can get a woman without your help." He'd come a long way since his teenage years, when he was the poor kid at a rich school and the girls didn't find him worth their time. Nowadays, if he wanted a woman in his bed at closing time, he'd have one willing to accompany him there. "Plus, I think that wedding ring on your finger might do more harm than good."

"You'd think, wouldn't you?" Mia fairly growled. "Didn't stop the barista at Starbucks from making eyes at him yesterday."

Noah chuckled and pressed a kiss to Mia's hair. He whispered something in her ear that made her blush, and Graham smiled and looked away.

His eyes skirted around the dim room and landed on a woman with curly blond hair. He perked up, thinking Claire had seen his text and decided to join them. But the woman turned, revealing a face that was attractive but unknown, and his excitement slipped away like an extinguished flame.

He loved Noah and Mia and enjoyed spending time with them, but they definitely fell on the reserved side. As in, perfectly content sitting at the bar, slowly nursing the one and only beer each they'd inevitably order, talking and people watching. Claire, on the other hand, matched his penchant for taking shots, telling crude jokes, and the kind of loud laughter that earned glares from people sitting nearby. She was always up for pool or dancing, and he just…had more fun when the whole crew was together.

Sitting here quiet and content to escape everyone's notice reminded him too much of the days when he did things like that on purpose. He hadn't felt the need to be invisible in a long time, and he had no intention of going back there.

Claire had been sleeping when he left for climbing that morning, so she wasn't working today. She was gone when he got home to shower, though, and hadn't answered his text about meeting at the bar.

What was she up to tonight? Mia was one of Claire's best friends—she'd probably know.

"Talk to Claire today?" he asked.

"Yep. She called me a few hours ago freaking out about what to wear on her date."

His eyebrows shot up. "Date?"

"Yeah. Someone from work asked her out."

Graham hummed and took a sip of his stout. It didn't bother him Claire was on a date, but he was a little surprised she hadn't told him about it, especially after their conversation on the porch last week. They used to help each other in the dating department, as a matter of fact.

Usually on a night like this, they'd be unstoppable. He'd steer her away from men he got a bad feeling about (after an incident four years ago with a guy who still lived with his mother, she welcomed Graham's intuition) and she'd scope out women who were funny and easy to talk to. They'd worked out a hell of a system, somehow making it clear they weren't a couple at the get-go, erasing any hesitation from interested parties to approach.

Mia's voice startled Graham out of his thoughts. "How about a wingwoman?"

"Sorry?"

"You don't want a wingman, but you and Claire seem to get a ton of attention together. I could pose as your sister. Tell them about my kidney transplant and how my wonderful, doting brother took care of me— Oh! Want me to tell them you donated the kidney?"

Graham blinked. "Uh, I don't think—"

"We look alike, actually," Mia said, holding out a lock of her dark hair. "We could totally pass for siblings."

Noah snickered, and Graham ran his palm along his jaw. "Thanks. But I'm good. I'm not looking to score a date tonight."

Mia frowned. "Why not? There are tons of women here."

Once again, Noah spoke quietly to her and she leaned into him with a smile. One more of those and Graham might need to relocate. He was glad they were happy and all, but he could only take so much.

"Noah and I worked hard today. I just want to relax tonight," he lied. He wasn't too tired to have fun, but the person he usually had it with wasn't here.

They stayed for another hour then parted ways, and as Graham approached the condo and prepared to turn into the driveway, movement on the porch caught his attention.

Claire stood there with a man. The overhead light cast a soft yellow glow across their shoulders, and by all appearances this was an end-of-the-date drop-off. Claire had gone all out for this one—wearing one of her nicest dresses and heels. For a girl whose standard work and home uniforms consisted of scrubs and a T-shirt with leggings, respectively, a dress was high praise indeed.

Not wanting to interrupt, Graham continued past the driveway and parked along the street just beyond as if he were a neighbor. He put it in Park but left the engine running, glancing at the rearview mirror. Claire's back was to him and the guy, whom Graham didn't recognize, was in plain view. He was tall and lanky with light-colored curly hair. Glasses framed his eyes and he smiled down at Claire with a sort of shy expression. Claire put her hands on his shoulders and he jolted forward a little, then paused, as if suddenly unsure what he was supposed to do.

Graham winced. This was awkward as hell.

Claire's date moved closer and put a hand on her back—way too high, if you asked Graham, and finally kissed her. It lasted all of two seconds before they separated.

Graham shook his head. If a woman was worth kissing, she should be kissed with conviction and purpose.

The guy made overly enthusiastic hand gestures as he said something, and nodded before hopping down the steps to his car, looking entirely too pleased with himself for the most pathetic good-night kiss in the history of ever.

Graham waited until the dude was down the street before he reversed and pulled into his usual spot.

When he walked in, Gertrude immediately leaped off the

couch to greet him, tail wagging. He bent to pick her up with a single hand, planting a kiss on the top of her furry head, murmuring, "How's my girl?" She wiggled in his grip, licking his face and tapping at his chest with her feet, and he set her down.

Claire waited in the kitchen with a glass of water.

She eyed him and leaned on the counter as he approached her. "I know you saw that."

"And now I know why you didn't come out tonight. You were on a date with Napoleon Dynamite."

"He doesn't look li—" She stopped and put her glass down, dropping her arms to her sides. "Dammit."

Graham chuckled. "So how was it?"

"It was nice."

"Nice?"

She shrugged. "Yeah."

"And that kiss?"

She looked away. "It was fine. First kisses are always a little awkward."

"They don't have to be."

Pursing her lips, Claire's brows rose. "You mean to tell me you nail all your first kisses? No one's that good."

"No, you're right. Some are awful. But with the right person and at the right moment, a first kiss can be pretty awesome."

She looked skeptical, and Graham tilted his head as he regarded her. "You've seriously never had a first kiss that knocked the wind out of you?"

"I guess not," she said, sounding disappointed. "It's probably me. I get in my head and can't focus."

Graham frowned. "Maybe it's the guys you're kissing. When I kiss a woman, she's definitely not thinking about anything except what's going on here." He tapped his lips and Claire's gaze followed his finger. He grinned. "Or…elsewhere. You know, depending on the situation."

She rolled her eyes. "You sound like an arrogant asshole, you know that?"

"Maybe," he allowed, enjoying the spark of challenge in her eyes. "But if I can back it up, what does it matter?"

"Good kisser or not, women don't like assholes."

"Some of them do."

"Fine. *I* don't like assholes."

He laughed and hopped up onto the counter, letting his legs dangle. "You've got four years to come to terms with sleeping with one."

A hint of insecurity crossed her features. "You seem awfully certain I won't be married by then."

"If you keep going out with guys like Napoleon, you probably won't. A guy like that isn't right for you."

"His name isn't Napoleon."

"What is it?"

"Marvin."

He choked on air. "No, it's not."

Her cheeks turned pink. "Don't make fun of him."

"You're not marrying a guy named Marvin. What's his last name?"

"That's not important." Yeah, that didn't make him less interested at all. "You don't know anything about him." Her voice lacked heat, but Claire wasn't the type to back down from an argument, no matter how small.

"Fine, I'm judging the dude based on appearance, a weak-ass kiss, and your less-than-enthused description of the date. But from that information alone I'd bet my next paycheck you were bored to death."

Her lips twisted to the side and she looked down at her feet.

"Am I right?"

"Maybe. A little." She sighed. "But it was a first date. Shouldn't I give him another chance?"

"If you want to. Or don't waste your time and come out with me next weekend instead."

Her eyes went wide. "On a date?"

He huffed out a laugh. "No. I meant, like, our usual. We're pretty good at finding people for each other. Remember that chef I scoped out for you last year? You were with him for a few months, right?"

"Sam? Yeah, until he ghosted me."

"Seriously? You didn't tell me that."

She snorted. "You want me to tell you every time a man screws me over?"

"Yes."

"Why? You gonna defend my honor?"

"Maybe. Friends do that, right?"

"I'd certainly punch Noah if he ever hurt Mia."

"He'd die before he hurt her."

Claire smiled softly. "I know. Anyway, I saw Sam not too long after he stopped answering my texts, and you know me… I marched up asked him what happened. Talk about awkward, but I wanted him to tell me to my face what went wrong. He said I was too outspoken and he realized he'd never be able to take me home to meet his mother."

"Dumbass," Graham muttered. His mom would adore Claire—all the more reason for them never to meet. He didn't need that kind of pressure.

He tried to remember anything else about that guy, but Graham had only spent time with him a few times when he'd tried to show off and cook dinner for the entire house. "His food sucked, anyway."

"No it didn't. It was fucking delicious."

She was right.

"Add that to the list of reasons men don't want me. I can't cook," she said.

"So?"

"Don't men want a woman who cooks?"

Graham waved a dismissive arm. "Who cares? There are dozens of places that deliver within a five-mile radius of here. I say it's better to support local businesses."

"Well. You're a minority in that, I think." She looked at him for a moment before pushing off from the counter. She nudged his knee and gave him a small smile. "I'm gonna head to bed. Thanks for trying to make me feel better."

"Trying?"

"Okay, thanks for making me feel better. A little."

Gertrude growled from her perch on the armchair as Claire passed.

"Thinking about marrying me now, aren't you?" he called after her.

She didn't miss a beat.

"Not a chance."

# 3

One week later, Claire sent Graham a text message halfway through her shift that said, I hate you.

After she'd seen Marvin that morning, Graham's voice had been in her head all day. *A guy like that isn't right for you.*

She'd spotted Marvin across the nursing station and given him a little wave, thinking he'd come over. His cheeks had flushed and he glanced away before looking back to smile at her. For a second it seemed he might approach her, but then he turned and went in the other direction, his navy scrubs billowing around his thin frame as he speed-walked down the hall.

He was incredibly nice. Sweet. Gentle.

And like Graham said, definitely *not* her type. It wasn't that she didn't like nice guys, or even sweet guys. She just wanted a little more...assertion. Fire. Confidence. It hit her as she watched Marvin walk away and pictured in her mind what would happen if she caught up with him and suggested they meet for a little rendezvous in the supply closet later.

He'd probably turn bright red and decline without looking her in the eye, mumbling something about it being inappropriate.

And yeah, it was inappropriate. But it was also hot and exciting and she'd always wanted to do it.

Then another image popped into her brain: how Graham would react in the same situation. He'd grab her hand and drag her down the hall to take care of it *right now.* As soon as the door shut, cloaking them in darkness, he'd grab her by the pockets of her scrubs and pull her against his body, knocking gauze and tubing off the shelves as he kissed her with the raw passion of a man consumed by his need for her.

Which immediately pissed her off for two reasons:

1. She didn't want Graham to be right, and she would have been excited to go out with Marvin again if Graham hadn't pointed out how incompatible they were. (Probably. Maybe.)

2. Since when did she entertain thoughts of kissing Graham?

It was probably the sex pact. She certainly hadn't thought about kissing him before that conversation, and even if they ended up going down that road, it was years away from becoming reality.

Hence the text message, and the lingering irritation she still felt hours later when she heard Ruthie mention something about a firefighter being brought in.

Claire perked up from where she sat at the nursing station, charting while waiting for lab results for a young woman in pod 12. Ruthie and another nurse stood several feet away and Claire tilted her head, trying to hear better. When she heard the words *multialarm fire* and *firefighter injured*, she immediately pulled her phone from her scrubs pocket.

Graham had yet to answer her text from earlier. She'd sent it three hours ago.

Did he work today? She racked her brain to remember if they'd talked about it, and she flipped through her photos to find his schedule. He typically worked twenty-four-hour shifts, but the dates weren't consistent and she'd never been able to keep it straight. He brought home a schedule every month and posted it on the fridge, and she'd gotten in the habit of taking a photo for reference.

Shit. She had the image of May's schedule, and today was June 2.

What did multiple injuries mean? Community injuries or firefighters? Or both?

Fear shot through her and suddenly she was eleven years old, standing on the airfield in that split second when she realized something wasn't right, and the ice-cold sensation that filled her then spread its tentacles through her veins once again.

She startled when Ruthie grabbed her elbow. "Claire?"

"Did I hear you say a firefighter is coming in?"

"Yeah, I was gonna put him with you in pod 7. Can you handle that? I know you've got three others, but Jimmy's full and Brooklyn's on her break."

She worked to steady her breathing. It could be a simple check-and-release per protocol. "I'm good. I'll take him. ETA?"

"Should be any minute. Fire wasn't too far from here."

Neither was Graham's station, which meant his department likely would have responded, especially if the incident was major.

It was on the tip of her tongue to ask if Ruthie knew anything more about the patient—like his name or if he was a tall, dark-haired, sarcastic asshole with a killer smile—but she'd already walked away.

Claire had just enough time to shoot off several text messages to Graham's phone before her new patient arrived.

Are you at work?

If you're fine and don't answer in the next five seconds I'm kicking your ass when I get home

I don't actually hate you, if you're punishing me for that

When he didn't respond to her machine gun messages, she gave up and called him.

Nothing.

"Dammit," she muttered, his lack of response like kindling to the burning anxiety beneath her sternum. Most days she was able to remain neutral and keep memories of the tragedy she'd witnessed as a kid from affecting her day-to-day life, probably because the trauma patients she cared for at work were typically strangers. But when something might have happened to someone she knew, it was as if her brain immediately recalled every heightened instinct and emotion from that day.

In that moment, a stretcher came through the ambulance entrance carrying a man in a familiar navy uniform. The body filled it out differently and she knew right away it wasn't Graham. He was awake and talking, and already had his protective gear off.

This guy didn't seem badly off and a touch of her worry melted away.

Ruthie intercepted the paramedics and directed them to the assigned pod, and Claire once again tucked her phone away before grabbing a supply cabinet and rolling it toward the curtain. One of the paramedics came out and gave her a quick rundown—too much water had brought down the ceiling and the patient had taken a blow to the head. He'd been knocked unconscious and dragged out of the building, then came to shortly thereafter.

They'd stabilized his spine and kept him awake during the drive, but would leave the rest up to the doctors.

"Thanks," Claire said, taking the handover document. "I'll take it from here."

The paramedics left and Claire pulled back the curtain and pushed her cart inside. The man's neck was immobilized by a brace placed by the paramedics, so she sidled up next to the bed and leaned over so he could see her. "Hi, I'm Claire, your nurse. The doctor will be in soon but I'll start an IV and ask you some questions first. I know they took your vitals in the ambulance, but I'll take them again if that's okay. What's your name?"

He gave her a smile. "Javier. Can I take this thing off now? My neck is fine."

Claire fought a smile. That's exactly what Graham would have said, eager to be cleared and get the hell out of the hospital. Just as quickly as the thought came, concern for her friend and roommate flooded her once again. Had anyone else been hurt?

"Not until the doctor says so, and odds are she's gonna want a scan first. Are you in pain?"

"It's not bad."

"On a scale of one to ten, with one being no pain and ten being the worst you could ever imagine, where would you rate it?"

"Four. Maybe four and a half."

She made a note and prepared the IV kit. "Are you nauseous?"

"I was on the drive in, but I tend to get carsick and the ambulance ride wasn't exactly smooth. It's already better."

She asked him a few more routine questions, and when she was confident nothing was so urgent she needed to run and grab the doctor right that second, she slipped in another question as she started the bag of fluids and strapped a blood pressure cuff to his arm. "Where was the fire?"

"Sixth and Pine. You know that multilevel apartment complex they're building?"

She knew exactly what he was talking about. "Yeah. How bad is it?"

"Damage is significant. Shit was falling everywhere. At least two other guys were in there when I got hit. They weren't from my station, I know that much, but I hope they're okay."

Her stomach dropped and she gripped her hands into fists. She hadn't heard of any other patients being brought in by ambulance. What if Graham had been hurt and they took him to another hospital?

*Focus on your patient.* "Do, um…? Is there anyone I can call for you?" she asked, attempting to mask the tremble in her voice.

"My phone's still on the truck," he said. "But the chief said he'd send someone up here as soon as he could. The paramedic called my wife and she's on her way."

Javier's gaze shifted over her shoulder and Dr. Singh appeared, offering a smile to the patient before turning to Claire for information. Claire outlined what she knew and what she'd done, then left the doctor and Javier alone.

She checked the clock as she sat at the computer to chart Javier's vitals. Half an hour remained.

Javier was wheeled away for imaging and other than calling Graham twice more, Claire couldn't have said what she did until the end of her shift. Her brain had gone fuzzy with the conflicting signals passing through over the last hour.

Unknown firefighter coming with unknown injuries: *freak out!*

Patient is fine: *relax*.

Patient isn't Graham: *seriously, relax*.

Additional unknown firefighters may have been injured: *freak out!*

Graham is unaccounted for: *RED ALERT!*

After she passed off to the overnight nurse, Claire jogged to her car. As she started the engine she suddenly realized she could have called Noah to see if he'd heard from Graham. Or Reagan, to see if she'd seen him today.

But she only lived a mile from the hospital and she'd be there in minutes. Either Graham would be home—where she'd promptly kill him—or she'd hopefully be able to locate his shift schedule for this month and find out if he'd worked today.

When she turned onto her street her gaze immediately landed on Graham's beat-up 4Runner parked in his usual spot in the driveway. The breath that whooshed out of her was thick with relief, and after pulling in under the carport she dropped her forehead against the steering wheel.

She took several deep breaths, willing her muscles to release the tension that had built over the last two hours. She couldn't remember the last time she'd gotten so worked up.

Was it because Graham was her friend, or because memories of her dad's accident had come screaming back?

Or both?

Either way, she had to calm down before she went in. That was the plan, anyway, which went to hell when she walked in the front door and found him in the living room, completely oblivious to the turmoil he'd caused her.

He was deep into some video game, sitting on the edge of the couch, shirt pulled taut across the muscles in his back as he moved. His dark, wavy hair was disheveled and his sleeves pushed up to reveal toned forearms rippling with each manipulation of the controller.

"Graham!"

His gaze didn't leave the screen. "Yeah?"

A flood of emotions rushed through her—agitation the most potent—and she marched around the couch and stopped directly in front of the television.

Graham leaned to the side in an attempt to see around her. "What are you doing? I can't see."

"I don't care! I've been calling and texting you all day. Why haven't you answered?"

He frowned, his eyes darting to hers in confusion before his attention returned to the portion of the screen he could see, his fingers continuing to toggle the controls. "You mean when you said you hated me? I didn't think that deserved a response."

"What about the others?"

"I didn't see anything else. I put my phone in my room to charge a while ago, though."

She pressed her hands against her temples. "Meanwhile I've been scared out of my mind thinking something happened to you. EMSA brought a firefighter in, and he said the ceiling fell on several of the guys trying to put out a fire at an apartment complex. I didn't remember if you were working and you never answered your fucking phone!"

This was exactly the kind of situation she'd always wanted to avoid. The fear and constant worry... She couldn't live like this on a regular basis. She'd watched her mother do it for years.

And they'd experienced their worst fear come true.

Graham stilled for a beat, finally seeming to hear her, then dropped the controller to the carpet and jogged around the couch to his room. Claire followed him, and within seconds he was on the phone. The conversation was short, and when he hung up he wrapped one hand around his neck and tossed the phone onto his bed.

"Everyone's fine," he said. "One concussion from Station 3, which is probably the guy you got. Everyone else has already been checked out and released."

Claire glared at him, anger and some other emotion she couldn't identify turning over in her stomach. "I didn't know that, Graham. I didn't know where you were or if you'd been there..." She trailed off at the strange look that entered his eyes.

Graham dropped his arm and tilted his head as he watched her. "Claire. Were you...worried about me?"

"No."

A tiny grin curved one corner of his mouth, drawing her attention there. "You were."

She rolled her eyes. "Well! Of course I was. You're my roommate. If you die I have to find someone else to help pay rent in this overpriced condo."

He took a step forward, his grin widening as he shook his head. "No, I think it's more than that. You were worried about Graham, the person. Not Graham, your roommate."

She didn't blink as he took another step closer. "Don't flatter yourself."

She'd quickly lost control of the situation and desperately tried to think of how to get it back.

He was right; she had been worried about him.

But it was more than that. She'd never told him the details of her dad's death and didn't intend to talk about it now, but the truth was that history made her hypersensitive to situations like these.

"Admit it," he continued, his voice softening as he stopped about a foot away. "You care about me, Claire. A lot."

His brown eyes held a spark and a challenge, which was

familiar and welcome in her flustered state. This back-and-forth felt normal, and it hit home just how much she needed this and how important Graham was to her. After the emotional whiplash of the last few hours, the realization caused something inside her to snap.

She was pissed off, but she was so happy he was *okay*. Ever since she'd heard the words *firefighter injured*, she'd battled images of Graham coming through the ER doors on a stretcher. She was mentally and emotionally spent and had very little filter left, in voice or action.

She would later blame her state of mind on what happened next as she lurched forward, grabbed his rough cheeks between her palms, and kissed him.

Graham sucked in a sharp breath and froze, his body going taut. She pulled back, the separation of their lips sending a faint wet sound echoing in the silence. Before she could fully process what she'd done and take it back, claiming momentary insanity, his face came into focus.

All awareness slipped away with her surprised exhale.

The way Graham was looking at her...

His ever-smiling mouth was slack and devoid of the quick, sarcastic words she'd come to expect. His pupils dilated and his usually playful eyes were dark and ominous.

Her heart pounded as his gaze dragged down her face, from her eyes to her lips, where they lingered for a long moment before slowly scrolling back up. A muscle ticked in his jaw as he stared at her, brow furrowed, as if seeing her for the first time.

Time stopped as they stood inches apart, his breath warm against her lips, chest brushing hers with each inhale. Heat rippled through her as she felt *want* rolling off him in thick waves.

Just when she'd decided she had to say or do *something*, Graham leaped into action. His mouth came back to hers, warm and hard and unyielding. His hands were in her hair, and his strong fingers threading between the strands sent a shiver racing down her spine. She gripped his shirt in her fists and pulled him along as she stumbled backward. She stopped when she hit the dresser and his body molded to hers, as if he couldn't get close enough. *Yes, closer.* Something fell and hit the floor with a crash, but he didn't seem to notice or care.

Exactly like she'd pictured them in the hospital supply closet scenario, damn him.

She definitely liked what he was doing and must have made some enthusiastic moan or murmur or something, because he hummed against her lips and slid one hand in the small space between the drawers and her lower back, arching her hips into him.

Her body threw caution to the wind and chose to ignore that which had just been discussed: Graham was her roommate, whom she decidedly did not care about.

Definitely not *a lot.*

He had great lips, though. She'd always loved his smile— one of those ridiculously wide ones that was nearly impossible not to respond to. Channeled James Marsden in *The Notebook* or *27 Dresses.*

As it turned out, smiling wasn't all his mouth was good for.

The man knew how to use it, and she melted against him with each passing second. Any moment now she'd come to her senses and push him away. Maybe slap him just to be contrary, even though she'd started it. But then his tongue slid across her lower lip and she trembled, opening her mouth and wrapping her arms around his shoulders.

Later. She'd put a stop to this later.

She bit at his lower lip and he growled into her mouth, grabbing her hips and lifting her onto the dresser. Of their own accord her legs cinched around his waist, pulling him closer. *Shit*, he smelled good. Like the outdoors and some manly bodywash.

Did he always smell like this? She hadn't been in this position before to notice. As in literally up against him, his tongue moving with hers and his body between her thighs.

Damn, those lips were really, really good. His chest pressed against hers as he ravaged her mouth like he was an addict and she was his drug of choice. Her brain had short-circuited and her pulse spiraled out of control. What were her hands doing? Shit, was that his ass (correction: firm ass) underneath her palm?

A rumble vibrated deep in his chest and he shifted his pelvis.

When she felt how turned on he was, awareness shot through her and she opened her eyes to find him looking back at her, irises black. For a long second they didn't move, lips still pressed together, gazes locked. It was too much, but she wasn't ready to stop, so she reached up and put one hand over his eyes.

He laughed against her mouth and pulled back, gently pulling her hand down. His chest heaved with exertion, and his voice held a trace of amusement. "What the hell are you doing?"

She swallowed and reached for her voice. "Is that about me kissing you, or me not wanting you to look at me while we do it?"

His eyes went wide. "Damn, are we about to do it?" He nodded enthusiastically and kept one hand wrapped around her thigh as he reached sideways to swing his door shut.

With the click of the latch, it hit her all at once.

She'd just made out with Graham. Her friend and roommate. Had let him—no, encouraged him to—hoist her onto a piece of furniture and grind his body against hers while her tongue tasted his mouth.

All with the door wide open.

Was Reagan home? What if she'd walked by?

Claire pushed him back and slid down, landing on unsteady legs, and swung the door open.

"No, we're not about to *do it*," she whisper-yelled. "Momentary lapse in judgment."

Graham's dark eyes held steady, still dancing with desire, but now with his usual hint of challenge. "It was pretty hot. Hotter than I expected. Don't you want to see if the rest is that good?"

Hotter than he expected? Had he thought about this before?

She worked to keep her voice steady and strong. "Nope."

"Liar."

If he tried to kiss her again, odds were high she wouldn't deny him. But despite the big talk and teasing, Graham wasn't the type to force a woman to do anything.

Not that he'd ever need to. He'd probably gotten laid based off that smile alone.

Shaking the thought away, she directed her gaze over his shoulder, unsure what she'd do if she looked at his lips again.

Something occurred to her then, and she frowned. "Where's your evil dog?" Usually when Claire came anywhere near Graham while they were home, Gertrude was never far, growling and making her disapproval well known.

He laughed lightly as if he knew why she'd asked. "She's getting her hair done. I probably need to leave soon to go pick her up."

He grinned and Claire's stomach flipped.

She needed to get the hell out of there.

"Here's the deal. We're gonna forget what just happened. I'm glad you're okay, but I'm pissed at you for making me worry. I get to control the thermostat tonight—" She held up a hand when he opened his mouth to protest. "It's fair punishment so don't even try to argue. Turn on your fan, sleep naked, whatever the hell you need to do. But it's going to seventy-two and I don't want to hear a peep."

He arched a challenging brow. "I'll definitely be sleeping naked. You know, if you change your mind about exploring this a little more…" He gestured between them with his index finger.

Clearing her throat, she smoothed out her scrub top and before spinning around to leave, made one parting comment—pact be damned.

"Believe me, Graham. What we just did? I can say with one hundred percent certainty, it will never, *ever* happen again."

His laugh followed her out the door as she attempted to saunter away with confidence.

"We'll see about that."

# 4

Graham *really* wanted it to happen again.

He shifted between the sheets, wearing just a pair of boxer briefs. Yeah, part of him wanted to be prepared in case Claire changed her mind, but it was mostly because he was burning the fuck up.

Who could sleep in this inferno?

He'd even sent Gertrude to the dog bed in the corner of his room. Normally he didn't mind her sleeping at the foot of the bed, but she was a mini–space heater he didn't need right now.

It was possible thinking about kissing Claire was at least partly responsible for his elevated body temperature, but mostly it was the thermostat setting.

Probably.

Honestly, though. He couldn't stop his brain from replaying the scene over and over in his mind. So many things had flashed in her eyes in those minutes, and for a woman who spoke her mind so freely, there sure was a lot she kept hidden.

Here he'd thought he was the only one with secrets.

Claire coming home in a mood was nothing out of the ordinary. The fact that her anger was directed toward him wasn't even uncommon. But the source of it all being how much she cared about him? Had been worried about him?

That was a damn revelation.

As was the split second of heat that followed, then the shocking feel of her lips against his. It had only taken a moment for his body to catch up, and Claire was the last person he'd leave with a half-assed kiss.

After what he witnessed on the porch with Merlin or whatever his name was, it was basically his duty to redeem men everywhere. Even if he could only give her part of what she was looking for in a man, turned out he was very, very interested in assisting in that particular department.

He'd done a pretty good job, too. She'd tried to play it off, but she'd been into it. Maybe after sleeping on it she'd be willing to revisit the topic of their friends-with-benefits scenario. Why wait until forty if the chemistry was there now?

★ ★ ★

Graham slept like shit and gave up around six. Gertrude had weaseled her way back onto the bed and had taken issue with his feet flailing around her spot, letting out several whines over the last hour.

"Sorry, girl," he muttered and swung his legs over the edge. He had plans to go mountain biking with a few buddies today and needed to be out of the house by seven, anyway.

He threw on a pair of shorts and padded to the kitchen to make a strong pot of coffee, Gertrude on his heels. He'd just poured himself a steaming cup when he heard a low growl, and turned to find Claire hovering in the hallway.

He gently nudged Gertie with his toe and leaned down. "We don't talk to her like that," he murmured. She looked up at him with innocent eyes, and he sent up a prayer he never had daughters. The thought was swiftly followed by how ridiculous a notion that was.

Odds were low Graham would ever have kids of his own. Birth control was extremely high on his priority list and he didn't see that changing anytime soon.

Claire straightened her back and entered the kitchen, shooting his dog a dirty look before going straight to the fridge. "Morning."

"Morning," he said with a smile and a wink.

Her hand paused on the handle and she glared at him even as her cheeks flushed. "Don't."

"Don't say good morning?"

"Not like that."

Graham lifted his eyebrows and turned his back to her, smiling into his coffee cup. "We still on for tonight?"

"What?" she squeaked.

"We're going out, remember? Reagan's coming, too. Unless…"

"Unless what?"

"I mean, if after last night you've changed your mind and just want to hang around at home, preferably in my bed, that's cool, too."

The fridge door slammed, and he turned to find Claire standing with a jug of orange juice in one hand, the other balled up and propped on her hip. "We're definitely going out."

He shrugged. "Your call." He took a long sip of the dark, bold coffee. "I'm going out on the trails, but I'll make sure I'm presentable by eight. Sound good?"

She rifled through the cabinet for a cup, feigning disinterest. "Sure."

Grinning, Graham lifted his mug to her and went back to his room.

By the time he pulled into the parking lot near his favorite mountain biking trail, he was ready to get out of his head and into the zone, where there was nothing but adrenaline and power. He'd had Claire on his mind all night and morning, and he needed to get his brain under control. The kiss had thrown him off, and he could give himself a little grace for temporarily focusing on it. He was a straight man, and she was an attractive woman, and their mouths had fit together surprisingly well.

Good thing adventure called today. His Cannondale paired with some fresh mountain air would be the perfect way to get his mind back on track.

His buddy Chris was already there, talking to another guy Graham didn't recognize. Graham parked next to them and got out, slapping his palm against Chris's in a handshake.

"Hey, man. This is Tyler. He came into the store last night and is new to the area, but not new to mountain biking. I told him he could come along and we'd show him the best trails."

"Awesome." Graham offered his hand to the new guy. "I'm Graham. I first met Chris at his store, too. Worked there all through college. Best outdoor gear in the state."

"Nice to meet you."

"Where are you from?" Graham asked.

"Arkansas. Moved here for a job a few weeks ago and they put me to work right away. With that and unpacking, I've been suffocating and dying to get outside."

"Between us and our buddies Hugh and Noah, you'll find someone in the mountains every weekend," Chris said. "Do you climb?"

"A little. It's not as popular where I'm from, but I'd love to learn."

"I'm headed to Eldorado Canyon next weekend," Graham said. "You're welcome to come and I'll show you around."

"That would be awesome. Thanks."

Tyler turned and worked the clamps to pull his bike from his roof rack and Graham did the same. Graham left the door open while he slipped on tall socks and his bike shoes.

"Are you a local like Chris?" Tyler asked, taking a swig from his water bottle.

Graham shook his head. "Moved here for college. I'm from Santa Fe."

"Never been. What's the outdoor scene like there?"

"Pretty awesome. Skiing in Taos and Angel Fire, obviously, but skiing has never been my favorite. Santa Fe National Forest is right outside the city and has great camping and hiking, and Valles Caldera has some of the best fly-fishing in the state. After my first camping trip with my dad as a kid I was hooked. It got even worse after my first climb in Pecos River Canyon. I was thirteen and had more confidence than sense, but I had a patient guide and somehow made it to the top. The second I looked down and saw what I'd scaled with my bare hands and a pair of rubber shoes, I never looked back. It was inevitable I'd end up somewhere like Colorado."

"I get that. I jumped at the chance for a job opportunity up here. Arkansas has some hidden gems, but I wanted more."

Chris clipped on his helmet and looked at Tyler. "So what's your standard level of difficulty? Would give us a good idea of where to start. This area is pretty versatile and has a little of everything."

"I stick to blues, mostly. The occasional green or single black depending on who I'm with and how I'm feeling."

Chris nodded. "Let's start with a blue and see how it goes.

There's a nice three-mile out-and-back we can do, but at the top it branches out into a black if we want to go that way."

"Sounds great," Tyler said.

Graham hopped up and rolled forward, clipping in as he headed for the trail Chris had referenced. "Let's do it."

They set off between the trees, and with each pump of his legs, Graham focused on the challenge before him and left everything else behind.

★ ★ ★

"Who needs another round?"

The club was crowded and the music ridiculously loud, drowning out Graham's question. He leaned across the table and reached out with both hands, nudging Reagan and Claire, who had their heads together, deep in conversation. When they looked up at him, he held up his empty glass and raised an eyebrow.

Claire nodded and Reagan shook her head. Graham shouldered his way to the bar to wait, wondering why Claire had chosen this place. It felt more like a meat market than the casual hipster bars they usually went to. He hadn't seen one guy who seemed anywhere near Claire's age, or worth her time.

And the women sending him seductive gazes had to have been at least ten years younger than him, if not more. To each their own, but he didn't usually go for women that far from his age group. He'd done his share of dating when he was in his early twenties, and at best it could be described as a complete shit show.

He could tell a thirty-five-year-old woman he wasn't in the market for a commitment, and she'd usually take him at his word. The last time he'd tried that with a twenty-five-year-old she'd cried when he'd said he had no intention of attending her family Christmas as her boyfriend.

Seeing how (1) he'd never broached the subject of precollege life with any woman and (2) the only one he'd (accidentally) introduced to his parents had left him the next day, serious events like holidays with his or anyone else's family were firmly off the table.

With drinks in hand he returned to the high-top near the dance floor and found it empty. Setting the glasses down, he looked around and found Claire and Reagan on the dance floor. The DJ was playing a Post Malone remix and they were laughing and having fun. Graham took a long pull from his beer and smiled.

Someone tapped Reagan on the shoulder and she turned, her face lighting up. She threw her arms around a woman Graham didn't recognize, and immediately went for a second woman a few feet away. Claire didn't seem to know Reagan's friends, so she kept her distance and kept dancing among the crowd, unbothered to be by herself.

Just as the thought of joining her crossed Graham's mind, a clean-cut man in a polo and chinos approached her. He leaned down to speak into her ear, and though Graham couldn't quite see her face, he figured everything was fine when Claire nodded.

Graham's phone vibrated in his pocket and he dug it out, finding a message from one of his coworkers asking him to switch a shift. It took him few minutes to check his calendar and reply, and when he looked up, out of habit he searched the crowd to locate Reagan and Claire.

Reagan was still talking animatedly with her friends and Claire was still dancing with Khaki Pants. But as they moved with the music and her body rotated a little, she swiveled her head around to catch Graham's eye. Her left eyebrow went up and in seconds Graham was moving, his beer forgotten on the table.

Years ago they'd arranged the signal—a raised eyebrow for her, a tip of the chin for him—that meant *save me*.

He was more than happy to step in to get Claire away from a guy who was too drunk or handsy, and it had come in handy for him over the years, too. Sometimes he knew within minutes he wasn't compatible with someone but didn't know how to politely end the conversation and step away.

Enter the chin dip, and enter Claire.

Tonight, it seemed he was up to bat.

Mentally stretching his muscles because it had been a while since he'd needed to do this, he tightened his jaw and hardened his gaze. With a smile that was anything but warm, he directed a cold glare at the guy as he approached and put himself between them. His arm went around Claire's waist in a possessive gesture, his hand resting low on her hip.

"Thanks for keeping my girlfriend company, but I've got it from here."

The guy paled and blinked, then took a big step back. "Sorry, man," he muttered, and disappeared.

"Your hand is on my ass," Claire muttered, though her voice held a trace of humor.

"Shut up and dance with me, sweetheart."

The track changed, and Imagine Dragons' "Dancing in the Dark" flowed through the speakers. A strangely sensual song somewhere between slow and rhythmic, it was an odd choice for a place like this, but Graham went with it. He rotated so he and Claire were face-to-face, and put both hands around her waist, sliding them a few inches higher now that his performance was over.

She gave him a look. "'Sweetheart'?"

"Seems like a standard endearment for couples."

"Sounded strange coming out of your mouth."

"Felt weird, too."

She laughed and relaxed against him, curling her fingers around his neck. "I don't know how to dance to this song. Is it fast? Slow?"

Graham pulled her a touch closer and rocked into her with the fluid, electronic beat. Her hips moved with him willingly. "This is probably best to make sure your suitor gets the point. What went wrong?"

"He smelled a little like cigarettes so I asked if he was a smoker."

Graham tipped his head back and laughed. "You just put it all out there, don't you?"

"That's a deal breaker for me," she said, unapologetic. She shrugged and smiled a little, and his eyes dropped to her lips.

Huge mistake.

His brain immediately reminded him how soft they'd felt moving against his, and the perfect way she'd used her tongue—firm and teasing without being overpowering. Her full bottom lip disappeared beneath her teeth and his gaze darted to her eyes.

She'd caught him staring.

He prepared himself for a set-down or snarky comment, to which he'd reply in equal measure. Instead, she lifted one hand and brushed her index finger across his brow with a frown.

"What happened here?"

It took him a second to catch up. "Just a scratch from biking today." Reagan and Claire had gone to dinner before they met him here, and the first time she'd seen him after his ride this afternoon was in this dark room.

Claire lifted to her tip-toes, angling her face to get a better look. "It looks pretty deep. Did it bleed a lot?"

He shrugged. "Some."

Irritation flashed across her face and Graham held back a grin. This woman was so easy to rile up.

"It could probably use a couple of stitches."

"Too late now, right?"

Her body stopped moving. "Not necessarily. Don't you have a suture kit with your camping stuff? For survival emergencies or whatever?"

He did, but he put light pressure against her waist to resume dancing. "We're not leaving so you can come at me with a needle."

Her lips pressed in a determined line. "I could probably do it while you're playing one of your video games and you'd barely notice. You don't have feelings, anyway, so I don't see what the problem is."

He refused to allow the barb to burrow any further than skin-deep and raised his brows. "Whoa, coming at me like that after I swooped in to rescue you?"

"If we're counting, I've intervened on your behalf way more than the other way around. Unlike you, I don't have a problem speaking my mind and telling a man I'm not interested."

"Why'd you call me over tonight, then?"

She hesitated, though he couldn't tell if she didn't know how to respond or if she simply didn't want to. "I'm…not sure, actually."

"Hmm." He had an inkling.

She stopped again. "Stop trying to distract me. I need to get a better look at that wound and it's too dark in here. Let's go."

"Claire, it's fine."

"Do you want it to scar weird? Or get infected?"

"No, but I cleaned it out when we got back to the car. Firefighters are also EMTs, you know."

"Yeah, well, I'm a nurse practitioner. NP trumps EMT. Let's go."

Just two weeks ago he could have argued, but she'd proudly displayed her license on the kitchen table for three whole days when the thing arrived in the mail.

He dropped his hands, frowning at the loss of her body beneath his skin, and sighed. "I'm coming."

# 5

After checking in with Reagan, who said she'd get a ride home, Claire and Graham grabbed an Uber back to the condo.

"How many did you have?" Graham asked, closing the front door and flipping on the light.

She stopped and faced him. "I'm sober enough to stitch you up."

He slid long fingers across his chin. "I'm afraid I need more convincing. This beautiful face is important to me and I don't want you to mess it up. How many live patients have you practiced on?"

"Six." Yeah, she'd been terrified for the first three. But by the fourth, she'd gained a decent measure of confidence. "And I'm not even drunk enough to kiss you again. How's that?"

"Wow, okay. Noted." He made a beeline for the fridge. "Totally unrelated, do you want a beer?"

Claire ignored him and pulled out a kitchen chair, then flipped on the fixture immediately overhead. "Sit down so I can get a good look."

He came back with two bottles and a hopeful gleam in his eye. He sat as instructed and tilted his head back.

She leaned down to inspect the wound, which bisected the outer edge of his right eyebrow, the one he often arched at her in consternation. Eyebrows were tricky. At least it wasn't his lips; lacerations there hardly ever lined up right when they healed. And also, for no other reason at all, at least it wasn't his lips.

"You cleaned it well," she admitted.

"Not my first injury."

She pressed her mouth together and inhaled deeply through her nose. "I could stitch it, or I think some Dermabond with a couple Steri Strips would be fine, too."

"Great. Glue me back together, nurse."

He stayed put while she went to the bathroom to get the supplies and wash her hands. When she returned, he popped the top off his beer and took a swig while she got everything set up and sidled up next to him.

They remained silent for a few moments while she worked. Then, he said, "You look nice."

She paused, ignoring the single butterfly that had the nerve to take flight behind her bellybutton. "What?"

"It was too quiet so I thought I'd tell you that you looked really nice tonight."

With a sigh, she resumed her ministrations on his cut. "What are you doing?"

"What do you mean?"

"It's the kiss, isn't it? It made things weird."

"A little."

"Make it go back."

"I can't right now. Not with your chest, like, two inches from my face."

"You're such a dick," she said with a laugh. She might have been angry at his comment, but she'd worn a low-cut shirt to the club and with the way she stood over him, her breasts were indeed invading his personal space. He literally couldn't look anywhere else unless he moved his head, which wasn't advisable.

"Sorry. I'll close my eyes." And he did, but kept speaking. "But I have to admit I'm feeling self-conscious about that kiss now. Have you not been thinking about it?"

She went with a half-truth. "I've thought about it once or twice."

"Thank fuck. I thought maybe I'd had an off night."

"Regardless, it can't happen again."

"Why not?"

"The obvious is because we're roommates and it's a terrible idea. But also because I'm not ready to give up on the idea of finding a real relationship. Do you and I have chemistry? Yeah. With the way we argue, it's no surprise we'd be good together in bed. But I want something more than physical."

"Until the time comes for the pact to kick in, you mean."

"If, in four years, I'm still single, I'll probably be lonely enough to discuss it." She finished up and inspected her handiwork. "Done."

"That was fast."

"I know. I'm good."

She put everything back into the first-aid kit. Just as she'd turned toward the hallway, he spoke again.

"You know, I'm still a little miffed you won't consider marrying me for convenience."

Claire turned to look at him, and at the hint of insecurity she saw on his face she opted to forgo sarcasm. "Don't take it personally."

His brow furrowed and he raked his fingers through his dark hair. "Is there another way to take it?"

She hesitated, unsure if she should say what was on her

mind. She glanced over his shoulder to the window, but there was only darkness beyond the glass. She looked back at him. It seemed he wasn't going to let this go, so she might as well tell him the truth.

"I decided a long time ago I'd never marry someone who has a dangerous job."

He cocked his head, confusion marring his features before understanding dawned. "Is…? Does it have something to do with your dad?"

All Graham knew was her dad had been a pilot and had died in a plane crash when she was a kid. She hadn't given details beyond that to anyone except Mia, and her best friend would never betray what had been said in confidence.

Claire nodded, reaching across her body to grip her upper arm. "He was actually an aerobatics pilot who did air shows. He performed those over-the-top stunts that make your breath catch and your heart stop. At first, I thought it was the coolest thing ever, and loved when he did a local show where I could watch. My friends loved it, too. He'd let us climb around in the plane and sit in the cockpit, and sometimes even took me out for a flight."

If Graham wanted to hide his surprise he was doing a terrible job. His eyes had widened and his mouth dropped open slightly.

"I noticed my mom never watched during a local show and paced during the away ones, waiting for him to call when it was over. It wasn't as bad when he was flying transport routes, which he did for a steady paycheck, but I could still see the worry in her eyes when she knew he was in the air. It consumed her. And no one can say it was silly or for naught, because it turns out she was right. Those maneuvers look dangerous because they are." Her voice cracked at the end and she hated it. Memories tried to force their way into her consciousness but she pushed them back like an unruly crowd at a metal concert. She swallowed and took a couple of breaths, willing the tears to stay contained. "I can't be that person, Graham. I won't live like that."

Graham gripped the back of his neck with one hand. "I— I'm sorry, Claire. I can't imagine how it must have felt to lose your dad. And while I'm not married, I know how it feels to worry about the people you love. The guys at the station are my family and anytime we go on a call or I hear about what happens when I'm off, I worry about my brothers and sisters in uniform." His dark eyes searched her face and he offered her a sad smile. "So I actually understand your reasoning pretty well. Still, I think I'm quite the catch for an arranged, emotionless marriage."

She let out a laugh, thankful that he lightened the mood a little.

And true to form, he didn't stop there. "Alas, I'm willing to accept arranged, emotionless sex instead."

"What's all this about emotionless? I experience several emotions when I think about you."

His grin slipped. "You do?"

"Sure. Irritation, exasperation, hostility. Take your pick."

"Hostility is probably best for sex."

"You think so?"

He nodded, his gaze locked on hers. She looked back at him for a few moments, feeling suddenly warm.

She blinked and spun around, and just before she entered the bathroom Graham called out one last thing.

"I meant what I said, Claire. You look amazing tonight."

★ ★ ★

"I kissed Graham."

Mia's fork hit her plate with a clatter. *"What?"*

Claire's forehead hit the table. "I know," she mumbled into the wood.

"How...when...why...how?"

Claire didn't move for a beat. When she raised her head, her best friend gawked at her, hand still poised in the air.

The low buzz of conversation throughout the restaurant was welcome. It gave Claire a few minutes to think without the urge to fill a dead silence. Why had she even brought it up in the first place?

"I don't know what happened. I was at work and a fireman came in with an injury and my mind immediately went to Graham. I didn't know if he was working, if he'd been at the same fire, or if he was okay. He didn't answer my texts and I sort of freaked out."

Mia's expression went somber. "Understandable, after what you went through with your dad."

"I know. But I've been friends with him for a long time, and he's been a firefighter for most of it. If something major happened in town and it was plastered on the news, then yeah— Graham would cross my mind. But not otherwise. That day it felt...different."

"Why?"

"I'm not sure. I've been asking myself the same thing. Before he and I were roommates, I think it was just an out-of-sight, out-of-mind sort of thing. But it feels different now, being around him so much more where I'm constantly reminded of what he does. I hear stories about the calls he responds to and I see him walk out the door in that navy uniform and find myself wondering if he'll walk back through it at the end of his shift."

Mia nodded slowly, her eyes soft. "That would be hard, even for someone who's just a friend." She emphasized the word *friend*. "Have you...been feeling *more* toward him lately?"

Claire's phone buzzed on the table, and Graham's name appeared.

"Speak of the devil," Claire muttered, swiping across to see what he wanted.

Graham: What's your email address?

Claire: Why?

Graham: I'm ordering a new body carrier for Gertrude and get a discount if I invite a friend to their website.

Claire: No

Graham: Come on, please? It'll save me like thirty bucks.

Claire: I don't even have a dog.

Graham: Don't you have an email you never use for shit like this?

Graham: Trade—I won't touch the thermostat for a week.

Claire: Fine. PinkSparkles91@zzmail.com.

Graham: You fucking with me?

Claire: I WAS TWELVE

Graham: Apologies, Ms. Sparkles. Thanks

Claire rolled her eyes and dropped her phone to the table. Mia wore an amused expression on her face.

"Sorry about that. And to answer your question, no. That's

what's weird. I'm not interested in dating him. You and I both know he's allergic to commitment, and I want to find the person I can settle down and build a life with. But when I got home after that shift, I was out of my head with worry, and the second I saw him and realized he was all right, something in me shifted. I just did it without thinking."

"That doesn't have to mean anything, though," Mia said. "I mean, I'd probably kiss you if I thought you were in serious danger and then saw you in person, safe and whole."

Claire appreciated Mia's attempt to downplay the situation, because that's what she wanted. But it wasn't the same. "But would you lift me on the furniture and put your tongue in my mouth?"

"Shit, no." Mia winced. "No offense."

"None taken."

Mia leaned in with wide eyes. "He lifted you onto the furniture? Where?"

"His dresser." Claire dropped her forehead into her palm. "It was so hot, Mia. The best kiss I've ever had. He's, um, very thorough."

Her friend's eyebrows shot up and she offered an appreciative nod. "Well, all right then."

"But that's weird, right? He's my friend and I don't want to be in a relationship with him. We're roommates, we fight all the time, and we want completely different things out of life."

"You don't have to want to be in a relationship with him to want to hook up," Mia pointed out. "And the fighting might be like…kindling."

Claire couldn't help but laugh. "That's what he said."

"It could be fun."

Claire's eyebrows went up. "You're encouraging me to kiss Graham? To *keep* kissing Graham?"

"Why not?"

"I thought I just explained that pretty well."

"I don't know." Mia picked up her fork. "Noah and I think—"

"Noah and you? You two have talked about us?"

Mia snorted. "Of course."

"The hell?"

"What? You two together are, like, the embodiment of foreplay."

Claire scrunched her nose. "Ew."

Mia rolled her eyes. "Not for *us*. I mean you two always put off this vibe like…you don't like each other but at the same time you want to rip each other's clothes off."

Claire stilled. Blinked.

Was that true?

Things had gone from zero to sixty pretty damn fast in his room that day. She could see herself getting carried away with him.

"There have been a few times I've wondered if you two had hooked up and you just hadn't told me. Like that time we rented that cabin last year and you shared a room."

Claire scoffed. "You seriously think I wouldn't tell you?"

Mia shrugged. "It's a little different now that we don't live together. I mean, I hope you'd tell me, but I'd understand if you felt weird about it, since it's Graham." She looked up, her dark eyes flashing. "But if you told Reagan before me, I'd be pissed."

"You're my best friend no matter where you live. You're the first and only person I've told about the kiss. Promise."

"Good." Mia twirled pasta around her fork and, before taking a bite, wagged her eyebrows. "So what happens next?"

Claire took a long, slow sip of wine and pressed her back against the booth. "Nothing? He wanted to keep it going, but I already told him I didn't want that kind of an arrangement right now."

"But you liked kissing him."

"So? There's a lot of things I'd probably like but won't do. Like spend my savings on a loaded luxury car or eat ice cream three meals a day—" Claire held up a hand when Mia opened her mouth. "That day sophomore year doesn't count. I was hungover and you know it. Sometimes we don't do things out of self-preservation."

Mia allowed that, but tilted her head a little. "Why is not kissing Graham a form of self-preservation? Are you worried you'll develop feelings for him?"

"No. I just figure if I've got someone to take care of the physical stuff, I won't be as motivated to go out and meet new people. What if I miss an opportunity with a great guy— maybe even my future husband—because I stayed in to get with my commitment-phobe roommate?"

"I guess that's true. But it could also take some of the pressure off. Maybe you'd be a little more relaxed when it came to the dating scene, and wouldn't waste your time on guys you didn't really like. Plus, it's not every day a hot man offers to be a woman's plaything. Seems like a waste to not at least give it a try."

Claire's eyes went wide. "Who are you and what did you do with my modest best friend?"

"She got married and discovered what it's like to have a hot-man plaything." Her cheeks flushed. "I highly recommend it."

"I bet you do."

Mia laughed, fanning herself. "You could join an online dating site and have a good time with Graham until the program matches you with your future husband. Just think about it, okay?"

"Why?"

"Because you could use a little fun and something tells me Graham is the perfect person to give it to you."

★ ★ ★

When Claire got home that night, she found Graham and Reagan in the living room watching *The Office* reruns.

"Hey, Ms. Sparkles," Graham greeted.

"Shut up."

Reagan grinned. "Ooh, new nickname?"

"Don't ask," Claire said, then glared at Graham. "Shouldn't you be thanking me? I did you a favor."

Graham sobered. "You're right. Thank you for doing that."

"It worked, then? I'm not sure I even remember the password to that account anymore. I don't know if it's even active."

"Yep, got my discount code."

"Good." Beers would be on him next time they went out.

She joined them for an episode, then decided she'd better get ready for bed. It was Friday night, but she worked tomorrow and had to be at the hospital before seven. She stood, but her "good night" was interrupted by the shrill ringtone from Reagan's phone.

Reagan scooped it off the coffee table. "Sorry." She answered the call and stepped onto the porch.

Claire glanced back at Graham and found him looking at her. She paused for a beat, thinking about everything she and Mia had discussed tonight. Offering an awkward smile, she escaped to her room. After changing into a tank top and leggings, she stepped back out and into the shared bathroom to brush her teeth. She rinsed her mouth and straightened, pulling her curly blond hair over her shoulder, staring at herself in the mirror.

*What do you want?*

With a heavy sigh, she turned to head back to her room and ran smack into Graham's chest.

"Whoa, sorry." He grabbed her arms lightly at the same time her hands went to his waist.

Damn, he was firm.

And he smelled good. Again. How was it she was just noticing this?

He released her and cocked an eyebrow. "You done in here?"

She nodded and moved to the side so he could pass. She went to her room but left the door open, and when he came out of the bathroom she called out before she could talk herself out of it.

"Graham?"

He appeared in the doorway, eyeing her perched on the edge of her bed. "Yeah?"

"Could, um, could I talk to you for a second?"

"Sure." He walked in and sat beside her, leaving a perfectly respectable distance between them.

Claire tucked her hands between her knees. "I told Mia that we kissed."

His brows shot up. His cut was healing nicely. "You did?"

"I'm sorry, I should have asked you first. I hope that's okay—"

Graham laughed lightly. "I don't care. I'm just surprised. I didn't think you wanted anyone to know."

"I tell her everything. She'll probably tell Noah."

He shrugged. "That's fine. Thanks for telling me, though, so I can be prepared." He adopted a terrible impression of Noah's voice. "Hey, man, I heard you and Claire kissed. What's the deal?" He angled himself as if talking to someone else. "Yeah, I told her I wanted to do other stuff but she turned me down. I cried. A lot."

Claire punched his shoulder. "You did not."

He laughed, a rich, deep sound, drawing her attention to his mouth. She thought, not for the first time, how handsome he was when he smiled.

She swallowed and told herself to be assertive. She was a strong, independent woman, and could tell a man what she wanted. "That's actually what I wanted to talk about. The, um, turning-down part."

"What about it?"

"Is this a 'no take-backs' situation? Or is the offer for a friends-with-benefits arrangement still on the table?"

"When you tell me no, I'll respect it. Always. But you can one hundred percent take it back."

"Really?" Mia's suggestion about the online dating service popped into her head. Situations like what she was proposing with Graham were only successful when both parties were completely honest, right? "Even if I'm simultaneously on the lookout for the guy who's perfect for me?"

"Fine by me." His eyes held steady as he scooted a few inches closer. Slowly. "Are you taking your no back, Claire?"

"I—I think so."

He shook his head. "Not good enough. You need to be sure."

She paused, inhaling deeply and letting the scent of his toothpaste flood her senses. She leaned closer. "I'm saying yes, Graham."

His brown eyes darted between hers.

Did he not believe her? Think she wasn't certain she wanted to do this?

She resisted the urge to fidget or talk in circles and instead let her gaze roam his handsome face, hoping confident silence would speak more to her decision.

Would she really be able to touch this man whenever she wanted? In a way that wasn't just friendly? Her attention snagged on his mouth, and the way his lower lip went a little crooked when it stretched into a grin.

Like now.

Damn. That smile was devastating.

He reached up with one hand, tracing the curve of her jaw with his thumb. "Well, then." Her breath caught as he leaned in and kissed the corner of her mouth.

Her lips parted with a soft gasp and without thought, she lifted her hand to grip his muscular forearm. He brushed a kiss to her cheek, teasing her, somehow in perfect control despite having had no idea this would happen thirty seconds ago.

Claire, on the other hand, had thought about it the entire drive across town, and she was a nervous wreck.

Maybe that was the problem. She'd gone inside her head, which was the last place she wanted to be when Graham's lips were within kissing distance.

She pressed her palm to his cheek and angled his face to hers, slanting her mouth over his. He moved even closer, the warmth of his thigh flush against hers, and her other hand slid into his thick hair.

A tiny part of her had wondered if the other night was a fluke and the only reason she'd gotten so hot so fast was because of the situation with the injured firefighter.

Judging by the race of her heart and immediate pulse of desire shooting to her core now, that wasn't the case.

His strong fingers moved slowly down her back, leaving trails of heat in their wake, and the wet tip of his tongue traced the seam of her lips. The coil in her stomach released at the same time her brain registered the slam of the front door.

Claire jerked back and pushed Graham to his feet. Reagan walked past, eyes on her phone screen.

Wide-eyed, Claire just stared at Graham, who now had an amused expression on his face. Mixed with the rapid rise and fall of his chest and the dilation of his pupils, he made quite the picture.

"I'm sorry," she said in a low voice, smoothing her hair. "I, um..."

"Don't want Reagan to know?"

She shook her head, thankful he kept his voice down.

"That might pose a problem, seeing as how we live with her."

"I know. But I can be discreet if you can."

"She was there when we discussed this, you know."

"That was when we were waiting several years. At which point I figured we wouldn't all be living under the same roof anymore."

"Planning to get rid of me?"

"Gertrude nearly gets you kicked out of this condo on the daily. I have seniority and call the shots around here."

Graham wisely remained silent, but the corner of his mouth twitched.

"Reagan will be done with graduate school by then. Surely she'll have moved on. Anyway, that's not the point. I just... don't want to make a spectacle of ourselves, okay?"

Graham stuffed his hands into his pockets. "For this to work, the first thing you'll need to do is tell yourself it's not a big deal. That's how an arrangement like this works."

Claire smoothed her hair back. "I know that in theory, but...I've never done this before. I didn't think I had it in me, but tonight at dinner Mia convinced me—"

"*Mia* convinced you?"

The disbelief in his tone forced a knowing laugh from her. "I was shocked as hell, too. I'm the one who made the decision, though. I want to do this and give it a try, but I didn't mean for us to like...start now."

It had just been difficult to resist when he was sitting that close and smelled that good, and leaned in like that...

"The way you were looking at me said otherwise."

"Well!" She flung a hand in his direction. "Look at you!"

Oh, hell. That *smile*.

"Maybe this is a bad idea," she blurted out, suddenly worried about her ability to keep her hands off him. Two kisses and her hormones were revolting and demanding satisfaction.

Graham, that spectacular smile still lighting up his face, slowly shook his head. "You don't mean that."

"Maybe I do. I'm already stressed out."

"You weren't when it was just us and you weren't thinking about anything else."

Her eyes slid closed as she thought about it.

*Accurate.*

He kept going, probably so she didn't have even more time to do something as awful as think. "I'm going to my room now. When you're ready, just let me know."

"Reagan leaves next week to visit her family in Florida and she'll be gone for almost a month. I think I'll be more comfortable if it's just us."

Graham shrugged and turned, giving her a sexy wink over his shoulder as he went. "Sure, if you think you can wait that long."

# 6

Graham's roommate was having a negative impact on his sleep routine.

Not Reagan. She was nice and all, and probably cute, too, but she was more than a decade younger than him.

His brain didn't even consider going there.

No, it was one hundred percent Claire.

Sweet fuck, he wanted to touch her everywhere. He'd always found her attractive and respected her confident, take-no-shit attitude, which only made her hotter. He'd never seriously considered more than friendship, though, because he knew he couldn't give her what she wanted.

Not long-term.

Then, last year when she'd suggested that ridiculous marriage pact, it seemed like the perfect solution. He'd never have guessed she'd be down for an arrangement of convenience, simply agreeing to be someone's companion because they'd hit a certain age where they'd be considered past their prime.

Who set that benchmark, anyway? He was closing in on forty and still looked pretty damn good.

Either way, it worked perfectly for him since he wasn't looking for an emotional connection. He was all for committing to someone he trusted, liked (most of the time), and was attracted to, as long as they understood he wouldn't be talking about his feelings and all that.

Thus far, women hadn't seem interested in that.

So Claire's idea was a perfect solution. Because despite his disinterest in a serious relationship, he still preferred not to be alone. He enjoyed the company of others. Thrived in it, actually. And while he was all for getting Noah and Mia together back then, he'd thought she was serious about their part, too.

With everything she'd been through with her dad, he understood why she didn't consider him marriage material. He really did. Ever since she mentioned it, he'd wondered if things would be different if he'd chosen another career path. But after seeing how the firemen worked tirelessly trying to save Nathan the night of their accident, and stabilized Graham and Noah until the ambulance arrived, he'd never wanted to do anything else.

Plus, his job wasn't the only dangerous thing he did.

Case in point: on the agenda today? Rock climbing with Noah, Chris, and Tyler in Eldorado Canyon.

Graham would climb anywhere—indoors, outside—and on any surface—sandstone, granite, ice. He'd climb with anyone—trad climbers, sport climbers, a first-timer, or a world champion. Give him a rope and a harness and he'd be there.

He'd camp, hike, and mountain bike anywhere, too.

In the winter he enjoyed skiing, though it was the adventure he was least experienced with.

Point being, he spent his free time pushing his body in a multitude of dangerous pursuits, and he didn't see that ending anytime soon. He didn't have to think about anything except strategy and how his body moved, and the associated risks never held him back. Especially not when it came to climbing—his favorite—the higher and more difficult the better.

Today wouldn't be one of those since they were taking Tyler, but still. There was always risk. So Claire had a point, and he didn't see that changing until he was too old to get out of bed.

Graham picked up Noah on his way, and Tyler had planned to meet Chris at the store and ride with him to the canyon.

"Hey, man," Graham greeted through the open window.

Noah tossed his gear in the back before settling into the passenger seat. "Morning."

They rode the first half hour in comfortable silence. Noah, who was quiet at baseline, was even less inclined to converse early in the morning.

When they skirted the outer limits of Boulder, Noah took a long drink of coffee and turned to Graham.

"We're taking a beginner out today, you said?"

"Yeah. His name's Tyler. Chris met him at the store and learned he was new to town, so he brought him out mountain biking with us last week. Tyler said he likes to climb, too, but doesn't have a lot of experience."

"That's cool. We haven't taken it easy in a while. Might be kind of nice."

"I told Chris we'd meet them at the usual spot. He said he'd pick the climbing routes. I'm assuming we'll stick with single pitches with a top rope today."

"Fine by me."

As they neared the park, Graham felt the telltale hum of excitement spread through his marrow. The day was almost perfect—sunny and warm, even if it was a touch windy. A few wispy clouds dotted the blue sky, and hopefully they'd get lucky and the rain he'd seen forecast in the afternoon would head south.

When they met up with Chris and Tyler, Graham introduced Noah to the new guy. The coffee must have finally kicked in because Noah engaged Tyler in friendly chatter as they walked to whatever face Chris had picked out to start the day.

"Graham said you just moved here?"

"Yeah, about a month ago."

"What do you think so far?"

"Love it. I've always wanted to live close to the mountains. My girlfriend's still back in Arkansas, though, so that part sucks. She's looking for jobs up here, so hopefully we won't be doing the long-distance thing for long."

"I don't know how people do that," Graham put in. He had enough trouble keeping things going with women who lived in the same city as him, let alone several states away.

"It's not easy," Tyler admitted. "It helps knowing it's temporary."

"And for the right person, it's worth it," Noah added.

Graham shot him a good-natured eye roll. "You would say that." He glanced at Tyler. "Noah's wife has him wrapped around her little finger."

Noah appeared unbothered.

"How long have you been married?" Tyler asked.

"A little over a year."

"Nice. Don't they say the first year is the hardest?"

"I don't know, but it's been pretty damn incredible if you ask me."

Graham groaned.

"Just wait," Noah said with a laugh, "one of these days you'll get it."

"Don't hold your breath," Graham muttered.

Noah was as loyal as they came and apparently still held out some fantastical hope Graham might settle down someday.

Unlikely.

A few minutes later Chris stopped in front of one of the routes popular for beginners. It wouldn't last long, but they'd come early enough they had the spot to themselves.

Climbing was one of the few things worth getting up early for.

Graham dropped his helmet, ropes, and shoes and uncapped his water while Chris told Tyler about the climb.

"I'm not sure if you've done multipitch routes, but just to be on the safe side I thought we'd start here. It gets a little awkward halfway up, but the bolts are in good spots and it's relatively even. We'll set up a top rope for belay." Chris glanced at Graham. "Wanna handle the anchor?"

"Sure."

"Climb it or you can get to the top on foot if you head around the north side."

He'd rather climb but it would be faster to hike, and they'd be waiting on him. He tossed his water to the ground, grabbing the equipment. He headed toward the path Chris pointed out but paused when Noah called out to him.

"Take your helmet for when you get up there," Noah said, holding it out. "Just in case. It's a decent height."

Graham didn't argue, looped one finger through the strap, and got moving. The mountain air filled his lungs as he hiked, the sounds of nature surrounding him.

Right on cue, he thought about Nathan.

Sometimes he wondered how different he might be if his best friend hadn't died. He and Noah would have had an extra man on every climbing trip, for one.

Would Graham have been a godfather by now? They'd been at Nathan's bachelor party the night of the accident, which meant he'd have been married for a decade and, knowing Nathan, would probably have had a kid or three by now.

Like Noah, Nathan had always been the relationship type. Neither had held the same casual, no-strings-attached dating style Graham maintained—one of the few things Graham and the Agnew brothers differed on.

Noah wasn't the kind of friend who pushed his opinions on anyone, so even if he joked Graham would settle down one day, he'd leave well enough alone if Graham asked him to. He let people be who they were and accepted them as such. Nathan, on the other hand, had always been sure his was *the* opinion and wouldn't stop until he'd made his case. Repeatedly. About women and anything else.

Would he have sold Graham on the idea of matrimony eventually?

Unlikely.

Graham brushed the thought away when he reached the top of the climb. Mostly because the guys would be able to see him from below and to avoid Noah yelling at him when he got back down, he put on his helmet. He grabbed four carabiners, a sling, and the rope and approached the edge.

Glancing down, he saw Chris and Tyler adjusting their harnesses. Noah glanced up and yelled something.

"What?" Graham called down.

"Anchor yourself!"

*Shit.* Usually if he placed a top rope he did it after climbing up and placing several pros along the way to catch him if he fell. Since he'd come up on foot he wasn't on belay and had no safety net.

Leave it to Noah to keep him in line.

Just as he spun around to double back to where he'd dropped his gear, a strong gust of wind whooshed past, knocking him off balance.

His foot slipped and his arms flailed, seeking purchase and finding none. His stomach plummeted as his back hit the rock and gravity took hold. Graham had one last thought before pain shot through his body and everything went dark.

*If I survive this, Claire's gonna kill me.*

# 7

Claire always tuned in at the mention of firefighter injuries. But traumas from the plethora of outdoor activities Denver and surrounding areas were known for?

Not so much.

They were just such frequent fliers in the ER she expected at least one per shift. Which was why when she heard Ruthie take the call about a climber coming by ambulance with several injuries, she'd caught very little other than to hear the patient would go straight to the trauma bay upon arrival.

Must be pretty bad, then.

Claire sat in front of her computer to chart and catch her breath for a few seconds. Two of the three patients currently assigned to her were high maintenance and she'd been running around for the last three hours getting medication, bringing ice chips and warm blankets, and providing written information on various potential medical conditions.

She hadn't even taken a break to pee.

Might be wishful thinking, but she hoped things would be

different once she was on shift as a provider. She loved being a nurse, always had, but had never been great at taking directions from other people. She'd still report to a physician once she officially made the move, but she'd also have more autonomy than she did now.

She didn't expect things to be less stressful, per se, but in most situations the more control she had, the better she fared. She'd take on more liability, but also had room to be part of the decision-making team. She'd be the one ordering medications rather than giving them, the one interpreting and responding to lab results rather than the one drawing the blood. Each piece was critical to do well, but she was ready for a change.

Progress in the love department hadn't budged in a long time, so she focused on taking a step up in her career instead.

Sirens in the distance edged closer and finally shut off when the vehicle parked outside the unit. The doors to the ambulance entrance burst open and the standard flurry of movement commenced. Paramedics barked information to the receiving staff, and the attending physician who had been alerted of the incoming patient shouted orders and demands to get out of his way as they wheeled the patient to the nearest trauma bay.

Claire glanced up briefly, planning to stay well out of the way at this point, but her eyes landed on a familiar face.

Noah stood just inside the doors, his face pale and eyes wild. It took her several long seconds to piece together why he was here, and why he'd come through the ambulance entrance. Fear shot through her like a bolt of lightning, and she jumped to her feet, catching a glimpse of the patient's lower half before the door swung shut to the trauma bay.

Pushing aside the unnatural angle of his right leg, her brain homed in on the green shorts—the same ones Graham often wore climbing.

She blinked twice before her brain caught up.

"Noah," she cried out, and his eyes found hers. She stumbled toward him, pushing off the counter, but with each step her lungs squeezed tighter. She tried to breathe but her throat was closing in. At the edge of the nursing station she gripped a chair and slid to the floor, knowing she might pass out if she remained on her feet.

Noah was at her side immediately, kneeling down and with one hand on her shoulder.

"It's Graham?"

He nodded, his expression grave. "I don't know what happened. He was at the top of a cliff to anchor the rope. We haven't top-roped in a while, but it's basic, beginner stuff and I've seen him do it a hundred times. I noticed he didn't anchor himself first, but I don't know why. I was at the bottom, waiting. We all were." He shifted onto his knees and squeezed his eyes shut. "Claire, when he hit the ground I thought he was dead."

Her stomach heaved and she whirled around to reach behind the counter for a trash can. By the time she'd emptied her stomach, Ruthie was there, her hand on Claire's back. "What's wrong? Are you okay?"

Claire shook her head and lifted a shaking finger to the room where they'd taken Graham. "That's my friend. My roommate."

"Shit." Ruthie's forehead wrinkled in concern. "Hang tight. I'll see if I can move your patients around, okay?"

Claire pressed a trembling hand to her forehead and nodded.

"But...you can't go in there right now." Ruthie's eyes were empathetic but stern. "Okay?"

Claire's whole body began to tremble, and Noah put an arm around her.

"Is there somewhere we can go?" he asked Ruthie. "While we wait?"

Ruthie finished tying the plastic bag and pulled it out of the trash can, then glanced around the ER. "Take her over there to pod 7. You can pull the curtain. I need to speak to a few people and I'll be there soon, okay?"

Noah helped Claire to her feet, though as they crossed the shiny linoleum floor, she wasn't quite sure who was supporting who. His skin had gone past white and was now tinted a shade of green, which could have been from witnessing Claire getting sick, or everything hitting him now that he was out of the enclosed environment of the ambulance.

He deposited Claire into a chair against the wall and pulled the curtain before he sat in the chair beside her.

She stared straight ahead at the clean hospital bed in the center of the room. "What did they say on the ride over?"

"A lot of stuff I didn't understand," Noah said. "Broken leg, but not through the skin. Likely concussion. Thank God he was wearing a helmet. They put a tube in his throat..." His voice cracked and he dropped his face into his hands.

They had to intubate him? Another wave of nausea crashed over her, and she slumped over and pressed her forehead to Noah's shoulder. "Did they mention his blood pressure? Give him any medications?"

"I don't know. I don't think so."

If they'd been required to give vasopressors to maintain blood pressure, Noah would have noticed. That was good. Hopefully it meant Graham hadn't gone into shock, or lost so much blood he wasn't perfusing.

Panic decreased a tiny, tiny notch.

"Was he awake?"

"Not when I first got to him. But he came to, seemed really confused, then passed out again." Noah shuddered and pressed his palms to his eyes. "I—I can't… This is too much like what happened with Nathan—"

Claire immediately put a firm hand on his shoulder. "Did you call Mia?"

"Not yet."

"Call her. You need her."

He sniffed and nodded, then pulled out his phone.

While he spoke to Mia, Claire stood and peeked out from the curtain, eyeing the room Graham was in. A few people came and went, and they weren't running. Or covered in blood.

That was good.

Another tiny improvement in her mental state, but she wouldn't completely calm down until she spoke to the doctor.

She needed answers, and needed to know exactly how bad it was.

★ ★ ★

Fractured tibia and fibula.

Concussion.

Bruised jaw.

Three bruised ribs and too many muscle and tendon strains to mention.

*It could have been worse.*

He'd spent several hours in the ER and was transferred to the ICU. Claire had been at his bedside for hours and so far ORL, ortho, trauma, and nutrition had been by.

For a man who liked attention, it was too bad he was so loaded on pain meds he couldn't enjoy it.

Not that he'd be able to flap his gums at any of them, though—which would have been his favorite part. If he could talk, he'd say, "I'm fine" or "You shoulda seen that fall" or "No worries, I'll be back on the side of a mountain in no time."

But there would be no talking for a while. The doctors determined he didn't need airway support and extubated him, but in the brief moments when he'd been awake he'd had trouble talking. It wasn't common, but vocal cord injury from the tube was possible, and the doctor said even if he wanted to talk—which many people didn't for several days because of throat pain—he might not be able to for a week or two.

Graham was gonna be pissed.

The leg would be an even bigger problem. It was a complete fracture that required surgery, which they'd take him away for any minute now. He'd need a cast and wouldn't be able to put weight on it for several weeks. For the most active man she knew, Claire was certain when he came to and heard the news, he'd be devastated.

Over time he'd lose muscle and to regain function would need physical therapy. In fact, his ability to get back to the active lifestyle he loved was in question. He should be able to walk again, but doing things at the level he had before…it was possible he'd never be there again.

Patient rooms in the trauma ICU only allowed one visitor at a time, so Noah, Mia, and Chris were in the waiting room. Claire had rotated with the others at first, but finally used the excuse that as the only health care professional of the group she wanted to be present as the specialists came through. She knew which questions to ask and better understood the news they passed on.

But really, she just wanted to be with him.

Her gaze traveled down his broken body and she took in a shaky breath. His jaw was a little swollen from the fall and several lacerations marred his cheek, forehead, and right arm. His leg was temporarily immobilized with a splint until surgery.

She worked her way back up and paused when she got to his eyes. They were closed, but a slight furrow of his eyebrows made him look anything but peaceful. Was he hurting even now?

Claire scooted to the edge of the chair and eyed the monitor perched behind the bed. His blood pressure was a little high, as was his heart rate. Despite the medication lulling him to sleep, it seemed his pain wasn't controlled.

Just as she grabbed the bedside remote with the call button, a woman in scrubs knocked lightly on the door frame.

"Hi, I'm Nat— Claire?"

"Hey, Natalie."

Natalie, a surgery tech, blinked. She glanced at the ER scrubs Claire was still wearing. "What are you doing in here?"

"This is a friend of mine."

"Oh. I'm so sorry."

Claire nodded. "Thanks. Are you taking him?" If he was about to go under anesthesia, more pain meds were a moot point, so she put the remote down.

Natalie nodded. "Yep. Surgery should take a few hours, plus another half hour in recovery."

"Okay. Who's doing it?"

"Dr. Mackey."

"Good." He was the best. "Take good care of him, okay?"

"We will."

Claire rose and helped unhook various monitors and after Natalie wheeled Graham out of the room, went to the waiting room.

Three pairs of eyes looked at her when she walked in.

Claire fell into a chair opposite them. "They just took him for surgery."

"What do they do, exactly?" Noah asked.

"I only have a basic understanding of it, but they'll put the bones back into place using screws, plates, or rods, depending on the damage."

"And after it heals he'll be back to normal?" Chris asked.

"It's too early to tell. I expect it won't be the same, but hopefully he'll regain near normal function."

Noah blew out a heavy breath and Mia rubbed his back. "Being on this side of things is worse than being the one in the hospital," she said.

Claire couldn't compare since she'd never been admitted. She could only relate it to caring for patients in the ER, and this was way worse. At least when she was on shift, she was actively doing things. The helplessness of being a visitor at the bedside was difficult to wrap her mind around. She'd been there for Mia during her chronic illness, but Noah had usually been the one to barge his way in to guard the bedside while Claire took second, making sure everyone had changes of clothes, cell phone chargers, and snacks from the vending machines.

"Did anyone call Graham's parents?" she asked.

"I did," Noah said. "Found his dad's number in his phone. I got voice mail, so I left a vague message asking him to call back."

Claire nodded and slumped farther into the uncomfortable chair. Mia eyed her.

"When's the last time you ate?" Mia asked.

Claire opened her mouth, then paused, unable to remember.

Chris stood. "I'll go get her something."

"I'm not hungry," Claire protested, but he was already walking away. She pinched the bridge of her nose and closed her eyes. Several minutes of silence passed, and in that moment she was thankful for Noah's natural quiet and Mia's ability to pick up on the emotions around her.

The same emotions swirling through Claire were probably sifting through her friends' bodies, too. Maybe even more so in Noah's, who was arguably the closest to Graham and the one who'd known him the longest.

*He's okay. He's alive, and that's what matters.*

Claire repeated the words in her head. She knew they were true, but she also knew how difficult the road ahead would be.

And as his friend, roommate, and a registered-nurse/nurse practitioner, she'd be with him every step of the way.

Whether he wanted her there or not.

# 8

Everything hurt.

His leg. His face. His throat. His torso.

His dick felt okay, though, which was a nice surprise.

Graham swallowed, wincing at the sensation, like glue sliding down sandpaper, and a bolt of agony shot through his jaw. His eyes flew open, the pain bringing him completely awake.

As he gripped something soft beneath him, his eyes darted around his surroundings. White ceiling, a hospital bed, a dry-erase board posted on the opposite wall. A thick, white cast on his right leg.

Slowly, it all came flooding back.

Standing at the top of the cliff.

The fall.

The crack of his bone. Or bones…it was unclear at this point.

A few flashes of Noah's face, and others from inside the ambulance. One of Claire's blond hair, though he didn't know when or where. Maybe he was projecting, because a flicker of movement in the corner of his eye caught his attention, and her face suddenly hovered over him.

She spoke softly but quickly, her wide, hazel eyes reflecting an emotion he'd never seen there before. "Graham, don't talk, okay? I know that's the first thing you'll try to do, but you can't right now. You had a climbing accident. You had a tube in your throat for a while and it will hurt if you try."

Before he could even process what he was doing, he immediately opened his mouth to ask what the hell she was talking about, but the pain stopped him short.

*Shit.*

"I just said don't try to talk."

He turned wide eyes on her, his brain screaming, *What? What are you talking about? I don't understand what's going on!*

He swallowed again and grimaced.

"Take a breath."

He took two. Through his nose. His mouth felt weird. It hurt, but it also felt numb, like it was disconnected from the rest of his body.

Her small hand slipped into his. "Just blink to respond. Once for yes, twice for no."

Out of habit he tried to nod, but the sharp jab through his cheek rendered him immobile.

"Your jaw is bruised on one side, like you hit your face at some point. Nothing broken in your jaw, but that right side is swollen. Are you in pain?"

He met her gaze and blinked once.

Her expression didn't change. "I'll get the nurse, then I'll tell you what I know about your injuries, okay? Do you feel lucid enough for that?"

Another single blink. *Yes.*

Claire disappeared and after what felt like less than a minute, she was back with an older woman in scrubs.

"Good to see you awake, Graham. I'm Pam and I'm the night-shift nurse. Claire said you're hurting." She grabbed a laminated strip of paper with an illustration of ten faces, each with a number below it, demonstrating the various levels of pain. "Where would you rate it?"

He pointed to the eight, and Claire flinched.

"Dr. Mackey ordered morphine for severe pain," Claire said. "No known drug allergies. I checked."

Pam raised a brow at Claire's tone, then focused on Graham. "I'd like it if we can get it below a five and keep it there. Unfortunately, it's common to wake up in pain since we can't assess it while you're asleep, but let's work together to not let it get that high again. Hang tight and I'll be right back with your meds."

The nurse left and Claire scooted closer. "What do you remember?"

Graham frowned and motioned with his hands like he was swiping through his phone. She retrieved the device from the small table next to the bed and he opened up the Notes app, ignoring the plethora of missed calls and texts.

That wasn't a yes or no question.

"Sorry."

He tapped at the screen again, thankful his hands were fully functioning.

I remember falling. Not much after that. How bad?

"Tib-fib fracture in your right leg. They took you to surgery and placed several screws. You need to stay off the leg as much as possible for the first four weeks. No weight on it, so you'll use crutches when you absolutely have to get up, like

to use the bathroom. As long as everything goes well you can start putting weight on it at around four weeks and physical therapy will start. Hopefully you'll be back to walking without a cast or crutches in two or three months."

He had to stay off his leg for four weeks? He focused on taking steady breaths so he wouldn't panic. There was no way he could live like that. He couldn't stay in bed that long. It was impossible.

Maybe she'd heard wrong. The doctor would be back to talk to him at some point, right? Surely they could work out some sort of deal. Maybe two weeks would be enough? He was in excellent shape, and maybe his body would heal faster than others.

Four weeks wasn't acceptable.

"The EMT intubated you in the ambulance. It's rare, but you have a mild vocal cord injury from the procedure. Not only will it hurt if you try, but they said you probably won't have a voice for a week or two until they heal. So no talking." Her eyes flashed with something, and she swallowed. "I know that will be hard for you."

*Fuck.* Graham closed his eyes. His brain spun, trying to keep up with the information. How much worse would this get?

He'd been so careless to not anchor himself at the top of that rock as soon as he got up there. He usually did, but the area seemed flat and steady, it wasn't his first rodeo, and it had just slipped his mind.

A hint of overconfidence and here he was, unable to climb for who knows how long.

"Otherwise you're just bruised up," Claire continued, eyeing him carefully. How much of his inner turmoil showed on his face? Normally he'd be smiling and joking around to fend off further questions about what was going on in his head—his superpower, really—but his default response was impossible right now. Once the nurse got back with the damn meds maybe he'd reassess. "It could have been a lot worse, Graham. These first few weeks will be hard but you'll get through it and be back outside before you know it."

Hard? It sounded like a nightmare. He shifted his gaze to the phone he still held.

Does the fire department know?

He exhaled carefully and kept his gaze between the phone's screen and Claire's face, trying to focus on anything but the pain.

"Yes, Noah called them. Several of the guys have already asked when they can come see you. He called your dad, too, but had to leave a message."

When can I leave?

"The hospital?"

He blinked the affirmative.

"They're ready to discharge you as soon as your pain is controlled on oral meds. I was able to take a few days off to help once you get home."

He cocked an eyebrow (good to know he had at least one cheeky move with functionality) and she looked away. Pam bustled back into the room and Graham's attention shifted to the woman who had the power to reduce the throb in his jaw and the burning sensation in his leg.

"This is two milligrams of morphine. It should work pretty quickly." She connected the syringe to his IV line. "I'll be back in fifteen minutes to see how you feel."

Pam remained in the room for a few more minutes to check

his vitals and ask some questions, most of which Claire answered on his behalf.

When Pam left, his gaze caught on the clock over the door. It was almost midnight, and Claire was still in her hospital scrubs.

Have you been here the entire time?

She nodded with a half shrug, like it wasn't a big deal. "I was in the ER when they brought you. It seemed best for me to be the one to stay. I know how things work around here and can make sure nothing slips through the cracks." She rested her forearms on the edge of the bed. "Chris was here for a while, and Noah and Mia stayed until visiting hours were over. I'm sure they'll be back tomorrow."

Graham swallowed thickly and his heart thudded with a foreign sensation, one he usually only felt after surviving some dangerous multipitch climb he probably shouldn't have attempted in the first place.

He shifted his gaze to the wall straight ahead, blinking the sensation away. He lifted his hand in a thumbs-up and closed his eyes, waiting for the soothing drugs to lull him to sleep.

★ ★ ★

They discharged him two days later, though his bedroom at the condo didn't feel any less like a prison.

The drive from the hospital to the condo had been almost cruel in its brevity. Claire had let him sit outside for a half hour while she got everything settled, then demanded he go inside to rest.

His ass had been in bed for less than an hour and it was already too long. He took stock of the room with a more critical eye, previously never having spent time in here except to sleep when he was alone and…*not* sleep when he had a guest.

Claire had done her best to prepare it for him, probably.

And when he was a little less pissed off about the situation, for which he had no one to blame but himself, he'd thank her for her efforts, maybe.

At the moment he didn't have it in him to be gracious.

With Noah's help, she'd rearranged the furniture so his bed faced the TV. His medications were lined up on the dresser and she'd set out several V-neck T-shirts and elastic-waist shorts to make dressing as easy as possible. She brought in the end table from the living room so he had more surface area beside him for his laptop, drinks, and…well, not food, because his throat hurt so much all he could tolerate was liquids.

He. Was. Starving.

She'd also brought in a chair from the kitchen table and put it next to his free weights. One of his first questions to the doctor had been how he was supposed to keep fit while staying off his leg. Dr. Mackey recommended maintaining upper body activities as much as possible, and once he was out of the large cast he could do push-ups, sit-ups, and possibly even ride an exercise bike.

Graham had immediately texted Chris and asked him to bring over a bike training stand from his outdoor store so Graham could convert his mountain bike into a stationary bike. He could set it up on the porch and ride outside. Even if it was nowhere near careening down a mountain on two wheels, he'd take what he could get.

She'd moved the framed photo of Graham and his parents closer, to the bedside table. Maybe she'd thought it might make him feel less alone. He loved his parents, but all it did was fill him with guilt. His mom was no stranger to being in bed like this, and his dad, the rock of their family, slid into the role of caretaker with ease whenever she needed him. Graham hated the thought of burdening his dad with what had happened. The man had enough to think about.

His dad was terrible about checking voice mail, and Graham assumed he hadn't gotten Noah's message yet. If he had, Graham's phone would have been blowing up. He would at some point, though, so Graham knew he had to do something. He sent his dad a text, taking extreme care with his words to ensure his dad didn't get concerned enough to call. Someone else—Claire, probably—would have to talk to him, and there was no way she'd say only what Graham instructed her to.

Hey, Dad. I had a minor climbing accident, and Noah left a message for you when I was in the hospital. I'm already out and doing great, so don't worry. Just wanted to let you know and I'll call soon to catch up.

He dropped his phone to the bed and Gertrude sidled up against his side. He rubbed her silky ears and wondered if his inability to speak was unsettling to her. His dog's presence improved his mood a little, even though Claire had tried to convince him to board her for a few weeks.

"Do you want her to jostle your leg when she jumps on the bed?" she'd asked the second he'd settled in, and with the usual disdain when she spoke about Gertrude.

He'd texted back. If this cast can't withstand a six-pound terrier, I'm concerned about its ability to protect me from anything else.

"Fine. But if she hurts you and you ask for your pain meds early, it's not happening."

Graham had just shrugged. Claire had been strangely accommodating and kind in the hospital. To him, anyway— she'd been ruthless when dealing with hospital staff, especially if she felt they were slacking on anything related to his care. Her presence had almost been…comforting.

Now that they were back at the condo, it seemed they'd returned to baseline. He could have blamed Gertrude, but he didn't think that's all it was. Based on the way she'd responded to the firefighter injury, she was probably pissed at him for getting hurt, accident or not.

She'd even barked at Reagan not to touch any of his medications.

Fine by him. He had a feeling he'd need their heated banter back and forth to keep him sane while stuck in this room. At least one thing about his daily routine could feel normal until she went back to work in a few days. He'd argued he would be fine, but through the first week, Noah had arranged to come hang out for several hours on the days Claire was gone. Beyond that, Graham hoped to be mobile enough to get around the house on his own and to start to consume a somewhat normal diet.

The urge to use the restroom hit him and he sat up, putting his weight on his hands while rotating his lower body. He didn't gauge the distance to the edge of the bed well and his injured leg bumped the wood frame before he got it all the way over. Cast or not, everything inside was still tender, and pain blazed up his shin and into his thigh.

Without thinking he clenched his teeth and a wave of agony tore through his jaw. An involuntary, silent groan of pain tried to rip from his throat. If he'd been able to, the word *fuck* would have left his mouth at a volume loud enough for the neighbors to hear. He slammed his fist on the bedside table, desperate for a physical outlet.

At the time, having a catheter while in the hospital had seemed unnecessary and he'd frankly been embarrassed to have one. Now, he realized he hadn't been prepared for the ordeal of getting up and getting to the bathroom.

And on a liquid diet, it was bound to happen often.

"Graham?" Claire rushed into his room, Reagan on her heels. "What the hell are you doing?"

Heat flooded his cheeks as he pointed a shaking hand toward the hallway.

"You're in pain. You can't get up." She checked her watch. "You're due for another dose of pain medication. Just…lay back down and tell me what you need. I'll get it."

"I can help, too," Reagan chimed in.

The mortification of this moment did nothing but piss him off. He pressed his good foot onto the floor for balance, and with jerky movements, grabbed his phone from where he'd left it on the bed. He tapped out a message and held the phone in Claire's face, glaring at her as she read.

I can take a fucking piss without help.

"I've got it, Reagan," Claire said, keeping her voice calm. "You've still got a lot of packing to do, anyway. Thanks, though."

"Okay, just let me know if I can do anything." Reagan offered him a sad smile before she disappeared into the hallway.

Claire handed his phone back and walked to the corner of his room. She reached into the bag she'd brought home from the hospital and pulled out a clear, plastic urinal that looked like a half-gallon milk jug.

"I grabbed one of these from the supply room. It might be easie—" She stopped when he shook his head.

He grabbed his crutches. The quicker he got this over with, the quicker he could take the meds.

"Graham, don't be ridiculous. It's obvious you're hurting

and this will be easier. I'm a professional, and there's no reason to be embarrassed."

He didn't look at her as he stood, using his core and arms to straighten and balance. He didn't look at her as he slowly ambled past, and he definitely didn't look at her when she positioned herself in the hallway across from the bathroom, arms crossed over her chest. He simply shut the door with his elbow, taking a small measure of satisfaction at the slam echoing through the walls.

★ ★ ★

With the exception of the alien from *ET* (because what the hell, that dude was creepy as fuck), few things scared Graham.

So it was a surprise to find sleeping in his bed, alone in his room at home, was one of them. More specifically, being unable to call out if something went wrong and he needed help. The doctor had talked about the risk of complications after surgery, like blood clots and shit. What if something like that happened and he couldn't breathe? Or talk?

At the hospital, not only had he been hooked up to various machines being monitored by other people, but he had a button to call for help. And even though Claire said not to, he'd tested his voice this morning. The doctor had been pretty vague about when it would return, so how else would he know?

So far, nothing. And yeah, it hurt.

Typical Graham would bitingly tell himself to shut up and quit worrying, and everything would be fine. But he'd never been quite so helpless or dependent on other people.

Claire would sleep in here if he asked her to, right?

That pesky fear of appearing weak and pathetic flared when he picked up his phone, but in the darkness and still a little high on pain meds, he pushed it aside.

Graham: You still up?

Claire: Yeah, need something?

Graham: Could you come in here for a sec?

She was in his room two seconds later, as if she'd already been on her way before he asked.

Gertrude immediately sat up and growled. Graham ran a soothing hand down her back and she settled back down but kept her eyes on Claire, body vibrating with a low, quieter rumble.

He adored his dog's sass.

Claire stuck her tongue out.

He kind of adored Claire's sass, too.

She took a few steps closer to the bed, passing her gaze down his body as if making sure he was all right. Her curly blond hair was piled on top of her head and the thin-strapped tank top and shorts she wore left an extreme amount of skin exposed.

Graham suddenly remembered the last conversation they'd had before his accident. Tomorrow, Reagan would leave for Florida, and he and Claire would be here alone. Which meant they would have...

He mentally slapped himself for getting hurt, then kicked himself in the balls for good measure.

"What do you need?" she asked.

She hadn't brought her phone, so he typed out a text and handed it to her.

I'm sorry about earlier.

She stared at the screen for several seconds longer than necessary, then her hazel eyes met his. "Don't worry about it."

He took his phone back, unsure what to say now. How was he supposed to ask?

His heartbeat sped up and he ran a hand through his hair, dropping his gaze to his legs and the bulky outline of the cast underneath the blanket. *It shouldn't be this hard. Just tell her you'd feel more comfortable having someone with you. Just for tonight.*

Graham lifted his eyes once more and found her assessing his face, her expression unreadable.

Words couldn't explain how badly he wished he could speak right now. He'd be able to spin it into some sort of inappropriate, innuendo-laden comment, which would get the point across but distract her from reading too much into the request.

Just Graham being Graham, trying to get a woman into his bed.

Then, she spoke. "Will your devil dog bite me if I pick her up?"

He wasn't sure, actually. Other than verbal abuse in the form of growls and trash talk, the two seemed to steer clear of each other.

Graham frowned, then shrugged. *Maybe.*

"I just thought maybe it would be best if I slept in here tonight," Claire said in her no-nonsense tone, walking around to the other side of the bed. She paused. "If that's okay. Just... in case you need something."

That same warm sensation he'd felt when she told him about his friends coming to the hospital circulated once more. He swallowed, then nodded. Quickly, he tapped out a message.

Five bucks says she leaves and pouts in the corner when you get in bed.

Claire put one hand on the mattress and leaned over to read it, then laughed. "That, or she goes for my jugular."

With a final challenging glance at Gertrude, Claire pulled back the covers and slipped under. Gertrude barked once, stood, and barked again, then looked at Graham as if to say, *Are we allowing this?*

He wanted to smile so badly, but his face hurt.

She leaped off the bed and trotted to the dog bed in the corner.

"Wow. I'd have expected her to fight a little more for you, Graham."

Women are fickle.

Another soft laugh, and Claire settled in beside him. The warmth of her body beside him immediately brought his anxiety down several notches.

He had no idea how, but someday he'd have to thank her for this.

# 9

Claire often struggled with insomnia and tonight was no different. Graham seemed restless but she couldn't blame him. The only option was to sleep on his back, and as a side sleeper herself, she could imagine how hard it would be to get comfortable. She gave him a dose of pain medication around three, which knocked him out for several hours, and Claire followed him under.

When she opened her eyes, dim sunlight streamed through the blinds and Gertrude sat like a creepy canine statue on Claire's side, staring at her.

Claire shot her a smug look. "I won this round, G," she whispered.

A hand tapped her back and she spun around to face Graham. The swelling around his jaw looked better today, and a slight upward tilt to his lips accompanied the humor dancing in his eyes. He held out his phone.

Don't heckle my dog. She's sweet if you get to know her.

"Right. The death glare she's giving me is very sweet."

Don't be so hard on her. She's jealous you got to sleep next to me, a feeling shared by all single women in the greater Denver area.

While she was glad he felt well enough to crack a joke, she couldn't just let it go. "Yeah, that heavy snoring rocked my world."

His shoulders fell and he looked away.

Claire laughed and sat up, looking over at him. His thick, dark hair was even more disheveled than yesterday but even with that and the dark bruise encompassing the entire right side of his face, he still looked handsome. "Don't be embarrassed. I'm sure it's just the swelling."

She stood and Gertrude was up like a shot, rushing across the blankets to Graham's side. He rubbed her ears fondly.

"I'm gonna go make coffee. Does a smoothie sound good? You need to take your antibiotics this morning and it's best to have something in your stomach."

He gave her a thumbs-up and pushed himself to a sitting position, the long, lean muscles in his arms flexing as he got up. He thumped across the floor on his crutches to the bathroom, slightly more efficiently than yesterday.

She heard him go back to his room while she prepared the coffee maker, then heard Reagan's voice speaking to him. Reagan soon joined Claire in the kitchen, pulling two suitcases behind her.

"You're sure you don't need a ride to the airport?" Claire asked. "Graham would be fine for an hour."

"Nah, Uber's almost here." Reagan pushed her bags to the door and faced Claire, waving a hand in the direction of Graham's room. "I'm sorry I'm leaving with everything going on. You sure you can handle it?"

Claire smiled. "I'm used to taking care of four or five patients at once, so I think I can handle one, no matter how difficult he might be. You've been dying to visit your family. Go, have fun, and don't worry about us."

"Keep me updated on how he's doing, okay?"

"You got it. Send me pictures of the beach. I'll show them to Graham so he knows what he's missing."

"You two are ridiculous." Reagan's phone beeped and she peeked out the window. "Ride's here. See you soon!"

"Have a safe trip."

When Reagan was gone, Claire grabbed fruit from the freezer and made Graham a smoothie with protein powder and almond milk. She filled a travel mug with coffee, hoping it would stay warm longer, and took both to his room.

She almost dropped everything when she saw him.

Graham sat on the edge of the bed in nothing but black boxer briefs. His shoulders hunched forward and his forearms rested on his thighs, his dark hair hanging in front of his forehead. His body was a beautiful expanse of long, curving muscles truncated by dips and valleys in between, and miles upon miles of golden, sun-kissed skin.

Even with the cast on his right leg and the scratches on his forearms, the picture he presented was so impossibly sexy it was hard to breathe. What she wouldn't give to go back to the night she'd told him she wanted to begin their arrangement, then told him they had to wait. There was no way in hell she would have pushed him away this time.

He must have sensed her presence because he straightened, cheeks flushing when he looked at her. He gripped the back of his neck in a move that was strangely endearing, and gestured to the floor with his other, where both crutches lay near his feet, but out of reach.

He was stranded.

Claire didn't get the feeling he was a man who was ever embarrassed about his body when he was with a woman. Because honestly, why would he be? But this moment wasn't on his terms. He wasn't seducing her, and he'd probably intended to be dressed before she came back in. This was a sort of weakness, which he wouldn't take well.

Claire cleared her throat, determined to treat him the same as usual in hopes it would lighten his mood. She walked forward and put the drinks on the dresser. "If this is a ploy to get me in bed with you, I have to admit it's tempting. But I'll have to ask for a rain check."

He cocked a brow and held up his hands, fingers splayed, slowly rotating them while he examined them. She marveled at his ability to shift from awkward to charming in mere seconds as he looked back at her with heat in his eyes.

Jeez, what was he doing to her? *Stay focused.* "Yes, I see your hands are in perfect working order. But when we go there, I'm gonna want a whole lot more than that."

He stilled and blinked a few times and she congratulated herself for shocking him.

"I assume you were trying to change?"

He nodded, and she wished he'd pick up his phone and communicate with her that way. She didn't want to have to keep looking at him, all undressed and stuff. *Seriously, wow.* She grabbed a shirt and pair of shorts from the top of the pile, then paused at the idea of rifling through drawers for underwear. "Were, um… Did you already change your…?"

She peeked behind her and he gave her a thumbs-up, his expression unreadable.

Thank God. She crossed the room and handed him the

clothes, then propped his crutches on the bed. "In that case, I can just give you these. Or I can help if you need me to."

He pointed to the door.

She shrugged and left, retreating to the kitchen to make her own breakfast. Her phone buzzed.

"Oh, now he wants my help," she muttered. "That didn't take long."

But Graham hadn't texted her and her hackles fell back into place.

Mia: How's he doing today? Noah wants the real answer because Graham just says he's fine.

Claire: He's not enjoying this. But otherwise, he's doing as well as can be expected. I slept in his room last night just in case he needed anything.

Mia: That was nice of you.

Claire wished she could see Mia's face or at the very least, hear her tone. As it was, she pretended it was a simple acknowledgment with no underlying questions.

Claire: Today's the first full day at home with just him and me. Check back in a few hours to see if we've killed each other yet. Last one standing: Graham, me, or Gertrude.

Mia: My money's on Gertrude. Hang in there and let us know if you need anything.

Claire ate a bowl of instant oatmeal and, after texting to make sure he was decent, went back to Graham's room to dole out his medications. He messaged her while she refilled his water.

Graham: I can handle my meds myself, you know. I'll remind you that I'm an adult and, again, that I'm an EMT.

She waited to respond until she was back in his room. She handed him the water and propped one hand on her hip. "Several of these cause drowsiness. You were out cold after the dose of hydrocodone last night, and the antibiotics and muscle relaxers need to stay on schedule. You'll be on your own soon when I have to go back to work, and I figured it would be best if I did as much as I could while I was here."

He tossed back the pills, keeping his gaze on her as he took a long drink. He picked up his phone again.

Graham: Fine. Can I make a request, though?

"Sure."

Could you always wear that?

She looked down, not even sure what she was wearing. It was a simple spaghetti strap tank top and shorts pajama combo she'd picked up on clearance at Nordstrom Rack. She hadn't thought anything of it when she popped in last night. But here in the daylight, she realized just how revealing it was. The shorts were almost to her ass, and the top left little to the imagination.

She turned on her heel. "You're an asshole."

Her phone buzzed in her hand, and she looked at it as she stepped into her own room to change.

And you're fine as hell.

Two hours later, Claire had made a grocery store run and, after checking on Graham, settled into the living room to watch *Schitt's Creek*.

Fifteen minutes in she realized how weird it was, sitting out here while he was alone in his room, probably doing the same thing.

Should she leave him be? She didn't want to come off as overbearing.

But this wasn't to lecture him on staying off his feet, or to measure out his meds. He was extremely social and didn't like being alone.

She knew because she was the same.

Huffing out a strangely irritated breath, she stood and went to his room. She peeked her head around first.

He was watching *Schitt's Creek*, too. Gertrude's growl alerted Graham to Claire's presence, so she took a few steps in.

She reached across her body and rubbed her upper arm with the opposite hand. "I was watching that, too. Want some company?"

He patted the mattress beside him.

She smiled and settled in, propping a few pillows up to lean against the headboard. "Your bed is ridiculously comfortable, you know that?"

He just winked, and she groaned.

Gertrude shifted closer to Graham, probably to get as far away from Claire as possible.

They watched two episodes before Graham texted her that he was bored out of his mind.

She looked around his room. "Did you do your exercises today?"

He nodded. He must have done it while she was at the

store, which irritated her. He didn't need to be trying to lift weights or do any of the non-weight-bearing leg exercises the doctor had recommended while he was at the condo alone.

"Want to play a video game?"

He scrunched his nose.

"Card game?"

He perked up at that, and sent her a text.

Strip poker?

Her stomach flipped at the mental image of Graham in his underwear this morning, but she'd never let it show. She cocked a brow and replied, "I already saw you almost naked this morning and it got you nowhere. I don't see the point."

If you were naked I definitely wouldn't be bored.

"Not happening."

He crossed his thick arms over his chest and she had to look away lest she change her mind. Nice arms were a particular weakness of hers, and the muscles of his forearms and biceps were so toned and perfect they could be sculpted and put on display next to a Michelangelo sculpture in Italy.

She cleared her throat. "You could borrow my Kindle if you want to read a book."

Graham's sigh was so despondent she had to laugh.

"You know, lot of people would be thrilled to have the opportunity to relax in bed for a few weeks."

Not me. I can't do this. It'll be even worse when you go back to work.

Claire racked her brain for anything else to suggest. "Have you ever tried writing? Like in a journal?"

He shook his head and his expression said he didn't intend to consider it now.

"I know it's not a common thing for guys to do, but my therapist recommended it after my dad died. I was only eleven, but I was in a bad place, and to be honest, judging by the look on your face today, there's a good chance you could get depressed as time goes on."

Smart-ass, nurse, therapist…is there anything you don't do?

"I mean it, Graham. Ignore me if you want, but I took her advice and it helped me a ton. I'd write about good things that happened to me and things I was thankful for. Not only did it pass time, but it gave me other things to think about and focus on. I still missed my dad, but my perspective improved."

Seems weird to me. Like writing to myself. What's the point if the thoughts are already in my head?

"You'd be surprised how different it comes out when you put it on paper. And you could write to someone else if that makes it less weird. Hell, you could write to me." She paused as soon as the words left her mouth, frowning a little. A journal was extremely personal. Not only that, but Graham was the last person who would ever write his feelings and share them with her. She wasn't even sure he acknowledged them to himself.

She thought quickly, hoping to spin it in a different way. Because the man really did need something to do when he was here alone. Without a way to pass the time, she could see him doing something foolish like home improvement projects or taking a drive. "When I'm at work and you're bored out of your mind, just write me a note and tell me what you'd rather be doing in that moment. Tell me places you want to go and things on your bucket list. If you don't have one, make one. You've got nothing but time."

He cocked an eyebrow and started typing.

You want me to sit here and write to you about all the things I want to do but can't? THAT'S depressing.

"It is if you want to think about it like that," she said, unable to hide the irritation seeping through her tone.

Graham just looked at her, and it was hard to tell what he was thinking. She was so patient with her patients at work, but evidently that didn't transfer to the home health sector.

"Look, all I'm saying is it might help to spend some time every day focusing on what's good. What's the first thing you'll do when the cast comes off? The first place you'll go for a beer? Where do you want to climb first when you're able to again?"

His gaze locked on hers for a second and he held up a single finger, asking her to wait as he went back to his phone screen.

Easy. I'll want to climb Eldo and have a beer at the Blue Lion. And because I'll never forgive myself for getting hurt when things were just getting good between us, the first thing I'll want to do when the cast comes off is you.

Claire sucked in a breath when she read that last line. Heat flared beneath her skin and she looked up to find his eyes on her. She took in his intense brown eyes and the lock of thick hair falling across his forehead. Holy hell, he was hotter than Clark Kent. Heart pounding, she swallowed.

"I look forward to it."

# 10

Claire slept in Graham's bed again.

He enjoyed having her beside him more than he should have. *Don't get used to it.*

While she was in the shower, Gertrude tugged her pillow off the bed. Which, for a six-pound dog, was quite a feat. Graham let it happen because at first, he couldn't figure out what Gertie was doing, and by the time he did he found it incredibly amusing.

He'd prefer two human women fighting over him but he'd take what he could get.

After breakfast, coffee, and meds, Claire scowled at Gertie as she tossed the pillow back on the bed, then settled beside him with the remote.

"What are we watching?"

He shrugged. He'd watched more TV yesterday than he had the last three months, and he was already over it.

She picked some Netflix Original he'd never heard of, and just when he started to get into it his phone rang.

It was his dad.

Claire glanced at his vibrating phone. "Want me to talk to him?"

Graham shook his head and declined the call. Thinking quickly, he sent a follow-up text.

Sorry, a little loud where I am so I can't talk. Everything OK?

It wasn't a complete lie. Claire had the volume up pretty loud…

Dad: We just wanted to check on you. I told your mother you said it wasn't a big deal, but she doesn't believe us.

Graham had sent it as a group text with his mom's cell, too, dammit.

Graham: I'm good. It's mostly my leg, but I'll be back to normal in no time. My roommate is a nurse, so she's taking good care of me.

Mom: I'm the queen of downplaying medical issues and I want more information. What kind of leg injury, and what kind of nurse is your roommate? Is this Claire or Reagan?

Why did he think he'd be able to slip this past them? He was in a different state so it shouldn't have been that difficult, but he'd never been good at lying to his parents. A twinge of guilt hit him in the gut but he stuffed it down because really, he *was* fine. He tried to be truthful but give as little information as possible.

Graham: I have to stay off it for a few weeks, which you know is driving me up the wall. It's Claire and she's an ER nurse, but is doubling as my babysitter and is keeping me on track. She could probably even get you to follow directions.

Mom: Sounds like a woman I'd like to meet. Why don't you come visit and bring her along?

Graham nearly choked. His mom was forever trying to get him to settle down.

The one time he'd brought a woman home had been a disaster, but that didn't deter her in the least.

As if she felt time was running out for her only child to get married and give her grandchildren, she'd been relentless these last couple of years. She'd clearly been paying attention anytime he mentioned his roommates, and taken note of their names.

Graham: Roommate, Mom. Not girlfriend.

Dad: She sounds like a great catch if she can keep you in line.

Graham: It's only been a few days and when it comes to pushing the boundaries of medical advice, I learned from the best.

Mom: My situation is completely different. Besides, you're my son and you should do as I say and not as I do.

Graham: Yes, Mother.

He dropped his phone to the bed and leaned his head against the headboard with a sigh.

"Everything okay?" Claire asked.

Keeping his head against the wood, he rotated his head to regard her, his dad's words scrolling through his mind. *She sounds like a great catch.* With those big, hazel eyes and wild hair that seemed untamable, she'd certainly caught his eye from the moment he met her.

She was also fun, independent, and tough. A force of nature.

So yeah, she was a great catch. Which was why he'd befriended her rather than dated her, because the latter was a surefire way to sever her from his life.

As he looked at her he tried to remember the last person he'd told about his mom. Or anything about his life growing up, for that matter. It had been several years…maybe even more than a decade. He'd learned quickly to leave that stuff off the table, especially with women.

But Claire was different, wasn't she? She was his friend, and a good one at that. They had an understanding. She didn't expect anything more from him, so what harm would it do to give her some? She wouldn't take it any sort of way, and he felt strangely calm at the prospect of telling her.

That was a first.

He unlocked his phone again and sent her a text.

Graham: I didn't tell my parents the details of the accident. I made it sound like it wasn't a big deal.

She read the message and frowned. "Why?"

I didn't want to worry them. My mom has multiple sclerosis and now that she's older, she has flares pretty often. She struggles with being sick and my dad does his best to take care of her on his own. They don't need the added burden.

He watched her face as she read. She looked over at him when she finished. "I'm sorry, I had no idea." Did he detect a hint of accusation in her tone? "MS is a terrible disease."

He nodded his agreement, careful to keep his expression even. Telling her was one thing; letting her see how much it tore him up inside was another.

"So what did you tell them?"

That I hurt my leg and I need to stay off it for a little while, but my roommate is a hot nurse/babysitter. Now my mother wants to meet you.

Claire laughed. "Taking care of you takes a hell of a lot more patience than when I babysat triplets as a teenager."

Damn. And here I thought you were enjoying my silent company.

Something flickered in her expression. Her gaze lingered on the phone screen for a beat, then she lifted her eyes to his. In her eyes and in her tone, sincerity shone through. "More than you know, Graham. Even though you piss me off, I'm happy you're still here to sit beside me."

Her chin trembled, the movement so slight he would have missed it if he hadn't been watching her so closely. Without thinking, he reached over and took her hand.

She let him, and his brain immediately screamed, *What are you doing?* And just as quickly he justified his reaction. *Easy. It just felt like the right thing to do. Comforting or some shit.*

From her place at the foot of the bed, Gertrude whined her disapproval. Graham tipped the left side of his lips up, which was as much of a smile as he could muster without pain.

Claire ignored her.

Graham ran his free hand through his hair and wrinkled his nose. He grabbed his phone again and tapped out a text with one hand, for once thankful for predictive text.

Graham: I hate to ask another favor, but…

She narrowed her eyes, but didn't pull her hand away. "If this has to do with sex, I swear…"

He shook his head.

Would you help me wash my hair? I've been able to do a decent job keeping clean otherwise, but that part's not easy with my current situation.

Her eyes flicked to his head and back down. "Sure. Now?"

It felt pretty greasy, and he'd sit here and think about it if they waited. He nodded.

"Okay." She thought for a second. "Let's try the kitchen. The sink's bigger."

She pulled away from him and stood, and he took his time shifting his legs off the bed. By the time he made it to the kitchen she'd pulled a wooden chair over, the back up against the cabinet.

He made his way to her and sat, propping up his crutches before he tilted his head back to test the height.

"This is actually pretty perfect. Sit back up for a second and I'll go get shampoo and towels."

Gertrude trotted in after Claire left. She hated getting wet and usually steered clear of anything she knew sprayed water, so she sat a few feet away and cocked her head, watching.

Claire returned and laid a folded towel along the counter where his neck would rest, draped one across his cast and handed him another one.

"Don't get mad at me if you get wet. I've never done this before."

He glanced down, contemplating, then carefully pulled his shirt over his head. He figured it would be easier to just dry his skin if she got water everywhere and hadn't really thought anything of it, but when he leaned back to settle in and caught Claire's expression, his body immediately tightened with awareness.

Her gaze started at his collarbone and slowly, slowly traveled down his torso. Heat followed in the wake of her gaze, which felt more like a caress than a perusal.

*Fuck.*

What would she do if he grabbed her by the waist and pulled her across his lap? He'd be a shit kisser right now, but as previously discussed his hands felt great. He just wanted to bury his face in her neck and breathe her scent into his lungs...

She swallowed and seemed to snap out of it, spinning around to the sink and turning on the water. It ran for several seconds before she switched to the sprayer and started wetting his hair. "How, um, how's the temperature?"

He gave her a thumbs-up, his brain and...other things still focused on the palpable desire that had just passed between them like a downed powerline sparking and slithering across the pavement.

*Tone it down.*

He tried to think of something—anything—else, but then she touched him. Fingers sliding through his hair, massaging, lightly pressing her nails to his scalp. Goose bumps broke out across his skin and he closed his eyes, leaning into her movements.

Holy shit, it felt good.

The clean scent of his shampoo filled his nostrils as she lathered, going from root to end, around his hairline and moving her hands to the back.

His body went hot and relaxed all at once. It felt so damn good. A thousand times better than whatever the barber did, though it may have been because the dude who cut his hair was, well, a dude, and easily in his sixties.

And this was Claire. His mouthy, sexy roommate, leaning over him and arousing every nerve ending within reach.

In this moment he was completely at her mercy. He wasn't even capable of washing his own hair, which was nothing if not a weakness. And yet he was strangely satisfied letting her do this for him. He'd asked her to, and took pleasure in how it felt as she performed this simple, basic task that he should be able to do himself.

Without thinking, he lifted his left hand and reached up to grip her waist. Her T-shirt rode up with the movement of her arms, revealing a thin strip of skin, and his thumb immediately went there. She felt soft, warm, and smooth against his own skin, which was weathered and rough from his constant outdoor activities.

She stilled her body, but kept her hands in his hair.

"Graham…" she chided lightly.

He squeezed his eyelids tight, dreading her next words, asking him to stop touching her. He waited, and she simply sighed and resumed the delicious massaging before rinsing his hair out.

As she went for the bottle of conditioner, he made a mental note to thank his barber for convincing him to use separate shampoo and conditioner rather than the combination products he'd always used before.

He sighed with pleasure as she went for round two, rubbing the thick cream through the strands. He moved his thumb back and forth across her hip bone, relishing the way his palm spanned the entire side of her hip.

Her breath hitched.

Graham's eyes snapped open to find hers focused below his waist.

He just stared at her, unashamed of the situation he had going on down there. What man wouldn't get hot while a woman he was attracted to attended to him like this? With his fingers mere inches away from her ass, no less?

Claire's eyes slid upward to meet his gaze, pink staining her cheeks. She pursed her lips, but just before she leaned forward to turn off the water and grab a clean towel, he could have sworn he saw them curve up in a smile.

# 11

Twenty-four hours had passed and Claire still couldn't stop thinking about washing Graham's hair.

It had been a basic hygiene request, and at the time she'd thought nothing of it. But now, the image of his large, shirtless body stretched out, long legs splayed and head back in a position that almost felt like surrender, would be forever burned in her brain.

She could still feel the gentle rub of his thumb across her hip, his fingers burning her through her clothes. She also wasn't likely to forget how very obviously he'd enjoyed the work of her hands through his hair, though as a woman who would give away half her savings for someone to constantly run their fingers through her hair, she couldn't really blame him. Few things in life felt that good.

After she'd finished up, an air of awkwardness descended, and she'd escaped to hide in her room for a few hours. She considered sleeping in her own room that night, but in the end decided she wasn't comfortable leaving him alone all night until his voice had returned.

The relief she glimpsed on his face when she padded into his room last night—wearing the frumpiest, most concealing set of pajamas she owned—told her he felt the same.

She had to go back to work tomorrow, and while he'd be fine and Noah would be here for several hours, she still wasn't thrilled about leaving Graham. They'd fallen into a nice little routine over the last few days. Get up, have breakfast and coffee, then he exercised while she showered. Watch television, text back and forth a little when Graham got bored. She'd even guilted him into playing gin rummy with her a few times when she told him it had been her dad's favorite card game and she missed playing it.

She enjoyed the routine, steady companionship of a man who appreciated her company. Things were a little quieter than she liked, but the desire to settle down with someone she could banter with, watch TV and play cards with, and sleep next to was more potent than ever.

Once again she remembered Mia's suggestion to try a dating site, and a voice in her head said now was as good a time as ever, because having Graham around wasn't a long-term solution.

Graham had fallen asleep after lunch, so she sneaked out with her laptop and settled onto the couch with a bag of chips. One of her coworkers had met her husband online, so she sent her a quick text asking what site she'd used.

Steph: TrueChemistry.com. You finally gonna sign up?

Claire: Thinking about it.

Steph: YES let me know how it goes

Claire went to the site and opted for the two-week free trial. She wasn't about to shell out any cash before she knew if it was worth it.

After selecting she was a woman hoping to connect with a man, she created an account and downloaded the app to her phone.

She'd just entered in general information like her age and city when Gertrude's click-clacking nails tapped across the hardwood. Claire glanced up to see the tiny asshole trot over to the front door and sit immediately underneath the hook with her leash.

"You know that haircut makes you look like you have a mustache, right?"

Gertrude blinked, looked up at the pink leash, then resumed staring at Claire.

Claire darted a look through the window at the beautiful day outside.

June in Denver was the best.

With a theatrical sigh, Claire closed her laptop and stood. "Look. I know Graham takes you on walks, like, every other day. And his house arrest is basically the same for you, and you tend to take your frustrations out on me. So, purely out of concern for the safety of my pillows and shoes, it's probably best we take a quick walk around the neighborhood. To be clear, this is for Graham and my personal belongings, not for you. Got it?"

Gertrude continued staring as Claire slipped on her shoes. When Claire grabbed the leash from the hook, she thought she saw a faint tail wag and leaned down to get a closer look.

But everything about G's tiny body was still as a statue except for those beady brown eyes, unrelenting and likely some form of evil.

Claire shrugged and clipped the leash to her collar.

She must have imagined it.

★ ★ ★

When Claire got into bed beside Graham that night with her laptop in hand, he raised a single brow at her.

She opened the lid and settled back. "I'm finally signing up for a dating website/app thing."

His other brow lifted to join the first.

"Don't look at me like that. My friend Steph swears this one's actually pretty good at matching compatibility. As you so astutely noticed, the last guy I went out with wasn't right for me and the only attractive guy at the club the other night—present company excluded—was a smoker. I might as well give this a try." She clicked to the site and logged in to pick up where she'd left off.

She felt Graham's gaze on her as she skimmed the questions she was supposed to answer. "I have no idea how to answer some of these."

Graham pointed to her computer and gestured for her to hand it over.

Claire laughed. "You want to help?"

He nodded, expression serious.

"Just don't hit Submit on anything," she warned, handing him the laptop. She scooted closer to see what he was doing.

He smelled good, which was unfair since he'd just been sitting in bed all day, and she regretted the move immediately.

Note to hormones: *snap out of it.*

Graham focused his attention on the screen for several seconds. He'd probably come to the same conclusion she had, and wouldn't know how to answer them, either.

But then, he started typing.

**Describe your perfect day.** *Sleeping until the sun wakes me up. Strong black coffee and a carb-filled breakfast on the patio at a* *local café. Maybe a little shopping, especially if there's a good sale. Would have to include a trip to Nordstrom Rack. A lazy afternoon on the couch binge-watching my recent Netflix obsession, then take-out dinner at home and wine on the porch until the stars come out.*

He stopped and shot her what was probably meant to be an arrogant smirk, but his smile wasn't quite there yet. She just stared at him, shocked as hell.

He sighed and mouthed, *Right?*

"That's pretty on point," she admitted. "Better than I could have come up with, and startlingly accurate. What else have you got?"

**Provide one random fact about yourself.** *I leave half-eaten bags of chips all over the house.*

He gave her the side-eye and she burst out laughing. "Yeah, sorry. But we're not putting that."

Graham rolled his eyes and hit the backspace key, then typed, *I take card games very seriously.*

She allowed that one. It was the truth, and it was probably best for anyone she dated to be aware up front.

**What's your biggest pet peeve?** *Small dogs.*
**What physical feature are you most attracted to?** *Forearms.*

Heat filled her cheeks. Had he noticed how often she checked out that particular body part on him? Hell, she'd just been watching the veins and flexing muscles as he typed.

Thankfully, he didn't look at her and kept typing.

**If you could choose a superpower, what would it be?** *Time travel.*

Her mouth dropped open and she shifted her gaze from the screen to his face. He was still typing, frowning in concentration as he went, as if that answer wasn't significant.

It was, though. Could have been, at least, if he'd chosen that power knowing she'd give anything to go back in time to see her dad again. Was it possible he'd just randomly picked it without thinking, or was he more intuitive than he let on?

By the time she looked back to the screen, he'd moved on to a Yes/No section and had answered several questions.

**Do you have any tattoos?** *No*

"Wait, how do you know?"

He gave her a look like she should know, and texted her. I've seen you naked.

"*What?* When?"

Come on. It was a couple of years ago, we got really drunk...

What the hell was he talking about? Her eyes must have been the size of grapefruits, because he bit his lip and shook his head.

I'm just messing with you. We all talked about it after Mia got hers, remember? You said you didn't.

She'd never been so relieved in her life. Not that she was opposed to Graham seeing her naked...but she wanted to be fully present for it. "I hate you," she muttered, and glanced back at the computer screen.

**Do you like to dance?** *Yes*
**Are you romantic?** *Yes*
**Are you adventurous**? *Yes*
**Do you believe in love at first sight?** *No*
**Do you believe in yourself?** *Sometimes*

Claire put a hand on his arm. Forearm, to be exact, and damn it was firm. And warm. And just...yeah. *Focus.* "Whoa. Some of these aren't right. I'm not romantic, and I'm damn sure not adventurous. Didn't I just explain one of my non-negotiables in a future husband is one who doesn't live dangerously? I don't do anything that falls in that category. And how do you know I don't believe in love at first sight?"

He picked up his phone.

You pretend you're not a romantic, but the episode of New Girl where Nick and Jess finally get together is always on the Continue Watching row of Netflix and anytime a guy has bought you flowers you keep them until all the petals fall off. Why do you think you're not adventurous?

"Did you already forget what you wrote about my perfect day? I'm boring. The opposite of adventurous. I hate roller coasters. I don't climb, mountain bike, or ski. I've never done anything like skydiving or bungee jumping. The idea of scuba diving makes me want to curl into a ball."

Agree to disagree on that one, but you should keep my answer.

Trust me. As for the love-at-first-sight thing—because you didn't fall for me the second you saw this face.

Claire scoffed, the last comment effectively distracting her from further arguing the response to the adventurous question. "You didn't fall for me."

I don't believe in it, either.

Their mutual attraction for one another confirmed, not that it needed to be, Claire asked him a more personal question than she normally would. He'd always seemed pretty locked down on the emotions front and was obviously commitment phobic. None of that actually meant he didn't have feelings, though. Just that he didn't show them. "Do you believe in love at all?"

He leaned back against the headboard and scratched at his scruff-covered jaw.

While he thought, Claire idly wondered if he'd ask her to shave his face next. Where would that fall on the sexy scale? More or less than hair washing?

More, probably, if she sat on the edge of the bathroom counter while he stood between her thighs, face inches from hers and head tilted just so, the distinct scent of shaving cream and pent-up desire filling the small space…

She nearly slid onto her back and begged him to roll on top of her, saved only by him finally tapping out a message.

Yeah. I love my family and my friends. As for the other kind, I guess I have to believe it exists because I've felt it. But while the first two kinds feel good, the latter mostly hurt.

Well, that sucked for him. Also, agreed.

"How did it hurt?"

He shook his head.

Was *that* why he was the way he was? He'd had his heart broken? Frustration seeped into her tone. "You can't just say something like that and not explain it. Who hurt you?"

Graham looked as if he wanted to smile. She saw it in his eyes.

Why, you gonna defend my honor?

They were the exact words she'd said to him weeks ago, and for some reason it irritated her.

"Maybe," she said, mirroring his response back to her. "Isn't that what friends do?"

He shrugged.

It was a long time ago.

"Not long enough for you to forget and move on, apparently."

How about this? If I ever run into her and you're with me, I'll let you know and you can have whatever revenge your little heart desires.

It had only been one woman, then. Was that better? Or did it just mean that single experience was so bad he'd closed off the road to his heart from that moment forward? Regardless, the thought of sticking it to whoever messed with him sounded vastly satisfying. She balled her hands into fists and pressed them to her smiling mouth. "I can? Really?"

It seemed the injury to his face was improving, because

he grinned. It was a little subdued and lopsided and wasn't a classic Graham smile, but it was better than she'd had since before the accident.

Something inside her chest thumped, and she frowned at the realization of how much she adored it. In a typical day, how many of her smiles were a direct response to one of his?

And if a partial Graham smile did this to her, how would it feel when he was able to give her the real thing?

He searched her face for a second and tilted his head.

What happened? You're frowning.

"What? No, I wasn't."

Yes you were. Tell me what you were thinking.

She shook her head.

OK. I'll assume you were picturing me naked and trying to figure out logistics of sex with a cast.

"Oh, my gosh, stop." She puffed up her cheeks and blew out a breath. "It might make you uncomfortable."

He considered that for a moment.

I can handle it.

"Fine. I was just thinking about how much I've missed your smile."

That's it?

"Yeah."

What's weird about that? I miss it, too. I've got a great smile.

There it was again, that half grin, and the desire to close the distance between them and kiss it off his face was so strong she almost couldn't stand it.

"Yeah," she said, unable to speak anything but the truth. "You do."

# 12

To: PinkSparkles91@zzmail.com
From: Graham.Scott27@zzmail.com
Subject: I don't know

Claire,

Well.

I'm desperate.

You went to work and I'm bored out of my fucking mind and Noah won't be here for another hour, so I'm trying my hand at your journaling suggestion. It still feels weird to write to no one so I'm writing to you, instead. Which only feels slightly less weird, but you said you never check this email so I figure you'll never see it, anyway. It'll probably just be a bunch of bullshit rambling but I'm not a fast typer so maybe by the time I'm done Noah will be here. Ooh, think maybe he'll take me on a drive?

Now I get why Gertrude gets so excited about the car.

By the way, she seems restless today. I think she misses you.

She wasn't even like this after that family gave her up. Do you remember that? I rescued her from a burning house and the family had to move into an apartment with a no-pet rule. First, I don't know how they could have ever given her up because she's basically perfect. Second, Gertie didn't even seem to miss them, so strike two in pet ownership.

My point is, if she's looking for you, she likes you. Have you been petting her while I've been asleep?

Speaking of sleeping… I think you had a bad dream last night. You seemed restless but I didn't want to wake you up. Or maybe it was a good dream, and maybe I was there…and we were doing stuff…

Anyway. Moving on. I just googled what to write about in a journal and here are the suggestions:

1. Inspirational quotes. That seems cliche, but I heard something once I try to live by:

> *"A ship is safe in the harbor,*
> *but that's not what ships are made for."*

I have no idea who said it. (Also, are you impressed with my formatting? I played around with it and went with italics and center alignment, and now I'm several seconds closer to Noah's arrival and getting out of this fresh hell that is journaling.)

2. Self care. I thought that's what the fuck I was doing?

3. Describe your current challenges. This one is pretty obvious, isn't it? I hate being stuck at home. I hate being alone. I hate not having full use of my body. Strangely enough, I never realized how much I depend on my health and physical ability. Remind me never to take it for granted again. Also, remind me not to take

you for granted again. You've been really good to me through this. I'll make it up to you when I'm better, promise (dirty stuff, in case that wasn't clear).

4. Write a time capsule memory. K, here goes: Hey, idiot—always anchor at the top when you're tying a top rope. If you had, you and Claire would have hooked up by now. Several times, probably, because you're that good.

5. Track the food you eat. Nope. Next.

6. Write a letter. HEY I'm doing that.

7. Write about things you want to let go of. Yeah, I don't think I want to do that one, either. In fact, that's probably enough for today. I'll pull out arm hairs until Noah gets here.

Also, Gertie just pushed your pillow off the bed again. Maybe she still hates you.

Graham

* * *

"If Claire finds out about this, she's gonna kill me."

Graham snorted and gestured between him and Noah with his index finger to say, *You and me both.*

"Yeah, but I'll leave behind a grieving wife." Noah's hands tightened on the steering wheel. "I shouldn't have let you talk me into this."

Graham gave him the finger.

Noah shot him a side-eye. "House arrest makes you grumpy."

Graham didn't feel bad for badgering Noah into driving him to the mountains. He had to get out of town and smell the mountain air. It was for the sake of his health.

Noah sighed. "Fine. But we're going to a touristy overlook with benches where you will stay seated and enjoy being outdoors. Safely. Got it?"

Cocking a brow, Graham knocked on his cast with his knuckles.

"Hey, I wouldn't put it past you to try to go on a hike or something, even with a cast and crutches."

Noah had a point. If anyone would try that, it would be him.

Graham sneaked his hand through the open window, letting the wind brush past his fingers as Noah took the exit. Man, it felt good to be out.

Noah followed through on his threat and found a scenic turnout on Highway 285, but Graham didn't care. It was kind of nice to see the Rockies from the exact location where some people experienced the mountains for the first time. While he preferred a more hands-on approach to the beautiful landscape, maybe it wasn't a bad idea to stop and enjoy the view every once in a while.

Graham lumbered out of the car and slowly made his way to a bench. He sat, propping his crutches up beside him, and Noah sat on the other side. Graham pulled out his phone and typed out a note, then handed it to Noah.

Thanks for making me wear my helmet that day.

He'd thought about it several times since—and how much worse it could have been if he hadn't been wearing it.

Noah shrugged and shoved the phone back in Graham's hand. "Don't mention it."

They sat in companionable silence for a long time, content to just be in nature.

Noah was the last person Graham felt compelled to force conversation with, which in a situation like this was perfect.

But in a rare moment of insecurity he wondered if Noah would prefer if Graham was a little less talkative in general, like now. Then he thought about Claire, and how frustrated she seemed sometimes when he couldn't just pop back at her when she said something snarky.

She missed his sass, even if she'd never admit it. Graham smiled at the thought, and as he did, realized his face felt great today.

He widened his smile, just to test it, and it felt normal. Reaching up, he lightly rubbed a hand across the right side of his jaw.

It didn't hurt.

Well, well, well. Claire was in for a treat tonight.

★ ★ ★

She came home in a shit mood.

She always came home hungry, which Graham had planned ahead for by ordering takeout from one of her favorite Mexican restaurants.

With an extra order of tortilla chips.

But the bad mood? He wasn't prepared for that. She didn't even notice the spread as she stalked past on her way to her room.

Thinking quickly, he grabbed two Coronas from the fridge, sliced up a lime, and added them to the table.

Damn, why hadn't he gotten her flowers? This was a thank-you meal, not an attempt to woo her, but still. He intended to make it known he was in perfect condition to kiss that lovely mouth of hers if she was inclined to let him.

With the way she was slamming drawers in her room, it seemed the odds for any messing around were low. Which was fine, but he'd still offer because getting a little action usually made him feel better and it might help her, too.

Selfless, right?

A few seconds later Claire reentered the kitchen, looking gorgeous and comfortable in sweatpants and a white tank top. Her arms were up, fingers gathering her hair at the top of her head, and she did some fancy maneuver with a band that somehow secured the unruly mass up there.

Part of him wished she'd leave it down, while the other appreciated the bared curve of her shoulders and lines of her slender neck.

She stopped at the table and regarded the food. "You're a lifesaver. Work was chaotic today. You won't believe what I had to deal with."

Graham arched a brow, a move he'd employed more in the last week than his entire life, but without the use of his voice, he'd learned the eyebrows were versatile communication tools. Tonight, for example, the simple muscle flex said, *Try me.*

"My first patient of the day caught his sheets on fire when he lit up a joint and dropped it. The next was a kid who ate twenty-seven LEGOs. And last but not least, I got a guy who kept taking off his gown. And on top of it all I was worried about you all day, which pissed me off."

Graham couldn't help it.

He smiled.

She was exhausted and irritated and he probably shouldn't have found anything she said the least bit funny. But she was just so lovely when she was riled up. It was his favorite version of Claire.

A small, silent laugh escaped his lips when her face lit up.

"You're smiling," she said, her own lips tipping up. "Your jaw is better?"

He nodded.

"Well. There's one good thing from this day, at least. Well, that and chips and salsa." She twisted her lips to the side and lowered her lashes a little. "I'm not sure which is better, actually. Thank you, Graham."

She continued to look at him, more at his mouth than anywhere else, and he took his chance.

His hips leaned against the counter, keeping him upright. He angled his head to the side and held out his hand, palm up, gesturing with his index finger. *Come here.*

Her brows furrowed and she approached him, stopping two feet away. He made the motion one more time.

*Closer.*

She took another step.

It was enough for him to keep one hand on the counter for balance, lean forward to slip the other around her neck and pull her flush against his body.

Her breath caught, her lips parted, and she turned those hazel eyes on him.

*Thank you*, he mouthed.

"For what?"

His hands were occupied, and with no other method of communication, he just looked at her, his gaze canvassing her face, enjoying the color rising in her cheeks. She probably knew, anyway.

She swallowed, putting a gentle hand on his chest and moving it in a soft, tiny circle. Her eyes dropped there as she spoke again. "Are we, um, starting our arrangement? Are you sure that's a good idea right now?"

He waited until their gazes locked and nodded, lowering his head.

*Yes and hell yes.*

Hesitation was nonexistent. She met him partway, lifting up and molding her mouth with his. Her body melted into him, and he wished he could wrap his other arm around her waist. But he couldn't risk falling right now and moving backward in his recovery.

Especially now that he'd gotten to this point. He might not be able to do everything he wanted with her, but if he could kiss her without pain, he was damn sure gonna do it. As much as possible. Because kissing Claire was like crossing the finish line and looking back to find you won the race.

Exhilarating, satisfying perfection.

This kiss wasn't as forceful as the first. The second one hadn't gone far enough to gauge, but this one was unhurried, thorough, and indulgent.

Her palms traveled across his chest, sending heat barreling through his veins as they continued up the sides of his neck and slid into his hair. Her nails lightly traced his scalp and suddenly he was back in that chair, shirtless, with her hands working their magic. *This* was what he'd wanted to do immediately after.

She'd wanted it, too.

Tongues slipped past lips and breath mingled. Hearts pounded and pulses raced, and Graham had to back off soon before he did something senseless like try to carry her to his bedroom, or twist around to lift her on the counter.

He brought his hand around to the front of her neck, his thumb tracing her collarbone as he pulled back.

*Damn.* He'd thought kissing her would be enough, but he wanted more.

He wanted it all.

He hated his broken leg more in this moment than any other.

The soft sound she made with her exhale nearly did him in. She must have caught the flash of need in his eyes, because she took a step back, giving them both room to breathe.

She chewed on her lower lip. "Well. Should we eat?"

It wasn't what he *wanted* to do next, but he nodded and gave himself a minute before he pushed off and took a seat at the table.

Claire chattered about her day while they ate. Graham was more than content to sit and listen to her.

Gertrude sat near his feet, giving him huge round eyes that he'd never been able to resist, and he periodically slipped her small pieces of his food.

When they got in bed that night they finished up her online dating profile and, after she'd spent ten minutes reviewing everything, hit Submit. She turned wide eyes on him and said, "This is it. I might have just started a connection with the man of my dreams."

Graham wasn't quite so optimistic. Yeah, he'd heard of success stories from online dating, but he'd also heard several shitty ones.

Maybe she'd let him review her matches before contacting them, sort of like how they worked while they were out.

Claire closed her laptop and set it on the nightstand. She turned out the lamp and scooted closer to him. He couldn't sleep on his side, but he turned his head to meet her eyes.

"It's probably weird to say this after setting up a profile to meet other men, and a terrible idea to suggest it when we're horizontal. But I'm the kind of girl who asks for what she wants, and all I want to do right now is kiss you again." She dropped her gaze briefly. "Feel free to turn me down. I won't be offended."

He reached out, tipped her chin up with his finger, and shot her an incredulous look. He wanted to tell her he'd have to be dead to not want to kiss her.

When she gave him a small smile that was...not quite shy, but not a standard, confident Claire smile, he leaned as far as he could to rest his hand on the small of her back and tucked her close against his side.

He brushed his nose against hers and she parted her lips, eyes falling closed. He wasted no time with pleasantries and sucked her bottom lip into his mouth. She let out a moan and enthusiastically returned his fervor, sliding one hand under his shirt as their mouths crashed together. His body went taut when she went up on her elbow to prop herself above him, pressing her breasts into his arm.

Not being able to flip her over, climb on top of her writhing body, and feel her pleasure beneath him was straight up going to kill him.

Just as the thought grabbed hold, another one popped up, this one unfamiliar and intriguing.

*Savor her.*

The concept was like a shock to his system, and he switched gears. Hot, urgent, and fast was for another time. A time when he had a voice, because he wanted to talk to her. Tell her how it felt, ask what she liked.

They were just getting started and learning about each other. And he couldn't ignore his physical limitations. A night like this was for intention. Touching. Tasting.

This experience with Claire wasn't a night out at a club downing shots and cutting loose on the dance floor. No, this was a trip to wine country with meandering bike rides down country roads and hours-long tastings and food pairings to satisfy the palate.

"Damn, Graham. I hope my future husband is as good at this as you are," she murmured against his mouth.

Her words gave birth to a strange, unwelcome sensation in his gut. He pushed it deep down, as far as it would go, and went in for more.

He was well aware of what they were doing and the boundaries, both spoken and unspoken. It was just…he was so comfortable with Claire, and this newfound discovery of their sexual chemistry was intoxicating. If she found another man she wanted to marry, he'd be happy for her and wish her the best.

But until then…what they had going was perfect for him, and part of him hoped that wouldn't change anytime soon.

* * *

To: PinkSparkles91@zzmail.com
From: Graham.Scott27@zzmail.com
Subject: Bored again

Claire,

Another Google suggestion for journal topics is the high and low of your day.

High: I woke up with you curled up against my side. Don't get weird about it, I'm not. I've just always liked sharing my bed with someone else. Women, preferably, but I won't lie and say Nathan, Noah, and I never cuddled for body heat when camping in the winter. Anyway, it was nice, and I'd like to make a motion we keep that up even when I get my voice back.

Yes, I realize I'll need to bring that up IRL at some point, because you'll never read this.

Low: You left for work. Again, don't get weird. I'm just bored and I hate being here alone. Gertrude is lovely company but she sleeps too much.

Oh, you want to hear what I've done today? K.

After you left I gave myself a sponge bath (if that mental image doesn't turn you on, I don't know what will) and stole some of your dry shampoo. THAT STUFF IS FUCKING AWESOME. Do they make it for guys? I may never wash my hair again.

You're always welcome to do it for me, though.

Then I "worked out." I don't think I'm supposed to, but I

did push-ups and sit-ups today in addition to weights. It didn't bother my leg in that behemoth cast so it's probably fine, right? By the time this is over I'll look like an ostrich. Huge on the top with tiny little toothpick legs completely devoid of muscle tone. But hairy. (Strike the sponge bath comment—that mental image should be what turns you on.)

K, so then I started some creepy show on Netflix and freaked myself out and turned it off. Then I sat on the porch for a while to get some vitamin D. I saw a Subaru coming down the street and for a second I thought maybe you got off early, but it wasn't you.

Obviously.

But then I was thinking about what I'd tell you if you were home, and here we are.

Some of my buddies from the station wanted to stop by this afternoon, but I said (er, texted) no. I feel weird not being able to talk to them. Come to think of it, I wasn't comfortable when Reagan was here, either. But with you and Noah I couldn't care less. Mia, too, probably. And maybe Chris.

Does that mean you're my people? Nathan was the first friend I ever had like that. He and I were so similar it was almost scary, and I knew within five minutes of talking to him he was different than the guys I grew up with (assholes, mostly). I got lucky that his brother was cool, too, and then got lucky again that a friendship with Noah meant I got to know you and Mia, too.

Whoa. OK, well, I didn't mean to get all sappy there. I think that's my cue to sign off.

Hope you have a good day today and we can make out when you get home. I really like kissing you.

Graham

# 13

Today was June 18.

Her dad's birthday.

Other than the recurring nightmare Claire often had about his death, she'd successfully avoided thinking about it the three days leading up to today. She worked three twelves in a row, and even though the heavy make-out session with Graham in bed that first night was incredible, she'd been too exhausted the next two nights for a repeat.

Today was her first day off, which would have been nice…

…if it weren't June 18.

Luckily, she had plans to take Graham to the otolaryngologist later, and as long as speaking was possible, he might be given the green light to use his voice again.

But first, she'd call her mom. They spoke every other week or so, but always talked on her dad's birthday. Claire figured her mom could use a friend on days like these, and she'd be lying if she said she didn't benefit from it, as well.

Graham was in his room lifting weights and she used the

phone call as an excuse to get out of the house. She grabbed her phone, a doggy bag, and Gertrude's leash, and the tiny dog came running.

"Is that a tail wag I see?"

The movement ceased.

Claire rolled her eyes and opened the door, anyway. "Let's go, you little jerk."

Once they'd descended the porch and Gertrude trotted several feet in front, prancing and sniffing the air daintily, Claire dialed her mom.

"Hey, sweetie."

"Hey, Mom. How are you?"

"I'm fine. Took the day off. I'm baking."

"Ooh, baking what?"

"I started with blueberry muffins, and a loaf of French bread is rising on the counter. Thought I'd finish out with some cookies later."

"I'll be by in a few hours."

Her mom laughed.

"I'm serious. I'll be out your way this afternoon."

Another chuckle. "I'll have a package ready to go for you. Will you stay for dinner?"

"Not this time. Graham hurt himself climbing and I've been helping him out. He'll be with me."

"Is he okay?"

"Dumbass broke his leg."

"Oh, no, poor guy. How awful."

"It could have been worse," was all Claire said.

Her mom didn't speak for a few long seconds. Some years they talked about her dad and some they didn't. This was the perfect segue if her mom wanted to talk about it.

"How's work been? Are you still happy with moving to the ER? Still waiting on the hospital to get your paperwork done?"

"Yeah, I'm still working regular nursing shifts for now. It's been busy, but I like it. I like being the first one taking care of the patients, but at the same time it's kind of nice to be able to leave work at the hospital when I go home." Claire paused when Gertrude found a mailbox particularly interesting. "When I was in the ICU, I was usually caring for the same patients weeks on end, and they'd be on my mind all the time. In the ER it's different every day. It can be hectic while I'm there, but it's better for my mental health when I'm not."

"That makes sense," her mom said. "What else is new, other than playing nurse for Graham? How are Mia and Noah?"

Gertrude determined the mailbox wasn't worth her time and they were off again. "Disgustingly adorable."

"Any special men in your life?"

"Not a one. But, and don't laugh, I signed up for an online dating platform."

"Why would I laugh? So did I."

Claire stopped, causing the leash to catch Gertrude's collar. The dog looked back and glared. *What?*

"Your mother can't join a dating service? I'm not that old."

Claire slowly started moving again. "I— Of course you're not. I just had no idea. When did you do this?"

"A couple of months ago."

"Why didn't you tell me?" Claire scrunched her nose at her own tone. She was surprised, was all. "For the record, I think it's great, Mom." Her mom had hardly dated since Claire's dad died, and those were mainly blind dates set up through friends.

"I don't know, I guess I didn't know what you'd think of it. But since you're doing it, too…"

"Had any luck so far?"

"Not at first. I went on one date, but we didn't connect. Then it matched me with a commercial pilot."

Oof. "Sorry, Mom."

Her mom cleared her throat. "It's fine. He might have been perfectly lovely, but I just couldn't."

"I don't blame you."

"Anyway, I've been talking to an accountant in Boulder through email, and he seems nice. We might meet soon."

An accountant sounded perfect for her mom. Maybe he had a son…

Gertrude paused to do her business in the front lawn of the nicest house on the street. "Let me know how it goes. I just finished my profile, so nothing yet. Maybe we'll find someone at the same time and we can have a dual wedding."

"What makes you think I'm looking for a husband? Maybe I just want to have some fun."

"Mom!" Gertrude startled at Claire's screech.

"What?"

"Are you serious?"

"No, but would that be so terrible?"

"Yes. But only because you're my mother."

"Fine. I'll keep my sex life to myself as long as you do the same."

Claire's stomach dropped at the thought of telling her mom about her and Graham's situation. "I thought this had been a lifelong unspoken understanding, but if we need to say it out loud, deal."

"Good." A chime sounded in the background. "Time to put my bread in the oven. Let me know when you think you'll come by, okay?"

"Okay. Love you, Mom."

"Love you, too."

★ ★ ★

Claire was so engrossed in the article she was reading on her phone that the low, scratchy voice in her ear nearly made her jump out of her seat.

"Do I sound sexy or creepy?"

Placing a hand over her racing heart, Claire glanced back at Graham, who had come up behind her chair. "You scared the shit out of me."

His face fell. "Creepy, huh?"

He'd straightened, which took him farther away from her ear, and she could barely hear him.

She shook her head and stood, then walked around the row of chairs in the waiting room. "Not creepy. You just startled me."

One corner of his mouth lifted. "So…sexy, then?"

She pursed her lips, unwilling to give it to him. "Just hoarse. Like you lost your voice at a football game or from a cold or something."

He snapped his fingers. "Damn."

"I guess that means the doctor said you were cleared to talk again?"

"Yep. Said I should go easy on it, though, and watch for signs of fatigue. As long as I don't push it, it should get better every day."

Claire patted his firm chest, the muscles flexed as he held himself up on the crutches. "Congrats. How does it feel?"

"Fucking awesome."

"I bet. One injury down, one to go."

He looked at his leg and blew out a breath. "I'm ready to be done with this one, too."

"You're off pain meds now. That's a good sign. Another three weeks and the cast might come off."

He groaned. "Three weeks is an eternity."

"Now that you can speak again, that's all I'm gonna hear, isn't it? Complaining?"

Graham leaned in, though with his current volume it wasn't necessary. "That and dirty talk."

"I'm not sure it's worth it."

"It is. Trust me."

Her stomach swooped, but she kept her face carefully neutral and grabbed her purse. "Are we ready to go?"

"Yep. After you, hot stuff."

"Don't call me that."

"No? I've had a lot of time to think up pet names and haven't had a chance to try any of them out yet."

She held the door for him and slowed her pace so he could keep up through the parking lot. "No pet names."

"Why not?"

"Because we're not in a relationship!"

Suddenly he was no longer beside her, and she stopped to look back. He'd paused between two cars.

"I know. But doesn't it feel a little different now? You're not just Claire to me anymore. You're not my girlfriend, but you're not just my friend, either."

She strained to hear him. "Are we in like…relationship purgatory?"

"I guess."

Unsure what to say to that, she turned and kept walking to her car. "Regardless," she finally tossed over her shoulder, "no pet names."

He didn't speak again until they were both in the car. She flipped the radio off so she could hear him. "I'll find one you like, you'll see."

"Doubtful."

He held up his hands in surrender. "Fine. Anyway, I'm starving. Wanna stop somewhere to eat?"

She eyed him dubiously. "You sure you feel up to it? I thought you might want to go back and rest your leg."

"I've tasted freedom. Never take me back!"

"You'd leave your dog?"

"Of course not. You can drop me off in the mountains somewhere and go back for her. We'll live off the land."

Claire let out a laugh. "Me, in the wilderness, with the two of you? Pass."

He pouted. "Fine. I'll settle for dinner out tonight."

She checked the clock. "A little early for dinner, isn't it?"

"Woman, I'm hungry and I can communicate again and I can see the sky. Don't ruin this for me."

With a snort, Claire turned onto the main road. "Right. Sorry. Let's go have dinner with the rest of the septuagenarians. I know just the place."

Graham smiled in satisfaction, leaned his head back and rolled down his window. His wavy, dark hair rustled around his forehead with the breeze and he rested his forearm on the window frame, opening his fingers to the air rushing by. In no time at all he went from teasing to content, lost in the open air and sounds of outside, even here in the city.

He really loved it, and Claire made a note to suggest they sit on the porch more often during the rest of his recovery.

Fifteen minutes later she pulled into the parking lot of Tagine, a new Moroccan restaurant.

Graham eyed the sign. "This is 'just the place'?"

"I've been wanting to try it. It just opened so it's been super busy. I thought maybe at this time of day it wouldn't be too bad." The parking lot was still surprisingly full, but at least the sidewalk was void of waiting patrons.

"What kind of food is it?"

"Moroccan. Couscous, lamb, vegetables, that kind of thing." Graham wasn't quite as adventurous an eater as she was. Claire loved all types of food and would try anything once. "They'll have meat kabobs or something you'll like."

"Promise?"

"No."

He reached into the back seat for his crutches and got out of the car with a grunt.

It was a beautiful day, and Claire asked for a table on the patio. Only one other couple was seated outside, and it was nice and quiet. Once they were settled, had ordered drinks, and Graham had found something acceptable on the menu, they fell into relaxed conversation.

"Heard from Reagan?" Graham asked.

"Yeah, she made it down there okay. Bitch said she's been on the beach every day."

Graham chuckled, though it came out more like a rasp. "You're more of a beach girl than a mountain girl, huh?"

Claire shrugged. "I love the beauty of the mountains. And I prefer cooler weather. But that summer I spent abroad in Barcelona hitting the beaches every weekend certainly wasn't torture. Tan skin looks good on me."

"I bet it does."

She loved traveling, and would do it more if she didn't require heavy doses of anxiety meds to get on a plane. "Did you travel much growing up?"

Graham shook his head just as a man burst onto the patio, gesturing violently with one hand while yelling into the phone held up to his ear with the other.

Graham leveled the guy with a look as he passed, but the man ignored him and paused at the railing just a few feet beside them.

"Even before my mom was diagnosed with MS we didn't really travel long distances," Graham said. Claire strained to hear his hoarse voice over the stranger's loud conversation. Graham glared at the guy's back, but kept going. "But my dad took me camping just outside town every chance he got."

"That's where it all started then, huh?" Claire asked with a smile. She'd never met anyone who loved being outside more than Graham. She could also count on one hand the number of times he'd mentioned anything about his life before she met him, and she wanted to hear more.

"Yeah. We—"

"*What?*" the guy yelled into his phone. "Come on!"

Claire held up a finger at Graham and stood, marching over to the asshole. She tapped him on the shoulder. He stopped midsentence and lifted his eyebrows.

"Yeah, hi. You seem pretty oblivious to anything beyond what you have going on there—" Claire motioned to his phone "—but there are people out here trying to have a conversation and all we can hear is you. Could you take it somewhere else or keep it down?"

The guy didn't take his eyes off her. "Shawn, I'm gonna have to call you back." He slid his phone into his pocket and grinned at her. "Sure, sweetheart. My apologies. But before I go, can I have your number?"

If his behavior thus far hadn't already made her dislike the guy, the lustful sweep of his eyes down her body would have done it.

"Definitely not." She turned on her heel and went back to the table. Taking a long sip of her water, she chanced a look at Graham, worried he might be embarrassed by her behavior. Why did she never consider that before she reacted?

But instead of a look of censure, she found that glorious, slightly crooked smile aimed in her direction. He propped his elbow on the table and rested his chin in his palm as if studying a piece of artwork up close. "You're something else, you know that?"

Suddenly self-conscious at his inspection and the warmth threading through her veins, she deflected. "Sorry. See? That's the shit I do on dates that usually cancels out the chance of a second one."

"I love watching you." His eyes darkened but his quiet tone remained playful. "So did that guy, apparently. If you're looking for someone who enjoys the mouth on you, you should go back and give him your number."

"Hell no. I have to believe there's someone out there who likes me for me, but also isn't an asshole."

"Once again, I'm out 'of the running."

"I didn't think you were ever in it?"

"I wasn't. You can blame Angela DiMarco for that."

Claire perked up. Now they were getting somewhere. "The girl who broke your heart is named Angela?"

He squinted. "You sound oddly disappointed."

"It's a little generic. I was imagining something with a little more flair. Porsche or Crystal or something. Angelas are shy girls, not the kind who go around breaking the hearts of big, brawny men like you."

"Maybe I wasn't so brawny back then."

"How long ago was this alleged heart-breaking?" Claire had met him when she was twenty-two and he was twenty-seven during a night out with Mia and Noah, and had cared more about having fun with him than getting to know him.

His dark eyes darted to the side, looking out at the street beyond. He swallowed. "You know, my throat's starting to hurt a little."

"Liar."

His gaze came back to hers, eyebrows raised. "Nurse Harper. You would have me go against doctor's orders just to learn about my relationship history?"

"You've only been talking, intermittently, for less than an hour. You're avoiding."

"Something I've been told I'm pretty good at."

Claire tucked hair behind one ear. "Fine, have it your way. I'll just talk your ear off for the rest of the meal."

"Sounds normal."

She flipped him off, fighting a grin. "It's probably best to save your voice, anyway. We've got one more stop to make after this and you're gonna need it."

"Why? Where are we going?"

"My mom's house."

Graham's eyes lit up and there was that smile again. Graham and her mom only saw each other once a year or so, as Claire didn't often have reason to bring her mom around her friends or vice versa. But every time they got together, they were like two peas in a pod.

"Claire Harper, you just made my day."

# 14

To: PinkSparkles91@zzmail.com
From: Graham.Scott27@zzmail.com
Subject: Your mom goes to college

How do I always forget how much I love your mom? That woman is the coolest person on the planet (and the best cook…how did you fall so far from that tree? Not judging, just wondering.). I can't believe we stayed there until almost midnight. For what it's worth, I felt bad when you had to get up and go to work this morning.

Also, what's up with that? You worked three twelves and only got one day off? That's bullshit. You'd better have a long stretch coming up to keep me company. And yes, I heard how selfish that made me sound.

I don't care.

Anyway, back to your mom. Any chance she'd keep making those cookies on a weekly basis while I'm down? I may or may not have finished them off this morning.

That's the first time I've been inside your house, right? It's definitely the first time I've seen a picture of your dad. He was a handsome dude and you have his eyes. Can I ask why you don't have a picture of him at the condo anywhere? (Of course I can ask, you'll never see this.) Are you mad at him for what happened? Or for doing something so dangerous when he had a family at home? If you are, I get that. But at the same time I get his side, too, that people like us who find our passion, no matter how dangerous it is, can't just give it up. It's like asking us to stop breathing. I've tried to keep the darkness away since I got hurt but I can feel it creeping in. I'd go to a bad place if I had to stay here permanently, I think.

I love adventure more than anything else, and probably always will. I've been thinking about it all day and realized it's one of the only places I feel things. Or maybe it's the only place I acknowledge them. I don't know. It's like, I go about my day working, hanging out, doing whatever…and sure, there are times when I'm content. But when I'm riding or climbing or skiing, there's so much more. Anticipation, joy, determination. I'm never more in awe of life than when I'm challenging it.

Does anything make you feel like that?

Want me to help you find what does? I feel like a damn expert therapist right now, with all that stuff I just realized about myself and helping you out, too. Therapists google, right? I just typed in "How to find your life passion."

Here's what it says:

Think about what you already love doing.

Well, after we have sex the answer will obviously be me, but we gotta go broader here. You love eating out. And dancing. Spending time with friends. You love binge-watching Netflix. I'm starting to think you love Gertrude, too. You didn't notice me, but I saw you loving on her the other day. She seemed pretty content, too, which almost made me drop my crutches and give myself away. As it was, I just lurked in the hallway like a creeper with little hearts for eyes.

What makes you lose track of time?

What can you talk about for hours?

What did you love to do as a kid?

If you could be financially secure, what would you do with your time?

What do you want to be remembered for after you die?

Damn. Those are good questions and I don't have a clue how you'd answer some of them (I want to, though. That's weird, right?). I also sort of wonder what my answers would be. Some of them I know, like what I want to be remembered for. I want people to remember me as the guy who experienced every-thing life had to offer, and I'd go anywhere or do anything to do it. That I was an example of living and loving life, and hopefully passed that passion on to others.

I'd think what you want to be remembered for might be dif-ferent than some of the other answers. And I think that's okay, because most of us have separate parts of our lives—what we do for others and what we do for ourselves—and there are only a lucky few who can combine the two. You'll be remembered for your role as a nurse, healing the sick and caring for the injured. You'll be remembered as someone who laughed and loved her friends and lived life out loud.

But if you didn't have to work, would you still want to heal people? What would you get lost in? What did you love doing as a kid?

I realize how ridiculous this seems, since I'm not actually asking you this stuff. But I just spent an hour writing this and searching the Internet for ideas. So while we're not actually conversing through these emails, (1) I'm killing time, (2) I'm learning a little about myself (unfortunate side effect), and (3) I might find a way to be sneaky and bring some of this up in conversation.

You're an interesting one, Claire. I've known you for a long time, but something tells me there's more to you than meets the eye.

Graham

★ ★ ★

An hour before Claire's shift ended, Graham texted her.

Graham: Want me to order in for dinner?

Claire: Nope. I already made plans.

Disappointment shot through him, which was startling, to say the least. He wasn't supposed to be this attached to his roommate or care what plans she had for dinner.

Or with whom.

He was probably just in a weird state of dependency because of the injury and it would pass when things were back to normal. When Reagan was home, he was back at work, and he could get out and expend some of this overwhelming energy that built on itself each passing day.

Graham: Cool. I'll find something for myself around here. Have fun.

Claire: What? I meant plans for us. I'm bringing something home I want you to try.

*Don't smile. Don't smile. Don't smile.*
He failed miserably, grinning at the screen.

Graham: That's cool, too. What is it?

Claire: It's a surprise.

Graham: Are you making me try something new again?

Claire: You liked the couscous, don't even try to pretend you didn't.

Graham: Fluke. You better be bringing pizza or tacos

Claire: Nope

Graham: Does it at least go with beer?

Claire: -ish

Graham: I'll make backup plans just in case

Claire: Wuss

Graham laughed and tossed his phone on the bed, startling Gertrude awake. He scratched her ears. "Sorry, sweets."

He turned on the TV and watched the news until he heard Claire come in. Gertrude barked and leaped off the bed and was out the door before he could even grab his crutches. He made it into the kitchen several seconds behind his dog, and pretended not to notice the sweet voice Claire spoke to her in.

"Nothing in here for you."

Okay, it wasn't exactly sweet. But she didn't call Gertie a "devil dog" or a "little jerk." Something good was happening there.

"Can't say I'd be heartbroken if you said the same thing to me," he announced.

"What are you, five? How about you try it before deciding you don't like it?"

He sighed and pulled out a chair. "You're right." He sat and propped his crutches against the table. "What do we have here?"

"It's a bunch of appetizers and desserts from this place I love in Capitol Hill. They use mostly locally sourced food and make everything fresh in-house, even the bread. It's to die for."

"That doesn't sound so bad."

"Told you." She pulled several boxes out of the bag and placed them on the table, pointing at each. "Charcuterie spread. Hummus. Stuffed mushrooms. Apple tart. Chocolate cheesecake."

"I call the cheesecake."

"What? You can't just call the cheesecake. We share."

Graham lifted his chin a notch. "How big is it?"

"I paid for this stuff and brought it home. You'd seriously take the best dessert and not let me have even a bite?"

"Okay. You can have one bite."

"Have I told you lately what an asshole you are?"

He couldn't remember, and busied himself opening each container to peek inside. "It's probably been a few days."

She turned on her heel and opened the cabinet, grabbing two plates. "Too long, then."

They loaded their plates with various appetizers and let the desserts be for now, though Graham made sure the cheesecake was closer to his plate than hers.

"How was work?" he asked.

"Another chaotic day in the ED."

"Any stories for me? You know I live for the good ones."

She spread hummus across a triangle of flatbread. "I've got a sort of good one and a really good one."

He could barely contain his excitement, indicative of just how boring his day had been. "Save the best for last."

She took a bite and grinned at him as she chewed. "Okay. The first one was a guy with a nail in his head. Like, sticking straight out of his skull like he walked out of that *Hellraiser* movie. Walked right in, awake, talking, cracking jokes with his buddy who accidentally hit him with a nail gun."

"Damn," Graham whistled. "Remind me never to let you near me with one of those."

Claire scoffed. "I'm excellent with power tools."

"Right. That's why you badgered me for weeks to put up the porch swing?"

"I could have done it. I just didn't want to."

He took a bite and just stared at her.

"Do you want to hear the best one or not?"

Graham nodded. Damn, that prosciutto was good.

"Okay, so this couple comes in, a man and a woman, and they're probably in their fifties. The man has some sort of issue going on down there and he's convinced his wife has been cheating on him and gave him an STD."

Graham scooted to the edge of his chair. This *was* a good one.

"Sure enough, his penis was red and swollen. Looked infected. The entire time he's being examined he and his wife are fighting. She's swearing up and down she didn't cheat but he wasn't having it."

"Did he have an STD?"

"Nope. Get this." Claire's eyes went wide. "Turns out he got a jalapeño seed stuck up there somehow and that's what was causing the problem."

Graham nearly choked on his food. He took a long drink of water. "A jalapeño seed?"

"Yep."

He blinked, his mouth ajar. "How... I... How?"

"Dunno. But when the doctor said what he found the guy's face sort of cleared up like *Ooooohhhh*."

Graham burst out laughing. "Shit. That's so messed up."

"Hey, everyone has their thing."

"That's one I think I'll pass on, thanks."

"I'm gonna go out on a limb and say I'd never have thought of that one in the first place."

He tipped his glass in her direction. "Same."

She rearranged the food on her plate and asked, "What did you do all day?"

"The usual. Worked out, watched TV, sat outside."

*Wrote you an email.*

"When did you say you can go back to work for light duty?"

"Next week. I'll be at a different station where administration is, just filing paperwork and stuff. But at least it's something."

They continued on in easy conversation while they ate, and eventually came to dessert. Feeling guilty, Graham pushed the cheesecake in her direction. "We can split it, I guess," he said grudgingly.

Claire put a hand over her heart. "Such a gentleman."

She took half of each and pushed them back to his side of the table. They spoke less during dessert, too focused on eating. Graham wasn't usually a fruit-dessert type person, but he had to admit the apple tart was pretty good. In fact, he'd liked almost everything Claire had ever introduced him to since they became roommates. Without her he'd still be on his old diet of pizza and chicken wings.

Gertrude had hovered around the table during the meal, hoping for a treat but unwilling to appear too eager.

Claire tossed her an extra piece of salami from the charcuterie spread. "There. Now stop staring at me with those eyes."

Graham's heart warmed at the nonhostile interaction between them.

"Did you have pets growing up?" he asked.

She sat back down. "No. My mom's allergic to cats and she was too much of a clean freak to have an indoor dog."

"You and your mom could not be more different."

"Are you saying I'm a slob?"

He took a drink. "Did you hear me say that?"

She pursed her lips. "What about you? Did you have a Gertrude when you were a kid?"

"Nah. We barely had enough money for ourselves, let alone to spend on keeping an animal fed."

He'd spoken without thinking as he put the last bite of cheesecake in his mouth, and didn't realize how out of character it was to say something so personal until he looked up and found Claire staring at him, fork poised halfway to her mouth.

Graham quickly dropped his gaze and put his fork down, leaning back and threading his fingers together behind his neck. "Well, and you know how much it pains me to say this, you were right. This was fucking delicious."

It was enough to break Claire out of her trance, and she grinned, finishing her last bite. "I'm glad you liked it." She stood and gathered the containers to the middle of the table.

As he watched, he noticed a speck of whipped cream near the corner of her mouth.

"Claire."

She didn't look up. "Hmm?"

"Come here."

Their gazes collided, and she straightened, moving to stand beside him.

Graham reached up and swiped his index finger across her lip, then brought it to his mouth, the creamy sweetness hitting his taste buds. His eyes didn't leave hers as he lifted his hand once more, gently rubbing his thumb back and forth across her perfect, full lower lip. Her mouth parted and she leaned forward, her knee bumping his thigh.

"Fuck it," she muttered, throwing one leg across his to straddle him.

Surprised, his hands went to her waist to steady her mere seconds before her lips crashed down on his. Her arms locked around his shoulders and she arched into him.

His mind went blank as her lips moved on his, his tongue sliding into the warmth of her mouth. Would he ever get over how perfect it felt to kiss her? How many friends slid into a dynamic shift as easily as they had? It wasn't awkward, it wasn't fumbling, it wasn't weird.

It was perfect.

Wanting her soft, warm skin beneath his fingers more than he wanted another piece of that cheesecake, he slid one hand beneath the drawstring waist of her pants.

"Shit, I didn't even change out of my scrubs," she said, and leaned back to tug the top over her head.

Graham's mouth dropped open at the expanse of bare skin and black bra suddenly in his face. He pressed his forehead to her collarbone, inhaling her sweet scent and releasing a groan. She grabbed his face and angled his lips back to hers.

He tried to lift up into her to ease the pressure building, and a bolt of pain shot down his leg.

He groaned, and not in a good way.

She pulled back. "What? Did I hurt you?"

"No." He gritted his teeth, trying not to let it show. Because fuck his broken leg and the throbbing pain of putting even a tiny bit of weight on it—he did *not* want to stop where this was going.

"You're lying." She jumped off his lap, concern marring her brow. "Graham, stop staring at my chest and focus. Is it your leg?"

"But you have very, *very* nice breasts."

"I know, but they're not more important than your broken leg."

"I disagree."

Claire growled in frustration. "Graham Scott. Look at me right now or I'll never take my top off for you again."

His gaze snapped to her face.

"Men," she muttered and crossed her arms. "Seriously, what happened?"

"I just put my weight on my feet for a second. Both of them. I wasn't thinking. There was a sharp pain but it's already fading."

"Are you sure?"

"Promise." He reached for her hand and tugged her close. "Get back over here."

She shook her head. "I won't risk you hurting yourself."

"I lost my head for a second. I'll be more careful."

She lifted one hand and threaded her fingers through his hair, giving him a sad sort of smile. "Isn't that the whole point? To lose your head? Maybe we should wait until you don't have to worry about your leg."

He ran both hands up her sides, his thumbs caressing each rib. Their gazes locked again and he swallowed. "Please, Claire. I'm going out of my mind over here. We don't have to have sex if you think it's too risky. But for the love of my sanity, please let me kiss you, and touch you, and make you feel good."

She shivered beneath his palms and leaned into him. "Are, um…" He'd never heard her voice so breathy. *More of that, please.* "Are you sure?"

"Very."

She hummed out a sigh when his hands moved higher still. Her chin lifted and her eyes slid shut. "Okay. But we're going to your room where you're off your feet." She seemed to regain focus and grabbed his crutches, handing them over. "And I want to make you feel good, too."

"I'll allow it," he managed.

She tossed him a saucy wink over her shoulder and crossed the room, hips swaying as she reached back to unclasp her bra before disappearing into the hallway.

"You're gonna kill me, woman," Graham said, nearly crashing to the floor in his haste to follow her.

★ ★ ★

To: PinkSparkles91@zzmail.com
From: Graham.Scott27@zzmail.com
Subject: Thought

You're asleep next to me and we just had the best non-sex sex I've ever had. And you know what I'm laying here thinking about?

My bed smells like you when you're not here.

And I like it.

That should probably concern me.

Graham

PS. Remember when we were at that restaurant and you told off the guy on his phone? I didn't want you to give him your number.

# 15

"I have a date tomorrow night."

Graham's head snapped up. They'd been on the front porch for an hour, and after spending the first half hour talking, had both allowed the warmth of the sun to lull them into states of half consciousness.

TrueChemistry alerted her of the match two days ago, and after reviewing the guy's profile, she'd sent him a message. They'd spoken back and forth through the app several times, and this morning she woke up to a request to meet.

Seeing it on her phone while curled up in Graham's bed, with his large, sleeping body pressed against her, felt a little strange.

Hence it taking her half the day to bring it up.

"You do?"

She searched for any hint of discomfort or jealousy in his voice and found none.

"Yep. We're meeting for coffee."

"Coffee, huh?" Graham leaned back and laid his head against the chair, the picture of ease. "Should I come?"

Claire snorted. "No, thanks."

"What do you know about him?"

"He's in real estate. Born and raised in Colorado Springs. Likes photography and checking out the Denver restaurant scene. Last show he binge-watched was *Stranger Things*."

Graham scratched at his chin, which sported a several-day layer of scruff. "Okay, sounds decent. How old?"

"Thirty."

He made a noncommittal sound. "Are you excited?"

"Yeah. I mean, I'm a little nervous. I feel like with all the prework to make sure we were compatible first, this could be the real deal. But what if...?" She trailed off, tucking her bottom lip underneath her teeth.

Graham's gaze was shrewd, as if he knew what she was thinking. But still, he asked gently, "What?"

"I haven't been very successful on the dating front. What if he doesn't like me?"

Despite Graham's voice returning to near normal volume by this point, she barely heard his soft reply. "He will."

She laughed humorlessly. "History would suggest otherwise."

"That's not all on you. Two people played a part in every past scenario, and sometimes things just don't work out."

"I don't know. Sometimes I think I'm just too weird. It's like...I became who I am early in life because my dad was this charismatic man who loved nothing more than giving people the thrill of their lives, and I started down that path, too. But then he broke me, and I just sort of stalled out."

Graham inched forward as if he might reach out to touch her, but his hands simply shifted forward on his thighs, gripping his knees.

Claire swallowed. "I'm loud and outgoing but I don't have

the lifestyle to back it up and no one knows what to do with me. Not even myself, sometimes."

He regarded her thoughtfully. "Are we back to the whole 'I'm not adventurous' thing? You better not have changed that answer on your profile, by the way."

She totally had.

"Just because you're not into extreme sports doesn't mean you're not adventurous. There's more than one way to meet that definition."

"What do you mean?"

"You do tons of shit I never would have if it weren't for you. You're always trying new foods, no matter what it is or where it came from. Remember the durian you picked up from the Asian restaurant? I thought I was gonna have to stay at Noah's the night you brought that home."

"Come on, it's a fruit that smells like rancid garbage but tastes sweet! How fascinating is that?"

"I have not, and will not, put something that smells like that in my mouth." He pointed at her. "In that, you're a hell of a lot more adventurous than me. And what about studying abroad for an entire summer? It takes a lot of guts to travel across the world by yourself and live in a city where you don't know a single person. Very few people would do that, Claire."

She blinked, taken aback. "I guess I've never thought about it like that."

"Well, start. You're more adventurous than you think. You don't give yourself enough credit. And while I respect your reasons for staying away from high-risk hobbies, I think you might be surprised how much you'd like a few of them if you ever tried. Like rock climbing." He grinned. "I mean, shit, you'd take it personally if you didn't make it to the top on the first try.

You'd call the rocks 'bitches' and rig up to try again, determined not to let a slab of granite best the badass that is Claire Harper."

A laugh bubbled up. "I totally would."

"See? You don't see yourself the way other people do."

That wasn't so easy to agree with.

"Claire, tons of people are unmarried at thirty-one. Thousands. Hundreds of thousands. Millions, probably. It's not always easy to find that person you're meant to be with. Not everyone grew up next door to the love of their life like Mia and Noah. And even for those two, it took a ridiculously long time for them to figure their shit out."

He had a point.

"Not finding your soulmate by now doesn't mean anything's wrong with you. Because believe me, there's not." Something in the way he said that made her stomach flip. "It just means the right guy hasn't found you yet. And I can guarantee he's looking."

Something inside her chest melted, which made her suspicious. "You're being really sweet," she accused. "And we're fully clothed."

He sat in the wooden rocking chair, legs splayed and palms on his thighs. When he lifted one hand to run his fingers through his hair in a move that somehow seemed deceptively lazy, Claire's gaze snagged on his rippling forearm. "I don't know why you sound so surprised. Sweet is my default setting."

How was he so sexy all the time? "More like sarcastic and foul-mouthed, but okay."

"You didn't seem to mind the other night."

"I did not."

His lids lowered a little as he watched her, their words hanging in the air. A low simmer of heat seemed to constantly burn beneath the surface when they were together, and the temperature rose by several degrees every day.

"Is this too weird?" she blurted out.

He arched a brow.

"Talking to you about my dating life while we're...you know."

"Nah. I knew what was up going into this. You want commitment and someone to share your deepest, darkest everythings with, and vice versa. That's not what I have to offer and I don't blame you for still wanting to find it." He shifted in his chair. "Is it weird for you?"

"It might be if I actually like this guy."

Graham glanced away for a beat. "Well, if that happens we stop what we're doing. I'm fine with it to a point, but the second you'd rather be in another man's bed instead of mine, we're done here."

His tone stung, but she tried not to let it get to her. "I understand."

Silence descended along with an air of awkwardness that didn't often exist between them. Graham seemed to dislike it as much as she did, and spoke again. "For what it's worth, I hope you like him. You deserve everything you're looking for and more."

The sincere words were a balm to her soul, and she wished like hell she could say something to return the favor.

If she were being honest, she wished she and Graham were two people who could make it work, because there were so many things she liked about the man sitting beside her. His humor, his desire to help people, the way she knew he wouldn't hesitate for a second to run into a burning building to save anything that breathes, be it a human or an animal, like the tiny dog curled up at his feet. She'd never had as much fun with anyone else, whether they were out on the town or at home playing a ridiculous card game. He could make something as mundane as a game of Old Maid fun…or sexy, depending on his mood.

That was the other thing. That pesky thing called attraction. She'd never connected with someone so well physically, including her most serious boyfriend, whom she'd dated for almost a year. She'd always sort of watched Graham from afar, proud to enter a room with him but never considering laying claim to him. They were friends and that was it.

She would have never guessed that kissing him on a whim would completely turn that on its head and take them down this path. But man, every time their lips touched, it was like lighting a match and throwing it on the campfire. The negative thoughts parading through her mind that said maybe she wasn't, and would never be, enough for a man went up in flames.

The same thing happened somewhere inside him; she knew it. But his wounds, though no deeper, were different than hers. She didn't know if anyone—certainly not her—would ever dig deep enough to heal them.

"You deserve that, too," she finally said.

His next words surprised the shit out of her.

"I know."

She stilled. "You do?"

He gave her a sort of sad half smile. "I said I know I deserve everything I'm looking for. That's why I go out every weekend looking for it."

Was he talking about women or being in the mountains? She was too chickenshit to ask, and Gertrude chose that moment to make her move, anyway. A woman with two large Rottweilers walked by, and Gertrude immediately went on

high alert, barking endlessly as if she stood a chance to defend this house against those monstrosities should they decide to attack.

Then, when they had turned the corner, Gertrude trotted over to Claire and leaped onto her lap, back straight and
tail wagging.

Graham's mouth dropped open. "What the hell?"

Claire glared at the dog. "You're not being cool here, G.
He wasn't supposed to find out about us."

The pitch in his voice went up an octave. "Gertrude?
Claire?"

Claire took a deep breath as if about to impart grave information. "Over the last couple weeks, Gertrude and I have
been..."

"What? Just tell me!"

"...going on walks."

Graham gasped. "No."

Claire nodded. "I'm sorry I didn't tell you. I didn't mean
for it to happen, but she kept standing by her leash all sad and
shit. At first I just did it so she'd get some exercise and maybe
not take it out on my pillows or shoes. And it's worked, by
the way—she hasn't chewed up anything since."

"But...going on walks was *our* thing."

"And it'll be your thing again, once you're better." Claire
ran a hand down Gertrude's soft fur. "She still loves you best,
Graham. You know that. It's just, well, I can give her something right now that you can't. It's just for a little while."

Gertrude whined, bringing both people's attention to her.

Graham collapsed back against the chair and flung his arm
across his eyes. "Just go."

"Are you sure?"

He sat up suddenly and reached for his crutches. "I'll go

inside to make it less awkward. Just…don't talk about it when you get back, okay?"

Claire couldn't help the giggle that escaped as he thumped into the house, shoulders rounded in dejection. She darted up to grab Gertrude's leash from just inside the door and turned to the little canine who, she had to admit, was pretty adorable in that moment.

"Well, G. Ready to go?"

* * *

The following evening, Graham appeared in her doorway while she stood in front of her open closet.

"You okay?" he asked. "I heard cursing."

"I don't know what to wear," she whined.

He gestured to her silk robe. "That looks pretty fucking hot."

He flashed that gorgeous crooked smile, which was the last thing she needed before going on a date with another guy.

*Please, please let me like the new guy's smile, too.*

Determined to keep character to convince herself as much as Graham, she rolled her eyes. "If you're not gonna help me, move along."

Graham moved farther into the room, eyeing the outfits she'd discarded on the bed. Putting his weight on one crutch, he gestured with the other. "What's wrong with that one?"

Claire scrunched her nose. "I decided it's too fancy, and a little too revealing." She ignored the flare of heat flashing through his eyes. "He just asked me for coffee, remember? I need to consider the setting."

Graham frowned as if the concept were foreign to him, but he didn't argue. "Okay, what are the other options?"

She pulled out a floral sundress that she'd always found cute and flirty and made her ass look great.

"You look really hot in that."

"I do?"

"Sure. You wore it last year when we went out for your birthday."

Her heartbeat slowed a fraction and she hooked the hanger on the back of the doorknob, trying to ignore the way her hand trembled slightly. She grabbed an emerald green silk tank top. "Um, I was also considering this one. With jeans."

"Also a good choice. Didn't that make it through an entire night at Dante's Bar?"

It had, and that night had been *insane*. "How do you remember what I wore that night?"

He didn't answer the question and instead asked his own. "What about that yellow dress you have? The one with buttons down the front?"

What the hell was happening?

*Don't call attention to it.*

She did a one-eighty back to her closet and mouthed *holy shit* to her clothes. Carefully keeping her expression neutral, she faced him again. "This one?"

"Yeah. I've always thought you look nice in that one. You know, goes with your hair and stuff."

It suddenly felt as if the walls of her room were slowly moving in. "Really?"

"Why are you looking at me like that? It shouldn't be news to you that I think you're beautiful."

A tingle spread along the back of her neck as if he'd touched her there. "Beautiful?"

He appeared dumbfounded. "Have I not made that clear?"

"I don't know... You usually use words like *hot* or *sexy*. *Beautiful* sort of feels like a different category."

"You're all of them. Hot, sexy, beautiful. Gorgeous. Stunning. A knockout. Take your pick and let's move on already. The guy finding you attractive is the last thing you should be worried about."

It took a second for her brain to trip over all the flattering words he'd just used to describe her and arrive at the second part. She stiffened. "Because once he gets to my personality I'm in trouble?"

"What? Hell no. I didn't say that. I don't understand why you're so convinced you're not the kind of woman men want. It's total bullshit."

Claire deflated. "I'm sorry. I think I'm just nervous."

"Don't be. I'm already mentally preparing myself for the chance you two hit it off and you come home engaged, and I may never kiss you again."

"Whoa, slow down. I don't believe in love at first sight, remember?"

He rotated so he could sit on the edge of her bed. "Right."

She regarded him for a second, hoping common sense would rouse her rarely used filter and prevent the next words from leaving her lips. No such luck. "Would it bother you to never kiss me again?"

Graham's chin dipped but his gaze lifted to hers, his eyes dark and conflicted. "I think it's best I don't answer that."

Claire could interpret that two ways. One, it would bother him but he didn't want to admit it. Maybe the thought freaked him out like it did her. Or two, it wouldn't bother him, but he didn't want to risk offending her and forgoing the chance to get laid in the near future.

Based on the Graham she knew, odds were it was reason number two.

He pushed to his feet. "I'd better let you get ready...unless you need help getting dressed?"

Definitely reason number two. "I'm good."

"Have fun tonight," he said, and tossed a lingering smile over his shoulder before he left.

# 16

To: PinkSparkles91@zzmail.com
From: Graham.Scott27@zzmail.com
Subject: I…like you?

Claire,

You just left for your date with Mr. Real Estate. You wore the yellow dress. Which makes me an asshole, because while you look damn good in it, it's the green top that would have made the guy lose his mind. And contrary to what I said, I guess I'm not ready to let this go yet.

I'm not sure what it is, but I'm inclined to blame you. You've been taking my dog on walks, for crying out loud. If there's a faster way to my heart I don't know what it is. Don't freak out (me—I'm telling myself that), I'm not professing my undying love or anything ridiculous. I'm just feeling…something. Something I haven't let myself feel in a long time, and I don't know why it's changing with you. For the most part I'm the same Graham around you as I am around everyone else, but lately I've slipped and said some things to you I don't normally talk about, like my mom's MS diagnosis or the fact that we were too poor to have a pet when I was growing up.

You didn't run away screaming or get all weird and awkward. It was nice.

AND, though I don't want to admit it, I've sort of liked these secret conversations we're having via email. Secret because you don't know about them, but on my end they're going well. I get why people do this (but I'll take that to my grave if you ever find out and ask me about it). It's sort of freeing to be able to say anything and put it all out there without fear of shame, embarrassment, or rebuke. None of which I particularly enjoy, but lived with on a daily basis before I left Santa Fe for college.

I went to a fancy private school, did you know that? Westfield. Only about two hundred kids between the middle and high school, so pretty close-knit group. Except for me, that is. At the beginning at least.

Up until sixth grade I went to a public school by my house and loved it. I had a ton of friends, played basketball, and made good grades. But the summer before junior high my dad got a job as the nighttime janitor at Westfield, and as an employee, he was able to send his only son to the prestigious school tuition free even though we lived miles from the district border. My parents were so excited about the opportunity that I went into it with a pretty open mind.

Yeah, that lasted about twenty minutes. Those rich-ass kids picked up my low-income scent in no time and I went through that entire first year a complete outcast. I was made fun of, picked on, and beat up on occasion. I was pretty small back then but wouldn't have had the guts to fight back even if I could have. I had one friend—the English teacher, Mr. Sikes. And my dad, who spent his nights mopping the floors and cleaning up after those punks.

In eighth grade we had a partner science project and I was paired up with Angela DiMarco. She'd always been decent to me, and by that I mean she didn't knock books off my desk or call me names. But during the project she actually talked to me, and naturally, as a thirteen-year-old boy I developed a huge crush on her. By the end of it I thought we were friends. She even talked to me in the hall where other people could see.

So I got up the nerve to ask her to the fall fling dance, which was so fucking stupid, but I was so gone for the first girl that had been nice to me that I wanted to go SO. BAD. I'd go to sleep thinking about walking in holding her hand, dancing with her, and maybe even kissing her in a corner somewhere.

Mr. Sikes had gotten me onto yearbook committee, and several days per week I hung out in the media room, where we put together photos and stories for that year's book. It was also where they kept recording equipment for announcements and this cheesy radio show the school played for people in the carpool lane.

So the day we turned in our science project I asked Angela to meet me in the media room after school. When she came, I let it all out and told her how much I liked her, waxing poetic about her kindness and how she was the prettiest girl in school. I don't know what happened, it was total word vomit once I started. At the end, I asked her if she'd go to the dance with me.

As I'm sure you can guess, since we hate Angela now, she said no in pretty spectacular fashion. Said she couldn't be seen going to the dance with the janitor's kid. Not only that, but having anticipated a potential opportunity when I asked her to meet me there, she secretly turned on the recording equipment and replayed my entire speech, including her rejection, the next day at school. This was junior high, mind you, so I'm sure you can imagine what my life was like after that.

I'll give you a hint: relentless torment.

Anyway. I'm not sure why I just told you all that, but it was my first experience telling a girl how I felt about her, and my heart was ripped to shreds and the pieces hung around the entire school for everyone to see. Embarrassing yourself in front of friends is one thing. Doing it in front of people who already hate you is another thing entirely.

So thanks, I guess, for not treating me that way. I've never felt judged by you.

Even when you say I'm an asshole. For some reason I find it endearing.

Graham

★ ★ ★

Graham slammed the laptop shut and glanced at the clock as the front door crashed open.

Either someone was breaking in, which he couldn't do a damn thing about, or Claire's date hadn't gone well. She'd only been gone an hour.

Gertrude barked her tiny head off and darted off the bed and into the hallway.

"Claire?" he called out, placing the laptop on the bedside table. He grabbed one of his crutches to use as a weapon if necessary.

Claire appeared in the doorway with Gertrude under one arm and her purse dangling from the other, loose at her side.

One look at her face and Graham's hackles rose. He released the crutch and pressed his hands into the mattress, sitting up straighter. "What happened? Are you okay?"

She dropped her purse and pulled Gertrude to the front

of her body, burying her face in his dog's fur. "His girlfriend showed up."

"His *what*?"

"Yeah." Claire was beside the bed now, and deposited Gertie near his legs. She swiped angrily at her eyes, color high on her cheeks. She still looked achingly beautiful, but he hated seeing her upset. "The bastard apparently has a girl-friend, and she happened to stop by the coffee shop with a friend. She saw us together and asked him who I was."

Anger burned hot in Graham's chest. "What an asshole. I'm sorry, Claire."

She threw up her hands. "Are there no decent men out there?"

"Not many."

She crossed her arms, the movement pushing her breasts up. His eyes dropped to the cleavage on display, because he was not a decent man.

"Graham."

His eyes lifted to find a tiny smile on her face. She raised her eyebrows.

He just grinned. "Sorry."

"Why can't more men be like you?" she asked.

Graham nearly choked. "Me? We don't need more of me. I'm fucked up and I was just ogling your breasts while you're upset. We need more Nathans and Noahs. Those are the kinds of guys women deserve."

Claire regarded him for a moment, her eyes passing over his face and chest. He couldn't decide if he wanted her to con-tradict him or not.

"Hmm," she said slowly. Thoughtfully. "I'm not sure I agree. You're not perfect, but you're a pretty great guy, Gra-ham. Whether you admit it or not."

He narrowed his eyes. "When you said you went to a coffee shop, did you really mean bar? Are you drunk?"

She shook her head and took another step forward. Before he knew what was happening, she climbed onto the bed and lifted the skirt of her bright yellow dress, straddling his waist.

With effort, he kept his arms at his sides. "What are you doing?"

"I want you, Graham."

He blinked. "Want me…how?"

Her hazel eyes flashed and she put her hands on his chest, leaning forward. "Do you think if I'm on top and do most of the work, we can…?"

*Yesyesyes.* "You're upset and not thinking clearly."

Her head was shaking before he even finished the sentence. "I've wanted to do this long before now."

Hard same.

She kissed him softly and he kept as still as possible. "Please?"

His blood was a freight train, ramming through his body to one central point. He locked eyes with her. "Part of me wants to say hell yes, while the other part demands I retain some dignity and say let's wait until I can participate more."

She traced a single finger along the skin above the collar of his shirt, raising goose bumps across his skin. "Which part is winning?"

"Right now it's about seventy-thirty in favor of fucking."

She arched her back and shifted her hips. "How about now?"

He groaned, unable to keep his eyes open as desire hit him like a spear through his midsection. "Ninety-ten."

Claire straightened, which put more pressure on his groin and forced a heavy breath through his lips. She met his gaze steadily and reached up to slowly undo the buttons at the top of her dress. "I think I can convince that last ten percent."

His voice was low, gravelly. "Please do."

She pursed her lips as if to stop from smiling, probably trying to keep the sultry look going. Surely she knew he wanted her either way, right? He'd been dying to finally arrive at this moment, like a kid in the back of the car on his way to Disneyland.

Did other men really not see how incredible she was?

He wanted her serious, laughing, teasing, bickering. He'd take them all at once or one at a time, savoring each shade and facet of her personality.

Current Claire—determined, confident, maybe projecting a little anger from her failed date—was sexy as hell. He was always happy to step up and ensure a woman knew how attractive she was and how much he wanted her, but he also loved when a woman went after what she wanted.

Her progress was achingly slow, the movement of her fingers tantalizing as she popped the tiny buttons from the holes, revealing more of her gorgeous body with each one.

"Touch me," she said, eyes still on his. She knew she was turning him on—there was no way she couldn't feel that—and knowing Claire, she basked in the knowledge and control it gave her. But a tiny hint of vulnerability in her expression told him maybe a small part of her needed that in this moment.

"You're bossy tonight." His back and head still against the headboard, Graham slid his palms up her smooth thighs and underneath the fabric of her skirt.

She was almost to midstomach and the dress gaped open at the top. His hands moved around to cup her ass and he pulled her closer at the same time he sat forward, and Claire abandoned the buttons as their chests connected. Simultaneous sighs escaped their lungs and in the split second before their lips met, Claire whispered, "I'm always bossy."

Their mouths came together with ease and familiarity.

Claire tugged at his shirt and he pulled back long enough for her to pull it over his head, then their lips met again. In seconds her dress pooled around her waist and her bra was tossed to the floor. Feeling her warm skin against his was like heaven.

Scooting her hips as close to his as they would go, Claire wrapped her legs around his waist and squeezed. Her arms wound around his back and her lips went to his neck, and he was in a cocoon of warm, soft, delicious-smelling woman.

This, right here, was one of the best experiences of Graham's existence.

"Don't move," he murmured. "Can we just stay like this all the time?"

"*Exactly* like this?" she teased, her breath against his neck.

"Well, maybe one or two parts could be rearranged. If you could just lift up a little, I could…"

She laughed, shifting sideways to shimmy out of her underwear. She settled back down, kissing her way up his rough jaw and meeting his lips for a deep kiss. His body heat rose with each touch, his skin like an inferno poised to set the room on fire.

Tracing his lips along the shell of her ear, he relished the way she trembled in his arms and whispered the things he would do to her if he could. With a moan that signaled she was getting to the end of her rope, she lifted up on her knees and wedged her hand between their bodies, working his zipper as he reached out to fumble blindly in the top drawer of his bedside table.

Seconds later, Graham was groaning into her hair, wondering if this thing with Claire might be the thing that healed him, or if he'd end up broken in even more pieces than before.

★ ★ ★

"I'm not a big fan of calling it fucking."

Claire was draped over his chest as he traced figure eights along her bare back.

"No?"

"No. It sounds so crass to me."

"Sorry. I just figured it was the best way to describe what we're doing." Graham tucked his free hand behind his head. "What do you want me to call it? Making love feels too flowery and boning just sounds juvenile."

She openly admired his biceps as she spoke. "Can't we just say we're having sex?"

"I guess. It's kind of clinical."

"Clinical would be intercourse. Or coitus."

Graham shuddered. "You're right, sex is better."

"Penetration?"

"There's no excuse to use that word. Ever."

Claire laughed against his chest and his heart did something funny, which he ignored.

They lay there a few moments without speaking. Graham couldn't stop thinking about what they just did, and how incredible it was despite him being in less than peak condition. What was she thinking about?

"I'm sorry your date was an asshole," he finally said.

She smirked at him. "Seemed to work out well in your favor."

He cracked a grin. "I didn't say I was sorry it didn't work out. I'm just sorry he was a dick to you. He didn't deserve even a second of your time."

"Agreed."

"In fact, I want all the seconds he got. Take them back and give them to me."

She put her hand flat on his chest and propped her chin there. "That's not how time works. I don't have the superpower you gave me."

"What did you guys talk about before you met up? He doesn't get to know anything about you I don't."

"You don't have to worry about that. You know way more about me than he does. You know more than almost anyone I know, actually. You and Mia are the only ones who really know how my dad died. Only you know I've watched the Jess and Nick episode of *New Girl* dozens of times."

"You know more about me than anyone else, too."

"Really? What's mine and mine alone?"

"Nathan knew about my mom's diagnosis. You're my only living friend that does. And I've never told anyone else we were too poor to have a pet."

"And yet you still won't tell me about Angela DiMarco."

*I did, though. You just don't know it.* "Don't be greedy."

"I can't help it. I like knowing you, Graham."

It took the words a few seconds to come out, as if his brain worried he was admitting to something more serious.

"I like knowing you, too."

★ ★ ★

To: PinkSparkles91@zzmail.com
From: Graham.Scott27@zzmail.com
Subject: The sex

Claire,

You've officially ruined me for other women.

How did you do that?

This was supposed to be just sex. I'm inclined to accuse you of having a magic vagina, but on second thought it seems far-fetched. Plus, there's the fact that I've had hints of this feeling every time we've kissed, and more that night we messed around. But tonight? It was multiplied by factors of infinity and I hardly did anything. You were so damn sexy and confident and I've never seen a woman so beautiful.

What will you feel like when I can move with you and use my

whole body? How will it feel for you when I'm on top, or when I push you against the wall? How will it feel to me?

Fuck, I hope I get the chance to find out. And not only because it felt good (and believe me, it felt GOOD), but there's something else, too. Something that freaks me out a little bit.

I don't usually look women in the eye when we have sex. Weird, right? I think it's sort of like Julia Roberts in *Pretty Woman* and how she didn't kiss on the mouth. It just feels so personal. I just don't really like letting people see too deep, you know? I opened up once with Angela, and that shit followed me for years. Never again, I promised myself.

So they see what I want them to see, which is a fun, confident, adventure-loving guy who doesn't care about much else, and definitely doesn't care about what people think of him. But I've always believed that saying that eyes are the window to the soul, and while I can control what I reflect most of the time, barriers fall down during sex. For me, at least. I figure I probably shouldn't be doing it if I can't let go at least a little. Still, I've always held on to a shred of emotional privacy, even when my body is for the taking.

But just now? With you? I felt myself slipping. My eyes kept drifting to yours even when I didn't want them to, and I couldn't stop looking at you. I desperately wanted to know if you'd let go and if I could see all the way down into the hidden corners of you, or if you were closed off in places, too.

Usually I don't care about that shit. I've never been in it for that. But that was before you.

I'm not gonna say anything yet, and you still don't know about these letters. This cast comes off soon, and then I find out where my recovery goes from there. And I hope that means you and I have more time and I can figure out what this is and what, if anything, I'm gonna do about it.

I can say one thing for sure, Claire Harper. You caught me off guard and I don't scare easy.

Graham

PS. Sorry I ripped your dress. I'll buy you a new one.

# 17

Claire sunk into the couch cushions with a sigh. "It feels so good to sit."

Mia, perched in the perpendicular armchair, tucked her leg underneath herself. "Busy day?"

"Very." Claire spread her arms along the back of the couch. "But I'm so glad you came over. Graham couldn't stop texting me today about how excited he was Noah was taking him out. I finally had to turn my phone off when the charge nurse kept giving me dirty looks."

Graham had started back at the station on light duty, which meant he was filing paperwork all day. While it was something, it wasn't enough. He'd already complained about needing someone to take him to and from work, and a desk job was the last thing he wanted to be doing.

Mia laughed. "I'm pretty sure Noah's just taking him to Wings To Go."

"Doesn't matter. The man would be happy with a trip to stand in line at the DMV right now." Gertrude leaped up and sidled over next to Claire's thigh. Claire absently scratched the dog's head and pulled up PostMates on her phone. "Is it okay if we order in? I'm too tired to go anywhere."

When Mia didn't answer right away, Claire looked up to find her friend watching her and Gertrude curiously.

"What's happening?" Mia asked. "I thought you and Gertrude hated each other."

Claire shrugged. "We've resolved our differences. Most of them, anyway."

"Huh."

Claire narrowed her eyes. "What's that tone?"

"There was no tone."

"Mia Agnew. You can't lie to me. When has that ever worked?"

Mia's eyes searched the ceiling.

"Never."

"Okay, fine! I was just wondering if your sudden change in relationship status with Gertrude has anything to do with what's going on with Graham."

Claire arched a brow. "What's going on with Graham?"

Mia crossed her arms. "You tell me."

The two friends stared at each other for a long moment, and both could be incredibly stubborn in their own right. She'd be the one to cave this time, though, because she wanted to talk to Mia about Graham. It was half the reason she was so happy Noah had taken him out and left her and Mia to hang out tonight.

"Can we order dinner first? I'm starving."

Mia rolled her eyes good-naturedly. "I guess. You're milking that measly twelve-hour shift for all it's worth, aren't you?"

"Yep. I'm in the mood for tacos, sound good?"

"Sure."

Claire found a nearby restaurant available for delivery and

placed their order. The second she set her phone on the coffee table she felt Mia's eyes on her.

Her friend wagged her eyebrows. "Spill."

Scrunching her nose, Claire picked at her fingernail. "I might have taken your advice."

Mia's sudden squeal startled Gertrude, who leaped off the couch with a glare in Mia's direction and slowly made her way to Graham's room. "I knew it!"

"Yes. We had the sex."

"And?" Mia's eyes were wide as she leaned forward, nearly tipping off the chair.

A slow smile crept in, along with a flush of heat as she thought about last Saturday night. And again on Sunday. "It was very, very good." How had she described him after their first kiss? *Thorough.*

Well. He'd certainly earned that badge of honor.

Thorough, attentive, consuming.

"Can't say I'm surprised."

"Mia!"

"What?" Mia shrugged. "You know I'm madly in love with Noah, but Graham's a good-looking guy, and if his body is like Noah's from all that climbing they do…" She fanned herself.

"You'll hear no complaints from me," Claire agreed.

"Not even with his cast?" Mia's cheeks flushed, which was more her style. "How did that work, exactly?"

"I was on top."

"Is there even another option?"

"I don't know… I don't think so. I can tell it bothers him, though. He feels like he's being lazy." She laughed, remembering what he'd said on Sunday when they were gearing up for round two. "He asked if this was how women felt all the time, just lying there while sweaty men grunt on top of them."

Mia gasped. "He compared you to a sweaty, grunting man?"

"Right? You know I didn't let that slide. He backtracked and…made it up to me in quite spectacular fashion." And how. "And I don't mind for now. I sort of like being in control."

"Why doesn't that surprise me?"

"I have no idea."

Mia grinned and twirled a piece of long, dark hair around one finger. "So you did it and it was good. How are you feeling about it?"

Claire tucked her hands underneath her legs. "That's a loaded question."

The thinly veiled avoidance attempt fooled no one.

"Okay, how about this: Has the change in your relationship with Graham also changed your feelings for him?"

This was a topic Claire hadn't let herself marinate on for long, and she wasn't about to start now. "I think about him more, but I've also been around him a lot lately. For the first week after his accident I was worried about him and constantly thinking about his next dose of medicine or if he would fall when he was in the bathroom. Now, I think about how much fun he is in bed, and I wonder how different it might be once he's recovered. I'll admit I look forward to seeing him, and I don't want to stop what we're doing."

"What would you do if he wanted to date you? For real?"

Feeling her shoulders tense, Claire shook her head. "I couldn't. It's not an option."

"Why not?"

"I can't live like my mom did. I want to have kids someday, and I won't subject them to the possibility of what I went through. As much as I like Graham, and even though we're having fun for the time being, he's just not the right guy for me long-term. Remember what happened after that firefighter got injured a few weeks ago? Seeing Graham, my friend, come through on that stretcher was a thousand times worse. The thought of facing that with a partner... I just can't do it."

"Does he know you feel that way?"

"Yeah, I told him about my dad."

Mia didn't try to hide her surprise. As a rule, Claire didn't discuss that topic often. "Really?"

"Yeah. He understands where I'm coming from, and besides, he feels the same. About serious relationships, I mean. I still haven't gotten the full story, but he's been burned and isn't interested in that level of commitment. I get the feeling he doesn't trust any woman, even me, not to hurt him eventually."

Mia nodded slowly. "I've gathered bits and pieces from him over the years, but even Noah doesn't know the full story. I guess I just assumed he was having fun living his life and hadn't found a woman he liked enough to settle down with."

"I'm sure that's true to a point. I just don't see any woman capable of getting inside that head of his."

"What's the status of the backup marriage pact?"

A laugh bubbled up. "Was I the only one who knew that wasn't a real thing?"

Mia's calm expression didn't budge. "Worked for Noah and me."

"That's totally different. You two are made for each other."

"What makes you think you and Graham aren't?"

Claire blinked. "Did—did you listen to anything I just said?"

"I just think you might be a better fit than either of you think."

"Unless big things change, including his job, extracurricular activities, and ability to be completely open about his thoughts and feelings, I don't agree."

"So he's the only one that needs to make a change, huh?"

"I... No." Claire frowned, rubbing at her forehead. "What's with all the questions? Obviously I'm not perfect, either. Otherwise I wouldn't be in my thirties and still single."

Undeterred, Mia pressed, "No one's perfect. Do you think Graham wants to change anything about you?"

Warmth settled deep in Claire's belly as she considered that. "I'm sure there are things he wished were different, but I doubt he'd ever say it. He's one of the most accepting people I know. Oddly enough the things other men seem to take exception to are the things Graham says are his favorite things about me."

"Hmm." Mia flicked invisible lint from her jeans, not seeming at all surprised.

Feeling suddenly uneasy with the direction this conversation was headed, Claire checked her phone. "Tacos are ten minutes out."

"Perfect." Mia extended her legs to rest her feet on the coffee table. "How are things going with the dating app? Anyone of interest?"

Claire had told Mia about signing up, but not about the total failure of a first date she'd had last weekend. When she thought back on that day, Graham was who she'd remember, not the douchebag she'd met for coffee. While the incident had been mortifying, the time she'd spent with Graham after she got home was more than enough to make up for it. She couldn't remember the last time she'd felt so beautiful.

Or so wanted.

She picked up her phone and pulled up the app. "Actually, I haven't checked in a few days." That first experience had sort of left a bad taste in her mouth. She tapped the inbox, feeling Mia's gaze on her. "I have two new matches."

Mia dropped her feet and was suddenly on the couch beside her. "Ooh, how do they look?"

They sat beside each other in silence for several minutes, reading the profiles.

"Are there photos?" Mia asked.

"Yep. Which one should we check out first?"

"Both sound promising, but I'm gonna go with the dentist. He sounded more like you."

Claire's eyebrows went up. She'd gravitated toward the high school baseball coach. "Why do you say that?"

"That question asking what he's looking for in a woman. He said independent, good sense of humor, and someone who loves going out to eat. That's you in a nutshell."

She had a point. Claire selected the dentist, Matt Foster. The photo loaded and they both leaned back.

"Wow," Mia breathed.

Claire stared. "Seconded."

If the photo was authentic and recent, Matt Foster was extremely hot. He stood alone on a bridge, hips against the railing and one ankle crossed over the other. She couldn't see much of his hair because he wore a baseball cap on his head, but a few blond curls escaped at the bottom. A strong jaw was covered in light brown scruff and a well-built body filled out the T-shirt and slim-cut jeans he wore. His nose was set below a pair of striking blue eyes, with slight lines at the edges that spoke of a man who smiled big and smiled often.

Which brought her to his mouth. Full lips stretched around straight white teeth in a smile that was almost as incredible as Graham's.

Almost.

"I was just thinking I needed to get my teeth cleaned." Mia reached for the phone she'd abandoned in her chair. "That's Foster, spelled *F-O-S-T-E-R*?"

"Actually it's spelled *N-O-A-H*."

Mia rolled her eyes. "You of all people know I'm madly in

love with my husband." She continued to pull up Google on her phone. "I also happen to need a new dentist."

Claire toggled back to Matt's profile and read more about him. He did seem pretty great, but she'd thought that about the real estate agent at first, too.

"You gonna message him?" Mia asked, eyes still on her phone.

"I don't know."

Mia's hands dropped to her lap and she stared at Claire. "What? Why not?"

An image of Graham's face popped into Claire's mind.

There was a moment on Saturday night when she'd caught him looking at her with something like tenderness. It had been there but was gone in an instant when he'd looked away, almost as if he couldn't take it. It wasn't until the next morning she'd thought back to it, and the intensity in his eyes, but she'd thought about it often since.

It probably wasn't the best idea to dwell on it given her commitment not to fall for him beyond that of friends with benefits.

"You're right," she said. "I should give him a chance, huh?"

Her friend gave her a strange look. "Wasn't that the whole point of signing up?"

"Yeah, of course." Just as Claire tapped the icon to start a conversation with Matt, a banner appeared on the screen to inform her their food had been delivered.

She jumped up and dropped her phone on the couch. "Food's here."

Later that evening, when she got into bed beside Graham, Claire realized she'd never sent a message to the dentist.

She could roll onto her side and send something quickly, but Graham's large hand closed around her hip, and thoughts of anything but him floated right out of her mind.

★ ★ ★

She didn't message Matt the dentist the next day, either.

Work was nonstop, and she was an hour and a half late getting home. She'd sneaked in a text to Graham that he should eat dinner without her, but had time for little else. Luckily a drug rep had left deli sandwiches in the break room and she swiped one on her way out. It was for Graham's benefit, really, because there was no telling what state of hangry she'd have been in by the time she got home otherwise.

She'd also received an email from the hospital's credentialing office that everything was complete and she could officially transition to her role as nurse practitioner. A second email from Dr. Singh followed, asking when Claire could meet to discuss an official start date. Other than giving Ruthie a quick heads-up that her nurse shift days were numbered, she hadn't had time to deal with it.

When she got to the condo she went straight to her room to change, wanting to fall right into bed. Graham's bed, that was…because she'd never gone back to sleeping in her room and had no intention of doing so.

She refused to think about what would happen next week when Reagan returned. She was dreading the impact that would have on her and Graham's…whatever it was.

Clad in yoga pants and a T-shirt, she padded to Graham's room and stopped short.

He sat on the side of the bed, shirtless, his shoulders hunched forward with one hand braced on his knee and the other in his thick hair.

"What's wrong?" she asked, unable to ignore how sexy he was in partial undress despite his obvious distress.

Graham straightened and looked up, shuttering his expression. "Nothing. I'm fine."

She frowned and walked around to stand in front of him.

She leaned her hips against the dresser and crossed her arms. "No, you're not."

He shook his head, the lines in his forehead smoothing. "You had a ridiculously long day. You must be exhausted. We can talk about it tomorrow."

"Graham Scott, if you don't tell me right this second—"

"Fine." He gripped the back of his neck. He paused, and finally his shoulders fell. "I just talked to my dad. My mom had a relapse. She fell and has been too weak to get out of bed for three days."

Her stomach dropped. "Oh, no." She took two steps forward and gently placed her hands on his shoulders, sliding her thumbs back and forth across his warm skin. "That's awful. I'm so sorry."

He leaned into her, resting his forehead against her rib cage. She slid one hand to his hair and he sighed heavily. "It's not the first time this has happened, but my dad hates to leave her to go to work when it does. When it looks like it'll be longer than a few days before she recovers, I usually try to go down there to help. But I can't fucking drive and it's expensive to fly."

The words left her mouth before she realized it. "I could drive you."

He lifted his head, dark eyes meeting hers. "What?"

"I mean, I can't take a ton of time off work, but I'm not on the schedule this weekend. We could go down Friday and stay until Sunday. I could probably switch shifts with someone on Monday if you wanted to stay a little longer."

Graham just stared at her, his lips parted slightly. "You'd do that?"

"Of course. You're my friend and you're worried about your family. They're important to you and you're important to me. I'd be happy to help, if you'll let me."

His expression altered a little, snagging on that last part with something like hesitation. "I've only taken someone where I grew up once, and it didn't go very well." He shook his head, the tips of his ears turning pink. "I didn't... That is, it's not very..." He seemed to struggle to find the right words.

"You know I don't care about where you lived, right?" Was that what he was worried about?

He shrugged, appearing strangely vulnerable.

"Graham, I want to go because you're my friend and because I want to be there for you, not because I give two shits about how much money your parents have. That means less than nothing to me." She cocked her head. "Is that what you mean by it didn't go so well? What kind of woman were you dating, Graham? Because she sounds like an asshole. You deserve better than that."

He just looked at her, searching her face. His hands had found their way to her waist and his fingers tightened their grip as his brow furrowed.

She moved her hands from his head to his shoulders. "Why are you looking at me like that?"

"I..." He blinked, as if trying to make sense of something. "I never thought I'd find something more attractive about you than your smart mouth. But that might be the nicest, most genuine thing you've ever said to me, and I've never wanted to kiss you more than I do right now. I'm not really sure what to do with that."

Claire's heart thumped beneath her ribs. Her legs wobbled a little and she leaned into him, lowering her forehead to his. "I think you do."

# 18

That was an invitation to kiss her if Graham had ever heard one.

With a tilt of his chin, their lips met in a kiss that was slow, deep, and searching.

Was she looking for the same thing as him?

He pressed harder, paying attention to her response, and she returned with a force of her own. Her hands pushed at his chest and he fell back, carefully lifting his legs onto the bed while she shed her clothes.

She carefully swung her leg over his hips and settled down exactly where he wanted her. Her blond hair, curly and unruly, framed her flushed cheeks like petals on a wildflower. Her lips were swollen from his kiss and her hazel eyes tracked her hands as she lightly trailed her nails across his chest.

He swallowed hard as he took her in.

She was so fucking beautiful.

Frowning, she asked, "Are you in pain?"

Several things hit him at once. Concern for his mom, frustration at his injury, and confusion over the depth of his feelings for this woman he couldn't get enough of.

Before he could filter his response, he nodded.

She went up on her knees, concern filling her eyes. "I'm so sorry, does the pressure hurt your leg? Where does it h—"

Graham settled a hand on her smooth thigh, easing her back down. He circled her wrist with his fingers and pressed her hand over his heart.

"Here." His voice came out thick. "It hurts here."

Her eyes went soft and she stilled as his heart beat steadily against her palm. "Graham," she whispered, then bent down to brush her lips against his.

They remained in that position for long moments, hands wedged between their hearts as they kissed softly. Reverently. Both knowing there were things he wanted to say but probably never would.

She brushed her nose against his and buried her face in his neck, just beneath his jaw. She inhaled deeply and sighed with pleasure, sending his body to a higher precipice.

"I love the way you smell."

He lifted his chin to give her better access, sliding his free hand down her back. He brushed her backside and squeezed gently before trailing back up her ribs. Her perfect lips covered his face with kisses, and his throat was so tight he didn't trust himself to speak.

But when he cupped her face in his palms and she sighed happily, he thought maybe that was okay. He looked her in the eye and arched up to kiss her, gaze unwavering.

He'd always preferred action to talking, anyway.

★ ★ ★

Claire slept like the dead beside him.

He couldn't stop looking at her.

Something was happening inside the hollow cavern of his chest and for the first time in a long time, he didn't have the urge to run away screaming.

Which worked out because he couldn't run even if he wanted to.

As a guy who hadn't been in love since the eighth grade, he wasn't usually one to wax poetic after sex. He wasn't a hit-it-and-quit-it kind of guy, but he didn't dwell on it long after the fact, either.

Sure, there were high points pinned in his memory as particularly good, but every single one paled in comparison to the past week with Claire. He wouldn't be surprised if the others started to fall off his radar completely.

He desperately hoped Claire felt the same. He still worried it wasn't as enjoyable for her because of his physical limitations, but he'd been creative in his endeavor to please her and so far, she'd voiced no complaints.

On the contrary, the sounds she made were...encouraging. To put it mildly.

What made these last few experiences stand out was how it felt everywhere, not just the usual places. The second she made eyes at him and he knew what was about to happen, his stomach dropped in anticipation. His heart leaped into his throat and his lungs constricted. It was hard to breathe or think about anything that wasn't her.

*Them.*

Carefully, so as not to jostle her, he pushed to a sitting position. He grabbed his laptop and propped it on his lap, turning the screen light to the dimmest setting.

★ ★ ★

To: PinkSparkles91@zzmail.com
From: Graham.Scott27@zzmail.com
Subject: Four letter words

Claire,

Fear isn't something I experience often, and I do a lot of dangerous shit. Only when I do something really out there do I get a whiff of actual crippling, bone-chilling fear.

But you? You scare the hell out of me, Claire Harper.

If you ever find these emails, or if I ever grow the balls to tell you about them, I'm sure you'll wonder why a single embarrassing event in the eighth grade had such an impact on my life and approach to relationships. While I don't think I can fully describe how devastating that moment was, or the utter humiliation of the months (yes, months) that followed, I can sort of see your point.

There's more to it.

That situation with Angela happened in the fall, and the rest of eighth grade was hell on earth. There were days I made myself throw up just to avoid going to school. But my mom was diagnosed that year, and my concern for her started to overshadow my own shame, and I didn't want to do anything to cause her or my dad more worry. So I sucked it up and finished the year.

Camping had always been like a reset for me. My dad and I had started going a few years before that, and even though trips were less frequent after my mom's diagnosis, we still went about once a month. Being out there and seeing how much bigger the world was outside of that small, judgmental school that smelled like money and arrogance was a shift to my perspective every time. It reminded me there was more to life than what happened inside those walls, and there were things I was good at.

Like rock climbing.

The summer after the year of hell I was on one of those trips, and just before night fell a kid from my school ran into our camp. He'd come out with a group of inexperienced climbers and one had frozen with fear on the side of a rock face. They were afraid he'd get tired holding on and fall, and even though he was on belay, they couldn't just let him stay up there all night. My dad and I grabbed our gear and followed the kid to the site. We were familiar with the area and knew there was a way to get to the top of the face on foot. My dad set the anchor and I climbed down to meet the stuck climber. Once I got there, I realized it was Blake, one of the most popular kids in my class and, incidentally, the guy Angela ended up going to the fall dance with.

Anyway, I talked him through getting off the rock, and by the following week the story had spread through town. I was in the newspaper and Blake, who turned out to be a pretty decent guy, invited me to his house the next weekend.

When I started high school, I was suddenly part of the "in" crowd. All the girls had heard about what I'd done and thought I was some sort of hero. Blake took me under his wing and his good word propelled me to the top of everyone's list, like my status as the poor janitor's kid no longer mattered.

I'd like to say I gave them all a "fuck you" and went about those four years with my pride intact, but I was a teenager. Nothing was more important than fitting in back then. So I went with it, slowly learning what it took to become one of them. You wanna know what rule number one was?

Don't let them see the real me.

It didn't take long to realize what mattered to those people. They valued confidence, which I learned to fake. Athletic ability, which I had. Power, which I had little of until I learned to make people laugh. I became the fun-loving jokester of the group, and that became my rightful place. And money, which was the one thing I had no hope of having. But with Blake's seal of approval, everyone else suddenly seemed content to overlook it despite years of bullying.

Things they didn't value: vulnerability, showing emotion, judging people by who they were on the inside as opposed to how they dressed or what they said. I never got on board with the last one, but I got pretty damn good at hiding the first two.

Once I got it, I was one of them. I belonged. People said hi to me, invited me to their parties, sat with me at lunch. They were "nice" to me. You bet your hot ass I went with it and became the person they wanted to see.

I didn't realize just how far I'd stepped into the role until I left for college. It's not so easy to turn back from someone you spend four years grooming yourself into, you know? I'm conditioned not to show weakness. Emotional connection? Fuck, no. Anytime I've gotten close, warning flags go up everywhere, telling me to turn around and go back. Not worth it, no one wants to hear it. People don't actually want to know you, they just want your fun side. The athletic side. The exciting side. The side that makes them feel good.

When I was twenty-one I came back to New Mexico for a camping trip with a bunch of friends and a girl I was casually dating. I couldn't be that close and not stop by and see my parents, so I planned to pop over to Santa Fe for lunch one of the days, and she tagged along. It was the most awkward thing ever. She just sort of stood in the middle of the room like she didn't want to be there, looking around like our home was roach-infested squalor rather than a, yeah, small and old, but *clean* home. While we were there my mom lost her footing and bumped into the cabinet in the dining room and this huge glass bowl fell off and broke her foot. At one point I almost cried, I was so upset seeing my mom like that—in pain and embarrassed because she thought she'd made a scene in front of a guest. My girlfriend wanted to go back to the campsite but we were in my car and I couldn't not go with my dad to take my mom to the ER, so we all went. She asked one of our other friends to come pick her up from the hospital and she broke up with me as soon as we got back to Denver.

That pretty much solidified that, even as an adult, letting people see the real me and meet my family just wasn't an option.

Then came you. A woman who I can be myself around and

who I'm actually going to let come meet my parents. And you know what I don't feel this time?

Fear.

Graham

# 19

Claire loved road trips.

Especially now, since she required heavy medication to get on airplanes. Her dad's accident may have taken her confidence in flying, but it hadn't stolen her desire to travel. She loved going new places and seeing new things.

And, as Graham had recently pointed out, trying new cuisines.

She wasn't sure what the plan would be for meals, and she'd be content to share them with Graham's family if that's how it worked out. But if they could have one or two out…she'd do some serious research and pick the most unique locally owned restaurant in Santa Fe she could find.

"You're, like, vibrating with excitement," Graham noted from his place in the passenger seat. She'd picked him up from the station at five o'clock sharp, bags packed and Gertrude in tow. After a quick stop at the gas station for drinks and snacks, they were ready to start the five-and-a-half-hour drive.

"I'm excited," she said, and immediately wished she could

take it back. She worriedly glanced over at him where he sat with Gertrude curled up in his lap. "I mean, not that your mother's ill. Gosh, that sounded horrible. I'm just excited to be getting away and going somewhere, even for a few days."

Graham squeezed her shoulder. "I understand. I am, too." He pressed his lips together and let out a heavy sigh. "I do have to warn you about something, though."

"Okay?"

"No matter what condition my mom's in, she's gonna try to get us together."

Claire flipped her hair. "Of course she will. I'm the dream daughter-in-law to mothers everywhere."

"Obviously. I couldn't do better."

"How do you want me to handle it? Pretend to be into you? We're just friends? This trip is all about you, Graham. I'm not usually so amenable, so you'd better take advantage while you can."

He trailed a finger along the side of her neck. "I intend to. You should definitely pretend to be into me. It's only a two-bedroom house, so we'll be sharing a bed in my old room, you know."

"We're not having sex in your parents' house."

"What? Why not?"

She knocked his hand away and tried to shake off the goose bumps. "Because!"

He just looked at her.

"No."

He crossed his arms. "Give me one good reason why not."

"Because you can't be quiet," she whisper-yelled.

"Why are you whispering? We're alone in the car."

No idea. She gripped the steering wheel tightly.

He chuckled beside her and slipped his hand back across the console to palm her thigh. She glanced down, loving the way his large hand wrapped all the way around her. "Let's just see how things play out, okay?"

"Fine," she whispered, just to be contrary.

He laughed again and the sound trickled into her skin like rain on a warm afternoon. His hand left her for a few minutes while he connected his phone to the Bluetooth in her car, returning it when music began flowing through the speakers.

They spent the rest of the drive talking and listening to music and enjoying each other's company. It was almost eleven by the time they pulled into the outskirts of Santa Fe.

Claire had never been there, and through the darkness she tried to look around as they went.

"What's that?" she asked, pointing. "Is it, like, a community college campus?"

Graham made a noise that was somewhere between a laugh and a grunt. It wasn't particularly happy. "That's Westfield. My old high school."

Claire turned in her seat to get a better look as they passed. "That's a high school?"

"Yeah. A fancy private one."

"Damn."

"My dad's the manager of building maintenance there. He started off as an overnight janitor, which is the only reason I went there. We're way outside the district line." He didn't look at her as he spoke, and faced his window instead. "You'll see."

It might have been best not to say anything here, but Claire had never done well with situations like that. "Hey, Graham? Money's not everything."

He didn't move. "At Westfield it was."

"They sound like a bunch of motherfuckers," she said, pulling to a stop at a red light.

That got a laugh out of him, and he finally looked over at her, his eyes happy. He quickly glanced through the windshield at the red light then back at her, and lurched across the car. His lips touched hers in a quick, hard kiss.

Before she knew it, he was back on his side of the car, re-settling a disgruntled Gertrude in his lap.

That didn't stop her heart from fluttering, or her lips from wishing for just a few more seconds of contact. "What was that for?"

He shrugged and smiled softly. "I'm just glad you're here."

She'd always been partial to Graham's wide, unabashed smiles. But this one might have just sneaked into the first slot in her favorites. It was sweet and just for her, like a secret whispered in her ear.

She threaded her fingers with his. "Me, too."

He continued to direct her, and twenty minutes later they pulled into a neighborhood. The houses were small and in various conditions. Some appeared well maintained while others had overgrown lawns and piles of junk lining the driveway. Graham told her to pull up in front of one she'd put in the former category. An older model pickup sat in the driveway and a single light bulb cast yellow light over the red front door.

It was hard to see in the dark, but the stucco was painted a lighter color and a tree several feet taller than the single-story house jutted from the middle of the grass lawn.

Claire parked along the curb right in front. "I bet you climbed the heck out of that when you were a kid."

Her comment seemed to please him. Had he been worried what she'd say about his childhood home? "I did." He opened the door and put Gertrude on the grass, and she immediately walked off, nose to the ground.

While he pulled his crutches from the back seat and got himself out of the car, Claire grabbed their bags. She met him at the passenger side and found a scowl in his face.

"I feel like a dick making you carry the bags."

She rolled her eyes and started across the grass, keeping her voice low. "Don't be ridiculous."

He caught up and reached the front door before her. "I told them we'd be late and not to wait up for us. My dad said he left a key under the mat."

Claire found the key and handed it to him, then knelt to pick up Gertrude.

Graham's gaze dropped to his dog in her arms, and that secret smile flashed across his face again.

Her heart squeezed and she frowned. What was he doing to her tonight?

Had coming here been a mistake? Too late now.

Graham opened the door and she followed him in, closing and locking it behind her. They were in what looked like a living room with a love seat and two faded recliners angled toward a small flat-screen television. A small lamp in the corner had been left on, illuminating a hallway in the back corner.

"Kitchen's through there," Graham said, pointing with a crutch. "Need water or a snack or anything?"

She shook her head.

"Okay. That way, then."

They crept down the dark, carpeted hallway and Graham gestured to the bathroom, which appeared to be the only one in the house.

He entered a room at the end and flipped on the light with his elbow. It was about the size of the bedrooms at the condo, maybe a little smaller. A bed was pushed against the corner and a desk with a sewing machine sat against the opposite wall.

"My mom made this her sewing room when I left," he said quietly. "My dad must have cleaned up in here, though. Usually the bed is covered in quilting fabrics and I end up sleeping on the couch."

Claire eyed the bed. "I'm happy to sleep on the couch if I need to."

Graham stalled. "What?"

"That bed looks kind of small for both of us, Graham. You're not exactly tiny, and that cast is like a whole other person."

He looked at her as if she'd lost her mind. "You've been in my bed every night for the last three weeks. I'm not losing you now. We'll make it work."

Who was this man—this impulse-kissing, sweet-smiling, sugar-speaking man—and what had he done with Graham?

Casting a hesitant glance back at her, he added, "If you want to, that is. If you'd be more comfortable being separate, you'll take the bed and I'll sleep on the couch. Would you rather do that?"

She bit her lip. "No."

He grinned. "Good."

Gertrude made herself comfortable on the bed while Claire dug through their bags for toothbrushes and something to sleep in. Minutes later she and Graham stood beside each other in the tiny bathroom with a mustard yellow toilet, trying and failing not to smile at each other as they brushed their teeth.

When she turned to leave he tapped her on the ass and winked. "Be there in a minute, sweetcakes."

She sat on that comment the entire time it took him to use the restroom and climb into bed beside her.

"Sweetcakes is a no go."

He straightened his arm and she went straight for the nook between his shoulder and chest as if it were the most natural thing in the world. "For the last time, what do you want to be called?"

"Claire."

"Claire Bear?"

"Nope."

"Honey?"

"If anyone gets that one it's you, Honey Grahams."

He groaned. "I didn't think this through."

"It's better than the first one I thought of."

"Let me guess. Graham Cracker?"

She put her finger to her nose.

"I'll definitely take Honey Grahams over that. But…do men usually get pet names?"

"Hell if I know. I've never had a boyfriend who demanded I have one in the first place."

He flicked her shoulder. "I'm not demanding. I just think it would be fun."

"Or…annoying?"

His chest lifted and he released a heavy sigh. "Fine. We can forgo the pet names for the time being."

"Thank you."

He lightly traced his fingers up and down her arm, sending a shiver through her. "I bet you're tired from the drive. We should go to sleep."

Claire nuzzled closer and buried her nose in his neck, inhaling his delicious scent. "Mmmkay. But can we make out first? Just a little."

He brushed his lips against her hair. "Sure. But I have to ask. Is it my fifth-place wrestling trophy or the photo montage of my good looks from first through twelfth grade turning you on?"

She shifted onto her stomach and propped herself on his chest, bringing her lips within an inch from his. "Actually, it's the Batman figurines on the bookcase."

One corner of his mouth tipped up. "I should have known."

Then he tilted his chin and pulled her in for a searing kiss, giving her exactly what she wanted.

★ ★ ★

Claire woke up alone.

She must have been tired if he'd been able to get out of bed and thump out of here on his crutches without waking her. Digging around for her phone, she tapped the screen and saw it was half past nine.

Movement under the covers forced a squeak of surprise from her throat before she realized it was Gertrude. She regarded the dog's tiny head peeking out from her cocoon.

"Graham left…and you stayed with me?"

Gertie put her head back down and closed her eyes.

Claire grinned, strangely pleased. As annoying as the little dog was, earning her allegiance was like a mark of honor.

She got out of bed and pulled on jeans and a white V-neck. Just as she was about to reach for the door it swung open.

"Finally." Graham winked from the doorway.

"Excuse me," she retorted in a low voice, "someone kept me up until one in the morning."

"It was your idea." He propped one shoulder on the frame, looking ridiculously sexy in faded shorts and a gray T-shirt.

Which was exactly why she'd let him keep her up till one in the morning.

She mumbled the worst excuse in the world as she knelt down to retrieve her bag of toiletries.

"I didn't catch that," he said, rotating with her as she slipped past him and into the hallway.

She glanced around to ensure her next words weren't the first ones his parents heard from her mouth. The hallway was empty and muffled voices sounded in the kitchen, so she looked back at him accusingly. "Maybe I'd be able to stop if you weren't so much fun to make out with."

His smile caused a short circuit in her brain and all she could do was stare at his mouth. "Stop looking at me like that," he ordered, "or my parents will wonder what happened to us."

"I need to brush my teeth first, anyway," she said, breaking out of her trance. "I'll be ready in a few minutes."

As she closed the bathroom door she heard him call out, "There you are, Gertrude, you little traitor."

The smile on her face quickly faded as nerves set in.

She was about to meet Graham's parents.

They weren't in a relationship, but it was still a big deal. No one from back home had met his parents. Not even Noah. Yes, he was restricted with his cast and wouldn't have asked her to come otherwise, but still.

Something about being the one he brought into this part of his world felt significant.

Shit, she hoped they liked her.

She'd have to watch her mouth, probably.

After ensuring she looked presentable, she opened the door to find him waiting for her in the hallway, Gertrude sitting primly at his feet.

"What did they say about the cast and crutches?" she asked. He still hadn't told them the extent of his injuries, but had said it was more important to see his mom than keep up the ruse. He'd thought it would be better to tell them in person, anyway, and show them he was in good spirits about it.

"My mom cried, then smacked me upside the head, and my dad called me an idiot."

Claire let out a surprised laugh and nodded. "Well. Sounds like we'll get along just fine."

# 20

Claire fit in with his family like the puzzle piece that had gone missing, but turned up one day between the couch cushions.

His mom felt well enough to get out of bed that morning and had been in the kitchen with his dad when he finally brought Claire in. Though, he'd been happy to have that hour alone with them first for several reasons.

One, he knew they'd be pissed when they saw the cast. He hadn't loved the idea of Claire witnessing his mother scold him like a ten-year-old boy.

Two, he wanted to remind them—his mother, especially— that Claire wasn't his girlfriend and they needed to keep matchmaking attempts to a minimum. He was warming up to the idea, it was true…but he wanted to talk to Claire about it himself, if he ever figured out how, without his parents around.

And three, because once Claire came into the picture, she stole the show, just like he knew she would.

His parents loved her.

Asking for seconds of the pancakes and eggs his dad had made was all it took for Claire to skyrocket to the top of his list.

Then she happened to mention something about *Schitt's Creek*, which apparently his mom had started this past week while in bed, and they didn't take a breath for like an hour.

Graham and his dad had just sat there quietly, drinking coffee and reading the paper, content to listen to them chat.

When his mom excused herself for a nap, Claire said she'd noticed a missed call from her mom, though Graham got the feeling she was trying to give him and his dad some alone time.

He'd always loved sitting with his dad. He was easy to talk to—straightforward and interesting, and few topics were off-limits. Every time Graham hung out with him, he learned something new about his dad's childhood or some outrageous story from his early twenties. They never got old and he hoped his dad never ran out of stories to tell.

Today, though, wasn't one for stories. They mostly talked about his mom and how she'd been doing. This relapse was worse than the last one, though she'd been doing well for a long stretch beforehand. Graham hated the unpredictability of MS, and how she could be fine one day and had difficulty seeing or speaking the next. She'd started a new drug last year which had improved things considerably, and she relapsed less often, but still. It sucked.

He'd do anything to take it away from her.

His dad tried to thank him for the money he sent and Graham quickly cut him off, cheeks filling with heat. His parents had done nothing but do their best by him and he owed them nothing less than the same in return.

"We'd rather have you than your money, though," his dad said quietly.

He sighed. "Don't try to guilt me. You know why I don't want to live here."

"Yeah. I do."

Graham had asked his parents to visit several times, but being away from home made both his parents nervous. If his mom started feeling bad while they were in another state or on the road, she'd be miserable. "I need to get down here to visit more often. I'll do better."

His dad nodded. "You're happy there. We know that. We're proud of you."

He sort of wanted to say it back, that he was damn proud of his dad and everything about the man he was and had taught Graham to be. But it felt like a weird thing to say, so he just offered a small smile of acknowledgment.

A few minutes later his dad stood, gripping the porch railing for support. It creaked and wobbled, and Graham glanced up.

"Bring a toolbox out here, would you?"

"With that cast?" his dad asked with a frown.

"I can fix it sitting down, old man. Stop worrying."

That was how he spent the next hour outside alone, and walked inside to hear Claire's loud voice in his parents' bedroom.

"Dammit, Nancy!"

Graham cast wide eyes at his dad, who pressed a fist to his mouth as if trying not to laugh.

"I wouldn't go in there if I were you," his dad warned.

Yeah, that wasn't happening.

Graham crossed the living room and swung open the door.

Claire sat in a chair at the side of his parents' queen-size bed, a deck of cards strewn across the comforter. His mom sat propped up in bed with…

…a huge smile on her face?

She fairly cackled with glee when she saw Graham. Claire, on the other hand, jerked her head around and glared at him.

"Your mom beat me three times in a row!" She lifted her

chin and narrowed her eyes at his mom. "I'm starting to think you've played gin rummy before."

"Never," his mom said, trying to straighten her expression. "Beginner's luck."

Claire pointed at Graham. "You. Should I trust her?"

He barely heard her over the blood rushing in his ears. His heart hadn't been this full in...well, ever.

He swallowed. "Definitely not."

Claire grunted and grabbed the deck to shuffle. "Up for another round, Nancy? If that is indeed your real name."

Graham laughed and shook his head as he walked back out, finding an identical smile on his dad's face.

"Told you," his dad said.

Graham joined him at the counter and turned on the faucet to wash his hands, trying to hide the slight tremble in his fingers.

His dad nudged his shoulder. "I like her."

"Dad."

"I'm just saying."

Graham sighed. "I like her, too."

★ ★ ★

His mom was asleep by six and his dad was glued to a baseball game on TV, so Graham asked Claire if she wanted to go out for dinner.

Her face lit up and she spent the next half hour researching local restaurants on her phone while he cleaned up and changed. His jaw nearly hit the floor when he walked into his old room and saw her. She'd changed into a casual T-shirt dress he hadn't seen before, and while there was nothing noteworthy about it, everything about her wearing it drew him in. She was the perfect mix of sexy and comfortable, and he wanted to bottle this feeling in his chest for safekeeping, proof to remind himself when he was old that there was once a woman who made him want to drop to his knees and give her the world.

He made his way to the bed and sat on the edge, tossing his crutches on the mattress. He reached for her and pulled her to stand between his legs. "I changed my mind," he said to the thin layer of cotton separating his lips from her skin. He ran his hands up her back and nuzzled her ribs with his nose. "I want to stay right here."

"Hmm." She sighed. "That sounds nice."

His body and heart lit up. "Yeah?"

"Yes. But first you have to feed me."

As if on cue, his own stomach growled. He mimicked the sound in his throat and tilted his head to meet her eyes. "Fine. You win this time."

"Oh, Graham," she said with a laugh, "I always win."

She walked to the dresser and grabbed her purse while he steadied his crutches back on the ground.

"Not when you play cards with my mom, apparently."

She pinned him with a faux stern glare. "Do you want to get laid tonight or not?"

"Very much so, yes." He decided against bringing up her earlier rule that they wouldn't have sex in his parents' house. Whatever had changed her mind, he wouldn't question it. "What I meant to say was, Claire, you are forever the winner of all time."

Flipping her blond hair over her shoulder, she continued out the door. "That's what I thought."

As if forgetting something, she stopped short and doubled back, nearly smacking into his chest. She went to the bed and pressed a kiss to his dog's head. "See you later, Gertie."

Fuck.

He was so screwed.

★ ★ ★

He didn't recognize the name of the restaurant she'd picked, but the area her navigation directed them to was an up-and-coming, hipster part of town that had been mostly abandoned warehouses when he was a kid.

The place didn't take reservations and they arrived to find a forty-five-minute wait.

Claire scrunched her nose at him. "Go somewhere else or wait it out?"

"How hungry are you?"

"Ravenous."

Shit, why did that response turn him on? He took a deep breath and told himself to rein it in. "How badly do you want to eat here?"

A sad look entered her eyes. "It looked really good."

The hostess cut in, "If it helps, we'll text you when the table is ready, and there are several adorable shops across the street. You can check them out and won't even notice the time pass."

Claire shrugged. "Okay."

Graham eyed the hostess. "Are they owned by the same folks as this place?"

Claire pursed her lips and turned apologetic eyes on the woman. "Sorry about him. Please put our name in, that sounds great."

She gave the hostess her cell number and they stepped back out onto the sidewalk.

Claire eyed his leg. "You don't have to come shopping if you'd rather sit down somewhere."

He shook his head. "I'm good. I'll come with you."

They browsed a local art gallery first, then went into a boutique with an eclectic blend of merchandise. They passed a section of kids' toys, kitchen gadgets, and wine, and made their way toward a small section of women's clothing and accessories in the back.

A woman with dark hair browsed in the corner, her back to them. When she turned, Graham stopped in his tracks.

Claire glanced back at him and, noticing his expression, frowned. "What?"

He tipped his head, wordlessly asking her to come closer. "That's Angela," he said in a low voice.

Claire whipped her head around, located the woman, then turned wide eyes on him. "*The* Angela?"

He nodded, jaw tight. He reminded himself Claire didn't know the entire story, because he'd only told her in an email she'd never read. But she obviously remembered the name.

If he was lucky, that's all she'd remember about that conversation.

Claire looked at Angela again, appearing to study her. How would she measure up in Claire's estimation? She was shorter than Claire by several inches, with sleek, dark hair that he'd bet money she spent a fortune on and clothes that spoke of money and class.

"Huh," Claire whispered.

"What?"

"She looks so…normal."

"What did you expect?"

"I don't know. Some tall, gazelle-like runway model. Who else would turn down a guy like you?"

He shouldn't take pleasure in that. "Lots of women, actually."

Claire rolled her eyes and glared at the other woman. "That handbag probably cost two months of rent at the condo." She wrapped her fingers around his forearm, sending spirals of pleasure across his skin. "I don't like her."

Something in her tone set off warning bells in his head.

"Let's just go," he said.

"Absolutely not." Claire tugged him forward gently. "You look ridiculously hot today and I want her to see what she missed out on."

"Wai—" he started to protest, but his brain snagged on the hot part. He wore the same shorts he'd had on earlier and had changed into a snug black T-shirt. He'd wished he could get jeans over his damn cast to look a little nicer for Claire, but it wasn't possible. "I do?"

The vehemence in her tone sent heat downward. *"Yes."*

*Claire likes shorts and fitted T-shirts.* Noted.

She stepped forward, closer to the rack where Angela browsed, and said loudly, "Oh, Graham! Look at this one." She grabbed a dress from the rack and held it up.

Out of the corner of his eye, he saw Angela turn.

Shit. He drew closer to Claire, wanting to be near her, as if she'd protect him from the strange feelings sprouting from the dormant soil of his memory. "That's, uh, nice."

"Graham?" came Angela's familiar, feminine voice.

His shoulders tensed and his gaze lifted over Claire's shoulder.

"Graham Scott? Is that you?"

Angela appeared on Claire's right side, her eyes wide as they tracked down his body.

Well, maybe Claire had been right about that.

Claire moved closer to him and wrapped her hand possessively around his bicep.

"Angela. Hey," he said, attempting to sound surprised to see her.

Rubbing her hand up and down his arm, Claire asked him in a voice sweeter than he'd ever heard come out of her mouth, "Who's this?"

Angela's shrewd gaze seemed to size Claire up. When he

didn't reply right away, she stood a little straighter. "I'm Angela. Graham and I went to school together."

"Did you?" Claire looked up at him. Those hazel eyes he adored were overflowing with mischief, and he wasn't quite sure which impulse was stronger: see how this played out or get the hell out of there. "I don't remember you ever mentioning an Angela." She shrugged and glanced back at Angela. "Nice to meet you, though."

Angela's tone sharpened a fraction. "Same."

"You two were at the same high school, huh?" Claire asked. She brushed a palm across his muscled chest and his breath shallowed. "Wow, what was that like? I bet all the girls were after him, weren't they?"

Angela shifted on her feet. "Um…"

Before Angela could say more, Claire kept going, "If not, boy, what a mistake that was, huh? Just look at this guy. And he's a fireman, too." She made a slow pass over his bicep as she lowered her voice conspiratorially and dipped her head in Angela's direction. "He doesn't mind wearing the uniform during off-hours, if you know what I mean."

"Claire," Graham muttered. "Fuck."

But she wasn't done, apparently.

"He's a local hero, too. Broke his leg saving an old woman from a fire in her apartment. Can you believe it? I guess I lucked out no one snagged him back then, though, because I wouldn't have had a chance. A man like Graham doesn't come around often. Sweet, kind, brave, and he's even hotter underneath." She winked. "Trust me."

Angela blinked, her gaze bouncing between him and Claire.

Claire's phone dinged. "Oh!" she said happily. "We'd better go, our table's ready. It was nice to meet you, Andrea."

"Angela."

"Right, sorry." Claire flashed a final smile and looked at Graham expectantly.

He was having a hell of a time keeping from laughing. He swallowed hard and forced himself to look at Angela. "It was good to see you."

Angela mumbled a goodbye as Graham and Claire turned to leave. When they got to the door he whispered, "Was that fun for you?"

"So much, thank you." On the street after the boutique door had closed, she clapped her hands. "That was the best thing ever. Did you see her face? She's regretting turning you down so hard right now."

Satisfaction, immature as it was, flared. "She is?"

"Yes. I guarantee if I hadn't been there she'd have given you her number." She suddenly paused, frowning up at him. "Wait. Would you... Do you want her to?"

He made a face. "Hell no. I'd pick you over her every day of the week."

A beautiful, genuine smile spread across her face, and she fell back into step beside him. "Good."

★ ★ ★

Once they were settled at their table with drinks and food between them, Graham used the opportunity to bring up some of the things he'd found on Google that day he'd been searching about passions in life.

"I have a question."

"Okay."

"If money was no object, what would you do for the rest of your life?"

Claire regarded him over her wineglass, then set it gently on the table. "Where'd that come from?"

Graham shrugged, the interaction with Angela leaving him feeling lighter than he had in weeks. "Just something I came across the other day. I've had some time on my hands, if you hadn't noticed."

She grinned and tucked a strand of blond hair behind her ear. "I know what your answer would be."

"What's that?"

"Disappear into the mountains. Maybe have a cabin near the best climbing spot, and have food and supplies delivered on a regular basis so you never had to leave."

Graham laughed and pushed his bread plate to the side. "That's pretty damn close."

Claire twirled her fork in her hand and glanced at her plate. "I'd probably go around finding the best cuisine in every city. Trying a bunch of places and then promoting the best. Even better if they were those hidden-gem, locally owned businesses. What I wouldn't do for people to recognize places like that instead of going to the same chains over and over again."

"I could totally see you doing that," Graham said, leaning back in his chair. "But you could do that now, you know."

"How?"

"Start a blog or Instagram page or something. Take pictures and write posts about your favorite places around Denver."

Her eyes went wide. "I'd have an excuse to eat out more..." She sat up and her mouth dropped open. "Oh, my gosh, if I had a decent following do you think places would give me free food?"

Damn, she was cute. "Probably."

He could practically see the gears working in her brain. Before she got carried away and created a website right here at the table, he asked another question.

"How about this one: When you die, what do you want to be remembered for?"

She gave him a little smile, tilting her head. "Graham. Did you do some soul-searching while you were bedbound?"

"It's your fault for going to work and leaving me to my own devices."

"I'm impressed. But that one's even harder." She searched the room for a moment, as if the other patrons would inspire her. "I have no idea. My work as a nurse, maybe? Healing people?"

"That's a good one," he said, but deep down he didn't think that was it. Claire would be remembered for more than her job. People would remember her light and laughter, and the way the world just felt bigger and brighter when she was around.

He couldn't seem to say the words out loud, though.

"Speaking of being a nurse, I won't be doing that much longer."

"Yeah? They finally got you transferred over in the system?"

"Yep. I'm officially credentialed as a nurse practitioner at the hospital." She dropped her eyes and her smile faded as she moved her hands to her lap, a wrinkle between her brows.

"Hey," he said, tapping her shoe with his foot. "What's up?"

She lifted her gaze and shook her head a little. "I don't know. I was really excited about the change—I mean, it's why I did the work to become an NP in the first place—I want to have more independence and a broader range to help people. And gosh, I loved clinicals. I know it's the right thing, but now that it's actually happening… I'm a little nervous."

"What are you nervous about?"

"I guess just thinking about being the one responsible for diagnosing and making the treatment plan…it's a lot of responsibility. What if I miss something? What if someone gets hurt because I make a mistake?"

"That won't happen."

"It absolutely could happen. I'm human."

Yeah, okay. "Fine, it *could* happen. But it probably won't, because you're damn good at what you do. You're smart, you're talented, and you listen to people. You care too much to skip over things and when you take care of someone, you make sure every angle is covered." He put a hand to his chest. "I should know."

The muscles in her forehead seemed to relax marginally.

"The fact that you're worried about it means you're going to be the best there is. You're compassionate and those patients mean something to you. I know you won't let them down. Plus, you're not alone in it. You'll still have doctors and all those nurses you work with, too, right? You're a team. It's not just on you, so slide some of that burden off your shoulders. I'm not running into a building on fire without my crew with me and a plan in place about how we're gonna tackle it together. But even then, I know we'll figure it out because we've trained for that moment. You have years of nursing experience under your belt, plus NP school on top of that. You've got all the tools you need to be the best one that hospital has ever seen. You're ready, Claire."

Cheeks flushed, she blinked at him for a moment, then dipped her chin. "Well."

He cocked his head. "Well, what?"

"That was…really nice. Quite a pep talk."

"It's easy when I believe every word. You think I'd have let just anyone else fix this gorgeous face?"

She rolled her eyes, still smiling. "I barely had to do anything."

"I see you didn't refute the gorgeous part."

"Obviously."

He grinned, wanting to kiss her, but settled for sliding his calf along hers under the table.

She arched a brow but didn't move her leg. "Anyway, what about you? What do you want to be remembered for?"

"Whether I want it to be or not, I figured mine would be for being adventurous. Or reckless. Could go either way."

She huffed out a single laugh. "Yeah. You'll be remembered for being an adrenaline junkie, no question."

He thought he detected a hint of something off in her tone, but she gave him a warm smile and he decided to leave it be.

Tonight was ending up damn near perfect, and he didn't plan on doing anything to mess it up.

★ ★ ★

To: PinkSparkles91@zzmail.com
From: Graham.Scott27@zzmail.com
Subject: Four letter words part 2

Claire,

I'm writing this from my phone while you sleep beside me. We're at my parents' house and I just had the best night of my life. I tried to show you when we got back how much you mean to me, and I hope you felt it. I hope you know. I'm sorry I couldn't speak the words out loud, but I have to say them somewhere. So here goes:

You. Are. Extraordinary.

You're an insanely beautiful, sassy, sometimes crass woman who takes no shit and isn't afraid to ask for what she wants. You've experienced tragedy in the worst way and yet you emerged strong and resilient. You refused to let your past steal your ability to laugh.

Your laugh is the most incredible sound, did you know that?

You have the most unbelievable eyes. I've never seen a color like that. And when they flash with...what word did you say you feel when you're with me? Hostility? That look wrecks me. I want to laugh, cry, and take you in my arms all at the same time. I lose all fucking control, Claire.

You've dedicated your life to healing people. You love trying new things, seeing new places, and you dance like no one's watching. You're a romantic but don't want anyone to know.

I know. I see you.

And I've fallen in love with you.

You make me feel things I usually only feel when I'm looking death in the face. I told you a while back that I spend so much time outdoors because I want to experience everything life has to offer, but this weekend I'm realizing I'm missing one key experience—true human connection and the joy that comes with letting yourself be completely vulnerable with someone.

People talk about reasons they fall in love and get married—things like physical attraction (check), enjoying each other's company (check), respect for one another (check), and having similar interests (check...sort of). But another one is opening up to share their lives with each other—wholly and completely—and I wasn't sure that piece was ever possible for me. It's the main reason I've kept that word out of my vocabulary for so long.

But I'm close, Claire. You've seen me at some low points these last few weeks, and I've shared things with you I've never told anyone. And while I realize much of it has been here, rather than spoken in person, it's a step closer than I've ever taken. Taking you to my hometown, introducing you to my parents, and showing you where I grew up is the most significant of it all.

I can't help but wonder if that will be the final piece that puts my heart back together. If so, know that it will be all yours, whether I can tell you or not.

I hope you want it as much as I want you to have it.

Graham

# 21

Claire spent the next morning vegging out in front of the television with Gertrude and Graham's dad while Graham hung out with his mom.

His dad made a damn good cup of coffee, and it was a lovely morning. Exactly how she loved spending Sundays.

Graham came out of his mom's room at one point and seemed to stop for a few seconds to take in the scene: she and Gertrude lounging on the love seat while his dad stretched out on the recliner beside her. The corners of his mouth tipped up and the expression on his face just looked so…full.

That look made her heart ache, and she wasn't sure if it was from pleasure or pain. Coming here had been a conscious decision and one she knew was a big deal. But she'd also told herself to tread carefully. Getting too attached to Graham would be a mistake of epic proportions.

Last night, against her better judgment, she'd thrown that viewpoint out the window. After the run-in with Angela the rest of the night had felt very date-ish, and instead of pulling back she'd leaned into it hard.

She'd loved how Graham was attentive in a way he wasn't on the regular. Or maybe he always had been and she just hadn't thought about it in a romantic sense.

After dinner they'd stopped at an ice cream shop and shared a cone while sitting on a bench, stealing sugar-laden kisses under the stars. They drove to his old high school and walked around while he told her more memories from his teenage years and paused to make out under the bleachers. After they got back to his parents' house and slid into bed, they met in the middle, and the way he kissed her had felt different. He'd held her face and traced her cheeks and lips with his fingers in a way that felt reverent, like she meant more to him than he let on. As if she was precious and adored.

In the darkness, she'd let go of her fear and hesitation. She'd given in and let herself feel him, soaking up each kiss, each touch, as if he was the oxygen to her fire. It had felt as if they'd laid down their swords and lowered their barriers to let each other in completely.

It had been their most incredible night together yet, and in the light of the morning she realized how comfortable she was becoming with this whole situation. She could get used to the regular attention of a man as incredible as Graham, and therein lay the problem. That wasn't the deal.

The deal: companionship and sex.

She wanted children someday, with a father who would be around and committed to staying that way.

She'd fallen off course in her search for that, just like she'd told Mia she feared might happen. She had to remember she and Graham were friends who had hooked up and nothing more. Being here with him in Santa Fe with his family and away from their day-to-day lives had made it easy to forget.

Just as she promised herself she'd send Matt the dentist a message when they got back, Graham's dad interrupted her thoughts.

"So you and Graham are roommates, right?"

She pushed thoughts of the dating app out of her mind and focused on the kind man next to her with salt-and-pepper hair and laugh lines around his eyes. If this was how Graham would look in twenty years...well, she wouldn't be mad about it. "Yep. It's been about a year, now. He wanted a place with lower rent and we were looking for a new roommate. Worked out perfectly."

"Ah." His dad pressed his lips together in a small, knowing smile that somehow still seemed sad. "That's when Nancy started her new injection. Insurance pays for some of it, but it's still several hundred dollars a month out of pocket. Graham insists on paying for it."

Claire's heart squeezed with affection. What was he doing to her? "Wow. That's...really sweet of him."

"We're lucky to have him as a son."

"He is pretty great. However, I feel it's my duty to inform you he's not the perfect roommate."

His dad chuckled. "Wasn't so great when he lived here, either. The shoes?"

"Yes! Always in the *middle* of the floor!"

Graham's dad nodded sagely. "He likes it cold, too. We used to fight over the thermostat before Nancy was diagnosed. He let it go after that, but walked around in his underwear half the time complaining how hot it was."

A mental image of Graham in his boxer-briefs filled her mind. Couldn't say she'd mind that. "Control of the thermostat is a reward tactic at our place." She scratched Gertrude's ears as she thought. "The video games until three in the morning?"

"Why do you think there's not a TV in his room? He'd never have put it down if we didn't regulate it somehow." His dad angled his head. "Offering to take him camping always did the trick, though. He'd jump at the chance to get outside no matter what."

"He's still like that."

"I'm still like what?" Graham appeared in the doorway and fell onto the love seat beside her, tossing his crutches to the floor. He put an arm around her and let his fingers trail down the skin of her upper arm. Her stomach flipped at the casual contact. *Simmer down.* "Handsome, funny, charming?"

She kept her eyes on the TV. "More like arrogant, snarky, and whiny."

"I'll admit arrogant and snarky but I draw the line at whiny."

"I don't envy you the job of being his nurse while he's injured," Graham's dad said.

"Hey!"

His dad shot him the side-eye, looking eerily like Graham in that moment. "Son, do you remember the time you dislocated your shoulder? Stopped us from hitting the parks for weeks. You're not normally a whiner, I'll give you that. But anything that restricts you from being active and you turn into a big baby."

Graham pursed his lips.

Claire took mercy on him and pinched his side, whispering, "You're not that bad."

He shot her a lopsided grin and leaned into her ear. "I think you've secretly enjoyed taking care of me."

She shrugged, unable to deny it but unwilling to admit it. He just grinned and settled back, his thumb tracing lazy circles on her shoulder, sending goose bumps up her neck.

At lunch, Graham's mom came out and the four of them ate

around the kitchen table while Graham and his dad relayed stories of camping and their various outdoor adventures while Graham was growing up. His dad told a story of Graham rescuing an inexperienced climber from the side of a rock face, during which Graham remained strangely silent.

While she still loathed the risks he took every time he met his buddies for some outdoor expedition, hearing him talk about it with his dad and witnessing their obvious bond helped her understand why it meant so much to him, and likely where his love for nature started.

"Do you still go camping?" Claire asked his dad.

"Not much," he admitted. "Only when Graham's home. I'm not much for going alone."

"If you'd take me up on my offer to find you a place in Denver, we could go every weekend," Graham said.

"I'm too old to move," his dad said in a tired voice that indicated this was a well-worn conversation.

Graham sighed and leaned toward Claire. "I'll convince them one of these days."

"I could be persuaded," his mom started. "If you ever got married and I had grandkids to see."

Graham choked on his water. *"Mom."*

"Do you want kids, Claire?" she asked.

*Stay calm. Graham warned you this would happen.* "Yes, I do. Someday."

"Well, if I may," his mom continued. "You two would have beautiful children. And I don't think the making part would be too difficult since you were practicing last night."

Graham groaned and dropped his forehead to the table with a thump.

Claire's face was hotter than the sun.

"Nancy," Graham's dad chided with a poorly contained grin. "You're embarrassing them."

She didn't look the least bit sorry. "Our room is right next door. Honestly."

Graham sat up and pressed balled-up fists to his forehead. He looked at his mom with incredulous eyes, and finally landed on Claire. "I think it's time for us to go."

"Oh, come on," his mom laughed, "I'm just teasing! Let an old, sick woman have some fun."

"There is zero fun here." Graham looked at Claire. "Are you having fun?"

It felt weird to admit, but… "A little. It's mostly awkward, but a tiny bit fun. Like, ninety-ten."

"What about yesterday when we played gin rummy?" his mom asked. "That was fun, right?"

"The one time I beat you, yes."

Graham shot his mom an impressed look. "She only beat you once? I haven't beat her yet! Teach me your secret."

His mom eyed him. "I don't think I will."

Graham threw up his hands. "I can't win around here."

Claire snorted. "Especially not at cards."

★ ★ ★

They headed back to Denver that afternoon. As they passed Westfield High in the daylight, Claire eyed the fancy buildings and football field, shivering as she remembered the way he'd pressed her against the wall under the bleachers and kissed her like it was his last day on earth.

He sat beside her, seemingly intent on looking anywhere but the campus, his large body filling the seat, dark head leaning back against the leather.

"Graham?"

"Yeah?"

"Would you tell me what happened with Angela?"

He stared at her for a long moment before turning his attention straight ahead, considering.

When he didn't speak for several seconds, she realized she'd never hear the real story. Disappointment burrowed deep, surprising her. It shouldn't matter, but she'd really thought they'd become closer.

She thought he saw her differently and trusted her enough to open up. She'd learned more about him in the last few weeks than in years prior and he'd brought her to Santa Fe, but apparently there was still a line he refused to cross.

Swallowing a thick lump, she sighed. It was probably for the best, since she planned to put some distance between them when they got back, anyway. "Never mind."

Out of the corner of her eye she noticed him tilt his head back, resting it against the seat. "I told you I was the poor kid at that school. That I didn't fit in." He ran a hand down his face. "In middle school every day was complete misery. I hated it so much, I can't even describe it. But my dad worked damn hard to get me there, and he and my mom were so sure with a good education I'd have a better chance at college and beyond. Neither of them went to college, so it was a huge deal to them. So I sucked it up and got through it.

"In eighth grade Angela and I were paired up for a science project. She was actually nice to me, and I thought we'd become friends. She talked to me in science class and even acknowledged me in the hallways. She was popular, attractive, and the first person to treat me like I wasn't complete trash. I fell hard for that girl, and out of some stupid boyish grandeur, I asked her to the school dance."

"She said no?" The words tasted like acid in her mouth.

The laugh he released then was harsh and clipped. "Not only did she turn me down, she did it in quite spectacular fashion. I became the laughingstock, and the rest of that year was even worse than before."

Claire gripped the steering wheel so tight her knuckles

turned white. Anger rushed through her like a Colorado river after massive snowmelt. Sure, it had been a long time ago. But she also knew how defining those middle school years could be, a critical time for self-esteem and influencing the way kids saw themselves and other people. Wounds inflicted in those awkward, should-be-gentle years of young adulthood seemed to heal much more slowly than any others she'd obtained.

Hell, she still remembered the name of her first boyfriend in sixth grade (Drew Nesbitt) and how he broke up with her (he drew a picture of a dump truck and asked a friend to pass her the note) just one week in. It had sucked, and that was with a ton of friends to lean on. She hadn't been a loner or had an entire class laughing at her expense.

It must have been terrible.

"I really, really wish I'd known the whole story before we ran into her last night," she bit out.

Graham turned his torso in her direction. "Why?"

"I would have come up with something so much worse than just rubbing your ridiculous sexiness in her face."

He grinned, and a little bit of her anger melted away. "I think your extreme sexiness is what bothered her the most. Isn't that how women's minds work? They care more about showing up the other woman than the man himself?"

"Sometimes, yeah. Dammit, I should have brought something sluttier. I packed for meeting your parents, not showing up the bitch that screwed you over."

"What you did was incredible, Claire. I've never had anyone stand up for me like that. Especially not a woman." He reached over and slipped his palm around the back of her neck, giving a light squeeze. "Thank you."

His tone held a hint of wonder, like he still couldn't believe she'd done it.

Unacceptable. "You know you deserve that, right?" she

asked, though it came out more like a statement than a question. "Someone who cares about you so much they'd fight for you and can't stand the idea of someone hurting you?"

His thumb rubbed up and down across her skin and she simultaneously wished he'd stop and never take his hand from her.

She'd definitely let herself get too close.

"I didn't." He swallowed. "I'd never felt that before. From another person, I mean. I never felt valued like that. Until recently."

She wanted to look at him longer than the few seconds she could without running off the road.

"I think I've changed a little. Since the accident. I've had a lot of time to think and reflect, and I've spent a lot of time with you. Something about you makes me feel worthy in a way I didn't know I ever could."

An alarm sounded in the rational side of her brain, warning her this was dangerous territory. A line she was apparently determined to leap over multiple times this weekend against her better judgment, and she was about to do it again.

But Graham didn't say things like that. Didn't use to, anyway. The admission was significant, and with his tendency to deflect from serious topics the last thing she could do was let it go. Even if things between them couldn't last, it wasn't because he wasn't a wonderful man.

It wouldn't be long before they got home and she retreated out of self-preservation, but for now, wasn't it more important to confirm his words than to protect herself?

# 22

Graham watched as she tried to decide whether to say what was on her mind. She always pressed the right corner of her lips together when she did that, as if trying to hold in the words until she came to a decision.

They usually came out regardless. With Claire, few things were ever held back.

He'd meant what he said—he felt different around her. Something he couldn't put his finger on...more confident, almost, but not in the usual way. He didn't need people to confirm he was attractive, funny, or entertaining. Hadn't needed that kind of confirmation in a while.

But belief in himself as a human? Like, a whole-ass man valued for who he was as a person—no matter what mood, no matter who else was around, no matter what he was going through?

That's what had changed.

Even so, the longer he waited for her to speak, rubbing his thumb up and down the soft skin below her hairline, old doubts creeped in. Maybe he shouldn't have said that, after all.

Her voice finally came, soothing him from the outside in.

"You're so worthy, Graham." She said the words slow, with intention. "I hope you never lose sight of that again because you're an incredible man. You're kind and sweet and funny. You're strong and thoughtful, and so inherently *good*. I actually don't think I've ever met a better man."

His fingers stilled as his throat tightened. "I wish I could explain how it feels when you say things like that to me."

He hoped she knew, and that somehow he made her feel the same. Last night in the darkness of his old room, the look in her eyes when he'd whispered into her ear gave him hope.

"That's the thing about feelings. They don't always need to be expressed. Some are just meant to be felt."

He'd avoided both for so long, it was nice to know it was okay to just sit with them sometimes. Feel, observe, soak it in. Maybe share it, maybe not.

He slid his hand from her neck and grabbed one of her hands, entwining his fingers with hers. "I definitely do."

She smiled, but it wasn't quite as bright as he'd like—could he put in a request for full reciprocation of the ridiculous infatuation thrumming through his veins? Maybe even a love declaration punctuated with a poem outlining highlights of his sexual prowess?

Fine, that was too much to ask, probably. It had been a long weekend, plus she had to stay alert and focused on the drive since he was zero help in that arena.

But speaking of sexual prowess...

"Also, I'm all for whatever slutty outfit you had in mind for the next time we see Angela. You can put it on tonight if it would make you feel better." He eyed her gravely. "For your sake, of course. I'm thinking of your mental health here, Claire."

She snorted. "I'm sure you are."

"Wouldn't it be fun to get dressed up sometime?"

"Got a problem with scrubs and yoga pants?"

Hell no. The woman was so pretty in blue it hurt. "Why does it always have to be about you? Maybe I'm trying to show off my ass in a pair of tailored slacks."

"Now we're talking." She cocked a brow. "Tux?"

He laughed. "You think I own a tux?"

"I don't know but I have a thing for bow ties."

"The mystery of your date with Merlin is finally explained."

She laughed and he felt it down to his toes. "What does that mean?"

"He's a bow tie guy for sure."

"See, you're trying to take a cheap shot at poor Marvin but all you're doing is making me want to see him in a bow tie."

"Fine, I'll wear the fucking bow tie."

"Good." She winked. "You're so easy."

He made sure her eyes were on him before he rolled his eyes. Also, he just liked the way she looked at him.

After a beat of silence, she asked, "So…how about you wear *just* a bow tie?"

"Thirsty?"

She did a little shrug as if to say *of course* and it made him smile.

"I can offer you a bow tie plus a cast. Final offer."

Claire didn't hesitate. "I'll take it."

★ ★ ★

A low, distressed cry startled Graham awake.

His eyes snapped open, blinking in the darkness as he oriented himself.

He was at the condo, in his bed, with Claire beside him.

Her body was tense and her head moved from side to side across the pillow.

"No no no…" she repeated, sounding closer to tears with each word.

Graham reached over and put his hand on her cheek, half twisting his torso and going up on his elbow while keeping his legs flat, wishing he could roll over and wrap his arms around her in a tight embrace. "Claire, shh. It's okay."

As he brought his palm down to her shoulder, gently stroking her hair, her lids fluttered open. Her gaze caught his and held. "Graham?"

"Hey."

"Are you okay?" Her voice trembled.

He frowned. Was *he* okay? "I'm fine. Are you? I think you were having a bad dream."

She stared at him for a moment and took a deep breath. The movement dropped his attention to the skin just below her collarbone, then he brought his eyes back to hers. She swallowed as she blinked up at him, looking as if she wanted to say something.

"What is it?" he asked, still running his fingers through her soft hair.

"I…" she started.

But instead of finishing her thought, she lurched forward and kissed him.

Unprepared, he fell onto his back and she followed him down, allowing their lips to part only for the barest second. She framed his face with her hands and he gripped her arms as she slid on top of him, kissing him as if she hadn't seen him in years.

"Hey, what—" he said into her mouth.

She raised her head the tiniest bit.

Something was seriously wrong with him to have stopped whatever she had in mind. "Are you okay? What happened?"

Pressing her forehead to his, she rotated her head back and

forth. "Graham, just…be quiet and kiss me." She paused. "Please."

Well. He wasn't gonna say no to that.

"Yes, ma'am."

★ ★ ★

The next morning, as Graham leaned his good side against the bathroom counter and stared at himself brushing his teeth, he made a choice.

It was time to put everything out there.

Things with Claire had been a little confusing lately. Sometimes he felt she was experiencing the same thing as him, as in…incredible, terrifying, big emotions that could be described as nothing other than the head-over-heels kind of love. Other times she seemed to withdraw and back off, and he worried he'd gone too far. They'd had an arrangement, after all—and love wasn't part of the deal.

But over the weekend he'd felt more encouragement about their developing relationship than not.

He'd told her more about his life growing up, introduced her to his family, and walked her around his old high school, touring the place where he'd become such an emotional mess. Being there with her had been a revelation. Like him, she hadn't fit there at all, and in the best way. She wasn't like they were, and he realized with a conviction he typically only experienced when climbing that he didn't have to be afraid of her.

Less important but still to be considered: Reagan was due back this evening. If there was a time to talk about how things had changed and what they were going to do about it, it was now.

Claire had taken the day off just in case they'd ended up staying through Monday, so she was still in bed. He regretted texting his boss last night to say he could come in today, but couldn't change it now. One of the guys would be by to pick him up any minute, so he quickly grabbed a Post-It note from the kitchen and scribbled out a note, sticking it in the middle of the bathroom mirror.

*Check your email, Ms. Sparkles.*

# 23

She had the dream again.

No, not a dream. This was a nightmare.

In the months following her dad's death, it had been so frequent and visceral she'd had trouble falling asleep. Most nights she'd crept into the living room—careful not to disturb her mom, who'd desperately needed rest—to watch television, hoping to distract her brain until she eventually fell under from sheer exhaustion.

With time and therapy, the realistic imagery came less often, and eventually became almost nonexistent. She'd even had some good dreams about her dad over the years, ones that had her opening her eyes with a smile on her face and a joyful memory on her mind.

Not this one. This particular dream was like a punch to the chest, forcing air from her lungs and sending her heart racing in panic. Her eyes would fly open, the sudden change of scenery disorienting and confusing until she realized she was at home. In bed. Not there, not in the fire. Not staring at her dead father.

Believe it or not, that wasn't even the worst part. It was always the split second of hope after she woke up and realized the whole thing had been a dream that her brain considered, *Oh, was the* whole *thing a dream? Is my dad okay? He's not actually gone?*

And Claire would come fully awake, lucid, and remember.

While it was just a dream, it was based on real events. Her dad wasn't okay. He was still gone.

That part was still real.

Everything about it was always awful, and last night was, too—but something had been different.

This time, she dreamed she lost Graham.

Usually she loved waking up next to him, rolling into his warm body. If he was already awake he'd tuck her into his chest, just lying with her for several minutes before one of them finally decided to get up (or make a move...these days it was anyone's guess). If she roused first, she'd snuggle into his side, breathing in his scent, content to feel his skin slowly move against hers as he inhaled and exhaled.

This morning, though, she was relieved to find herself alone as several tears slipped down her cheeks.

Before now, the subject of her dream had never changed. No matter how many times she'd suffered through it, even if tiny details changed—like the color of her shirt or how old she was when she found him—it was always her dad.

It felt like a betrayal to her dad, but the way she'd felt just a few short hours ago in the all-too-real moments of her subconscious, wrenching open that airplane door to see Graham's pale, lifeless face had been the worst yet.

It could have been because it was unexpected, or because

she'd so recently seen Graham injured. Maybe it was because even though she missed her dad immensely, she'd learned to live without him.

Whatever it was, grief and heartbreak had crashed down so hard she'd nearly collapsed into the grass next to the burning plane. Someone had touched her face, speaking to her, but nothing—no one—could ever fix her now. Not after this.

Nothing would ever be okay.

The soothing voice had kept going, though, the gentle touch moving to her hair, her neck, her shoulder. And then she opened her eyes and found herself here, in this bed, in the darkness—Graham's devastatingly handsome face watching her, brow marred with concern.

He said she'd had a bad dream and when she realized he was here and alive and touching her, she'd nearly blurted out, *I love you.*

She'd kissed him and made love to him instead, and now, in the light of the morning, she was thankful. Thankful she'd said it without words, because it was safer that way. For both of them.

She'd gotten in way too deep and let him do the same, and what happened last night was proof it would destroy her if she let it continue.

It would hurt like hell, but it was for the best. She had to put an end to whatever they were doing for both their sakes.

And she had to do it today.

* * *

Claire loved on Gertrude for a few minutes before getting out of bed. Just as she pulled on the tank top Graham had tossed onto the floor in the middle of the night, her phone dinged from the nightstand.

Mia: How was the weekend getaway?

Claire groaned and sat back down, sinking into the mattress.

Claire: I wouldn't call it a getaway. Graham was supporting his family and I just helped him get there.

*And he gave me a glimpse into his childhood, his life, and his deepest insecurities. I adore his mother and his dog is now my favorite. I realized I've fallen in love with him.*

Thank God for texting. It was so much easier to lie by omission when she wasn't looking her best friend in the eye.

Mia: Noah's been camping in New Mexico with Graham and still has never met Graham's parents.

Claire: Probably because it was a guys' camping trip. And I'm sure Graham would have taken him if Noah had asked.

*Maybe.*

Mia: Doubtful.

Claire: I'm sure Graham found it more fun to bring along someone he's sleeping with.

Another lie—a semiromantic companion was the last person Graham would have usually brought to his parent's place. Especially now that she knew his mom's penchant for matchmaking. And heart-stealing, for that matter. One weekend and Claire loved the woman.

Mia: So we're just gonna pretend this wasn't a big deal?

Claire: We're trying to, but you're not making it easy.

Mia: You won't give me anything? Not even a single tidbit of what happened down there?

Claire: His mom beat me at gin rummy.

Mia: Did she live to tell about it?

Claire: Only because that woman is a fucking delight.

Mia: Wow, what else?

Claire: Oh, his mom heard us having sex.

Mia: WHAT

Mia: NO

Mia: OMG

Claire: And that is why, no matter how badly you want something to happen between me and Graham, it never will because I can never show my face in that house again.

Claire: That's all you're getting. Gertie needs a walk.

Claire tossed her phone down and glanced at Gertrude, curled up at the foot of the bed.

"Let me change and brush my teeth and then we'll take a nice long stroll around the block, okay? I need some fresh air while I think about what I'm gonna say to your dad."

She put on a sports bra, a fresh top, and some yoga pants

before padding to the bathroom to pee and brush her teeth. It wasn't until she had the toothbrush in her mouth and glanced into the mirror that she saw the note.

*Check your email, Ms. Sparkles.*

She frowned, her brain briefly asking, *Who the hell is Ms. Sparkles?* before she made the connection. Why did he want her to check her old email account?

Coffee was the next priority, but Graham had gallantly left her half a pot warming on the hot plate. She idly wondered if he'd still do gestures like that after she cut things off. Was it possible for them to go back to the friendship they'd had before, or would it become stilted and awkward?

Good thing Reagan was due back today. They could use the buffer.

She poured a fresh cup and tossed a small bone to Gertrude to distract her while Claire sat down at the computer. It took her a few tries to get the password right, but when she finally got in her account, it was populated with several emails from two senders: *DogFaves@PetSavings.com* and *Graham.Scott27@zzmail.com.*

Graham had emailed her? What the…?

She opened the oldest one first, and her confused frown quickly shifted to a smile as she read.

You went to work and I'm bored out of my fucking mind and Noah won't be here for another hour, so I'm trying my hand at your journaling suggestion. It still feels weird to write to no one so I'm writing to you, instead.

She laughed into the quiet house, marveling that he'd actually listened to her for once. The first email was from several weeks ago, and she glanced at the most recent—this weekend. He'd been writing to her this whole time?

She pored over the words, shaking her head, snorting, and chuckling at his whining, sarcasm, and how very *Graham* the emails were. It was clear that at first, he thought the entire exercise was ridiculous.

But as she continued reading, his tone began to change, and she slowed down to process each thought. Every line. Some of the written revelations had recently come out in conversation, though not in as much detail. It seemed her experience with journaling was true for him, too—sometimes it was easier to work through things on paper first. Pride filled her as she realized he'd really made an effort to process things he'd never let himself dwell on before.

Like things that inspired him:

I heard something once I try to live by:

> *"A ship is safe in the harbor,*
> *but that's not what ships are made for."*

Realizing he had people around him who love him:

Some of my buddies from the station wanted to stop by this afternoon, but I said (er, texted) no. I feel weird not being able to talk to them. Come to think of it, I wasn't comfortable when Reagan was here, either. But with you and Noah I couldn't care less. Mia, too, probably. And maybe Chris.

Does that mean you're my people?

Acknowledging his need to feel emotions:

I love adventure more than anything else, and probably always will. I've been thinking about it all day and realized it's one of the only places I feel things.

And identifying when he stopped showing them in the first place:

That pretty much solidified that, even as an adult, letting people see the real me and meet my family just wasn't an option.

She rubbed a palm across her sternum as she relived his experiences, absorbing the whole picture of who he was all at once. A strange mix of fascination and sorrow settled low in her gut as she realized just how deep his passion for adventure ran and how important it was to him. How it had served as an escape and a gift to a man who needed something to prove he was worth believing in.

That he'd trusted her enough to share these things with her was momentous in itself, but then…he started to write about *her*.

Things that made her breath catch and her heart lodge in her throat.

High: I woke up with you curled up against my side.

PS. Remember when we were at that restaurant and you told off the guy on his phone? I didn't want you to give him your number.

I'm just feeling…something. Something I haven't let myself feel in a long time, and I don't know why it's changing with you.

I've never felt judged by you.

Even when you say I'm an asshole. For some reason I find it endearing.

Then came you. A woman who I can be myself around and who I'm actually going to let come meet my parents. And you know what I don't feel this time?
Fear.

By the time she made it to the final email, she knew what she'd find inside. She knew because he'd been different with her this weekend. It was in the soft way he looked at her and in the gentle intensity of his touch.

She knew because she felt it, too.

I've fallen in love with you.

I can't help but wonder if that will be the final piece that puts my heart back together. If so, know that it will be all yours, whether I can tell you or not.
I hope you want it as much as I want you to have it.

Tears streamed down her face as she stared, the words that should have made her heart burst with joy swimming in a blur across the screen. How long had she wished for a man to love and who loved her back, someone to share her life with? For a man who saw her as she was, flaws and all, and loved her all the more because of it?

What was the universe playing at?

Because as much as she cared for Graham and deeply wished things were different, she had to take a step back. It had been one thing when they agreed to just sex, because feelings hadn't been part of that deal.

She couldn't handle an attachment to a man who lived like

he did. Her reaction the day he arrived in the ER and then again after last night's dream made that fact painfully clear.

She swallowed a sob and leaned forward to bury her face in her arms. She'd already decided they needed to talk, and knew it wouldn't be easy. But now? After reading him lay his heart bare?

She didn't know how she'd survive it.

# 24

By midafternoon, Graham started to regret his decision.

He'd heard nothing from Claire all day. He wasn't sure exactly what he'd expected…but it definitely wasn't nothing.

Maybe he'd hoped for a text that said, *I got your emails. Can't wait until you get home*, followed by a naked picture?

A kiss or heart emoji at the very least.

What did her silence mean?

By the time Graham's buddy dropped him at home, his stomach was in knots. Suddenly he was thirteen again, back in that media room waiting for the girl he liked to show up.

He shook the thought away. *This is different. Claire's different.*

Maybe she couldn't figure out her password and never read the emails? The thought gave him a sliver of hope, but not much.

He walked in and spotted her immediately, sitting on the couch with her back to the door. Gertrude charged toward him in greeting, tail wagging, but he couldn't even look at his beloved dog. All he could do was wait for Claire to turn so he could see her face.

That's when he saw the laptop on the table.

He slowly made his way to her, the thump of his crutches on the hardwood echoing in the silent room.

She looked up when he sat beside her.

She lifted her lips in a small smile, but she wasn't happy. Pink splotches covered her face and her eyes were red-rimmed and puffy.

Somehow, she was still the most beautiful woman he'd ever seen.

Something dark and anxious tightened and twisted deep inside him. He inhaled her scent, wondering if this would be his last chance to do so. He meant to be patient and let her speak first, but the words crawled up his throat. "You read them?"

She nodded and squeezed her eyes shut. Her lips trembled.

His voice scratched and cracked. "You don't feel the same."

It wasn't a question.

She propped an elbow on one knee and dropped her forehead into her palm. "No. I do."

He leaned in, a tiny, foolish ray of hope peeking around the corner of his terrified heart. "What?"

"I do feel the same," she said, sniffling. "But that's the problem. This wasn't supposed to happen."

Had she just admitted she loved him, too? In such a morose, troubled way? Elation and trepidation hit him in a one-two punch.

Graham reached out to take her free hand, skin prickling when he touched her. "Is that such a bad thing? I know there are things we were both afraid of, but that was before. You've helped me start working through my issues without even knowing. Maybe I can help you, and we can come at yours together. Isn't love supposed to be able to overcome all fears? Or something?"

He was so bad at this.

She yanked her hand back. "What I have isn't an *issue*, Graham. It's trauma." She suddenly stood, making a wide berth as she circled the couch.

Gertrude retreated into the hallway.

Claire walked toward the sink and spun around, eyes full of anguish. "I was *there* that day. I stood there and watched that plane crash into the ground and burst into flames, knowing my dad was inside and there was no way he'd survived. I felt the chaos of the audience around me, but to them, it was a nameless pilot that had just died before their eyes. Don't compare what I went through with a bunch of rich assholes from high school."

Her pain sank in like a corkscrew in his gut. He couldn't comprehend how she must have felt in that moment, or in the years since. "I'm—I'm sorry."

Her hips fell back into the cabinets and she covered her face with her hands.

Graham grabbed his crutches and stood, but she immediately shook her head.

"Don't. Please," came her muffled voice.

"Claire," he croaked, continuing toward her. "I love you—"

A sob wrenched from her chest.

"And I can't just sit here and watch you cry. You might as well rip my heart out."

She let her hands drop, revealing tears streaming down her cheeks. "Mine's already in pieces. It shattered the moment I read the last email and I knew that, even after you'd come so far and finally, after twentysomething years, you'd finally opened yourself up to love, I had no choice but to break yours."

Silence descended, thick and heavy.

Words failed him at the finality he sensed in her statement. His world seemed to spin on its axis and he fell back into a kitchen chair.

Cracks and pops sounded in the streets beyond as people celebrated Independence Day one day early. Normally Graham wouldn't mind it, but the thought of anyone happy and laughing in this moment grated on his nerves.

There was no way his grief stayed contained inside his body. Couldn't they feel it? Didn't they know his world was coming apart at the seams?

"Please believe me," she said, flattening her palms against her stomach. His throat tightened as if a hand gripped him there. "There's a part of me that desperately wants to try, because I do love you, Graham. You mean so much to me. More than any man ever has. But I know deep down it's not the right choice for me. Even though the moments spent with you would seem worth any cost, I know in the hours you'd be at work, or climbing, biking, or anything you enjoy that instills a healthy fear in us mortals, I'd suffer. I watched my mom do it for years, and you wanna know the worst part? Because he couldn't give up his passion, my dad's death was the only thing that set her free."

Graham pressed heavy palms into his thighs, curling his hands into fists. Yes, he loved all those things, but none of that mattered. Not compared to her. "What if I gave it all up? The climbing and biking? Found a different job?"

She was shaking her head before he even finished talking. "I'd never ask you to do that—"

"You didn't."

"And I'd never allow it. It's who you are, Graham. Now, more than ever, I know how much the outdoors means to you. I couldn't live with myself if I took that away from you. I have to take me away instead."

He let out a humorless laugh. The way her eyes widened said maybe it was an inappropriate response, but twenty years of emotional suppression meant little practice in healthy reactions. "So, you're a martyr, then? You're making this decision without my input?"

Her expression tightened. She didn't like that.

"I used to have this recurring nightmare," she said. "I'd dream I saw a plane crash, but I was the only one around. I'd run to the crash site, and even though the plane was on fire I could open the cockpit door. Dreams, I guess. And I'd see my dad in the seat. The weird thing was he looked normal. Uninjured and unharmed, like he was just asleep. But even in the dream I knew he was gone."

She reached back to grip the counter. "I hadn't had the dream in years, but after the scare with the firefighter when I thought it was you, it started up again. And then, last night…" She winced, as if the memory brought physical pain. "When I opened the door, it wasn't my dad. It was you."

His chest tightened at the distress on her face and in her voice. It made so much sense now…the look she'd given him last night when he woke her up. The way she'd kissed him with raw desperation and something like relief.

"I wish I could take it all away from you." A futile thing to say, but it was the truth.

He'd do just about anything.

Her eyes locked with his. "I wish you could, too."

He said the next words gently. "You said you went to therapy back then. Did it help? Do you think maybe you should do that again?"

Her shoulders slumped. "I don't know. Maybe." She gripped her wrist with the opposite hand. "I haven't felt like I've

needed anything like that for a long time. I was doing fine...
until you."

It took a few seconds for her words to sink in. *I was doing
fine...until you.*

His muscles froze as his brain tripped over what she'd said.

Maybe he should be offended by the comment, but she
hadn't said it with malice. She was hurting.

He tried to take a breath, but it felt like he was twenty
thousand feet in the air.

The first woman he'd loved in decades, and ultimately he'd
only caused them both pain.

"I don't know what to say." The deep ache spreading from
the center of his chest was a stark reminder of why he'd avoided
this for so long. "I'm sorry I ever suggested we do this."

Claire straightened, shaking her head. "Don't say that. No
matter what, I'll never regret getting to know you. I'll never
regret being with you. Not any of it. I just think it's best we
put an end to things before they go any further."

He forced a swallow, choking on the memories of rejection
and embarrassment. He couldn't sit here any longer, watching her watch him so carefully, waiting to see what he'd do.
Feeling sorry for him.

Being unable to walk out the door and drive away on his
own was a particularly low blow. He slid his phone out of his
pocket and pulled up the Uber app.

He couldn't look at her as he stood. "Okay. Gertrude, come
here, girl."

Claire let out a shaky breath. "Graham..."

The front door swung open.

"I'm back!" Reagan sang, dancing in with her suitcases.
"First, notice this killer tan. Then tell me how much you
missed me."

When neither Graham nor Claire responded, she paused

and looked around, taking in the tense atmosphere. He picked up his dog and cradled her in his hand against his chest, tucking his crutches under his other arm.

"Um." She cleared her throat. "Should I come back?"

"No," Graham said.

He went for the door, casting one final glance at Claire as he went.

"I was just leaving."

# 25

She never said she was sorry.

Five days had passed and even though Claire replayed her conversation with Graham in her head a million times, she just realized she never told him that.

She was so, so sorry. She'd been out of her damn mind to think she and Graham, two friends with such volatile chemistry, could have a casual sexual relationship. It was like tossing a lit match onto a pile of dry pine needles and expecting it not to catch fire.

She couldn't quite find it in her to be sorry she'd kissed him, though. Or touched him, or slept with him. She could still feel his lips against hers, his rough hands tracing her skin. As long as she lived, she'd never forget the way he looked at her that last time they'd made love. Right then, she'd known. Known she'd lost control and things had gone too far for both of them. But seconds before she'd been in a dream where he'd died, and she couldn't seem to muster the self-control to stay away from him.

As she curled up in bed, she wondered what he was doing right this minute. According to Mia he'd been crashing on Chris's couch in the apartment above the outdoor store. At first, she'd thought it would just be for a day or two, but yesterday while she was at work Graham and Chris had come over to take most of his belongings from the condo.

Only the furniture remained.

She even missed Gertrude, for crying out loud.

Chris's apartment could only be accessed by stairs from the back hallway of the store—how was Graham maneuvering those with his crutches? His cast was supposed to come off Monday, something she'd initially planned to be present for.

She wished she could see his face when it happened.

A light knock sounded at the doorway and Reagan peeked her head in. "How we doing?"

Claire gave a thumbs-down.

The bed dipped as Reagan sat, turning to face Claire and crossing her legs. "Ready to tell me what happened yet?"

Her roommate had been patient. Claire had worked several days since Reagan witnessed the awkward conclusion of Claire and Graham's relationship, and on the days she hadn't, she'd pretty much stayed in her room. Claire would have been pulling her hair out by now if their roles were reversed and Reagan hadn't relayed the full story.

With a heavy sigh, Claire pushed herself up to a half slouch, half sitting position with her upper back against the headboard. She rubbed the heels of her hands over her eyes. She probably looked like a total mess.

"While you were gone, Graham and I sort of… Well, we kind of…"

"Hooked up?" Reagan finished, sounding unsurprised.

"Yeah. Well, it started as that, anyway. After his accident I started sleeping in his bed since he couldn't talk and I was worried he might need something in the middle of the night. Then he got better, and I stayed."

Reagan nodded as if that made complete sense.

"We talked a lot, too. Through texts when he couldn't speak, and then his voice came back about a week later. We spent more one-on-one time together than we ever have. He told me about his life and let me into his head in a way that was totally different than ever before. That, plus the addition of sex… It was inevitable we'd fall for each other. I mean seriously, I was so naive to think we could keep our feelings out of it." She paused. "Actually, that's not true. I was naive to think I could keep my feelings out of it. But the thought Graham might fall in love with *me* was never on my radar. This is all his fault, really."

"It usually is," Reagan agreed. "But, um, I need to make sure I'm understanding you correctly—are you saying you and Graham *fell in love*?"

She closed her eyes and nodded. "Unfortunately."

"Wow. I…didn't see that coming."

"I know!" Claire slapped the comforter. "Me, either. And now everything is awful, and it's my fault because I broke the heart of the one man who'd sworn never to give it away in the first place. He's sure as hell never gonna do it again. I basically just guaranteed he'll grow old damaged and alone."

Reagan raised her hand as if she had a question. "Okay, I'm lost. When we sat on the porch and you guys talked about the pact—which went from marriage to sex—you said the reason you wouldn't consider marrying him was because of his fear of commitment and intimacy. It sounds like he overcame that somehow with you, right?"

Claire's heart splintered at hearing the words from someone else's mouth. "He did."

"So why can't you be together?"

"There's more to it than that."

Before now, she'd told Reagan nothing about her dad's death, only that he'd died when she was eleven. So she started from the beginning and told her roommate everything about his job as an aerobatics pilot and how it affected both Claire and her mom. About witnessing his death, and the grief that hovered over their household for so long after. The recurring nightmares, and how old feelings of worry and fear resurfaced when Graham moved in and became even more visceral when she'd thought he was injured on the job.

Reagan patiently listened to everything Claire said, her expression oscillating between horrified and sympathetic. "Wow. I—I had no idea. That's so awful. I can't imagine what it could have been like to go through that."

Claire dipped her head. "I feel so selfish, but I can't put myself in that position. My mom was never able to turn it off, and her anxiety was through the roof anytime he flew. If I stayed with Graham, I'd be on top of the world when he was home and we were together. But I'd fall to the lowest low when he went to work or left for one of his daring climbing trips, like the ice-climbing expedition he did last year. For once in my life I want stability, you know?"

Reagan nodded slowly, her brows pinching together a little bit. "Yeah, I understand what you're saying."

Something about her expression gave Claire pause. "But?"

Squinting, Reagan scrunched her nose a little. "I don't want this to come out wrong, so feel free to tell me to fuck off or that I have no idea what I'm talking about. It's just...while I get you had this awful, traumatic experience and have every reason to be fearful, I also think maybe it's unhealthy to let it rule your life like that. Being afraid of flying or avoiding air shows for the rest of your life? Yep, get that. No question. But projecting that fear onto anyone you care about who wants to do anything with the slightest risk? I'm not sure that's fair. To them or to you."

Claire processed that for a moment, trying to repel her knee-jerk defensive reaction. "I don't think I project it on everyone I care about. And I don't expect Graham or anyone else to stop doing things they love because of my issues. I'm just saying those things affect who I choose to commit and start a family with. Is that so wrong? Don't we all have non-negotiables when it comes to searching for a partner?"

"Sure. I've always said I'd never marry someone who eats meat. I feel strongly about the reasons I've chosen to live a vegan lifestyle and I want to find someone who shares those beliefs. But can I promise with one hundred percent certainty that if the right man came along who happened to be a carnivore, I'd turn him down?" She shook her head. "Sometimes love likes to mess with us and remind us we're not the ones in control."

Claire frowned. "Love sounds like an asshole."

"Sometimes it is."

"From the very start I said I wouldn't marry Graham and I never said otherwise. Our feelings may have changed during the course of the last month, but that doesn't mean my decision did. All I'm doing is standing by what I've said all along. Is that so awful? Am I the most selfish person in the world?"

"Don't be ridiculous," Reagan said. "When someone falls in love with you, you're not obligated to respond in a certain way. It sucks to know you hurt someone, but you have to do what you think is right. I'm not saying you should be with Graham to appease him—even if he took a huge step out of his comfort zone. I'm just worried about you. You seem pretty miserable. Are you sure this is what you want?"

She *was* miserable.

But continuing on the path she and Graham were headed

down could foster a whole different kind of misery. One she'd lived through and never wanted to experience again.

A tiny voice in the back of her mind hinted it was too late. Relationship or not, Graham was the most important person in her life and she was already invested in his well-being and happiness.

"I don't know," Claire admitted, tucking her legs up against her chest. "I think so?"

Reagan cocked a single eyebrow.

Claire groaned. "Why couldn't I have just met another guy sooner? I joined a dating app and everything. Maybe if I'd found someone nice this never would have happened."

"You'd rather the last few weeks with Graham never happened?"

Damn Reagan and her shrewd questions. She was as bad as Mia.

"No." She'd always remember them. "Sure would have made things easier, though."

Reagan stretched her legs out and leaned forward to grab her toes. "A dating app, huh? Which one?"

"TrueChemistry."

"Didn't find anyone worth meeting?"

"There was one, but it was a disaster. And there was a dentist that looked promising, but I never sent him a message."

"Why not?"

Claire shrugged. "We matched right before Graham and I went to visit his parents. I told myself I'd do it after we got back, but I didn't. I let myself fall into my feelings with Graham, knowing it was a terrible idea. Seriously, I'm so messed up."

"You fell for someone you promised yourself you wouldn't fall for. This is the kind of stuff TV shows live for."

"It's like a daytime soap opera up in here," Claire said, pointing to her heart.

Reagan shuddered. "Ugh. I always hated those."

"Me, too. Now I know why."

After a few seconds of silence, Reagan said, "Why don't you message the dentist and just see what happens? It might help to take your mind off Graham for a little while, and maybe this new guy is exactly what you've been looking for."

"Or he could be a total weirdo."

"In that case, maybe you double back and reconsider your stance about Graham."

That rubbed Claire the wrong way. "I don't expect him to sit around and wait while I go out with other men."

"Who says he's waiting for you?" Reagan's tone wasn't harsh, but her words were still like a punch in the gut. "That doesn't seem like him."

Reagan was right: it wasn't like the old Graham. But hadn't he changed over these last few weeks? The emails seemed to suggest so, but what did Claire know?

"I'm not suggesting you go out with this guy to spite Graham, or even to compare them. Just a few weeks ago you were interested in meeting new people, so why not see it through with someone you're supposedly compatible with? It might help clear things up for you. Help you figure out what you really want, you know?"

Claire looked down at her hands. "Maybe you're right."

"Of course I am." Reagan stood and put her hands on her hips. "You know what else will clear your head? Alcohol."

"I don't think that's how that works."

Reagan laughed. "But it will temporarily make you feel better while simultaneously guaranteeing you'll feel like shit tomorrow."

"That's more like it."

"I say we go out and try to have a little fun."

Claire scrunched her nose and glanced down at the comfortable clothes she wore. "I don't know…"

"I was thinking we could go to that tapas bar. Have chips and salsa with margaritas?"

"You had to say chips, didn't you?"

"What can I say? I know my roommate."

"Okay, I'm in."

Reagan clapped and danced out of the room, calling over her shoulder, "Be ready in ten!"

Claire released a heavy sigh and didn't move. Her eye caught on her phone charging on the bedside table.

She grabbed it and opened the TrueChemistry app and found Matt was still active in her recent matches.

She selected his name, opened a new message, and started to type.

# 26

To: PinkSparkles91@zzmail.com
From: Graham.Scott27@zzmail.com
Subject: Do I hate you?

Claire,

How are you? Not gonna lie, I've been picturing you at least a little bit miserable. Maybe like, 25% miserable, 75% okay. Does that make me a jerk?

I'm more like 60/40 if that makes a difference, and I'd quickly shift to 80/20 if I thought you were out dancing and having fun every night and not thinking of me. Some of that's the anger talking, but mostly it's hurt. (Also, can we pause here and just acknowledge the things I'm saying right now? Apparently the emotion floodgates are open because I've just admitted to being miserable, angry, and hurt in the span of two paragraphs, something I haven't done in more than two decades.)

For what it's worth, I understand your choice. It doesn't make it suck any less, because I don't see myself coming back from this. Will I date other women? Sure, but the same way I dated women before I kissed you. I'll never come close to giving another woman my heart.

Because even if you don't want it, I'll never get it back. It's just following you around like a pathetic, lost puppy. Sort of like Gertrude that first week after I moved out. I really think she got attached to you.

We both did.

Anyway, sorry for going off topic. I was trying to say I don't blame you, and that while I still love you, I hope you find what you're looking for. I'll never regret the time we had together, and I'm so fucking grateful for everything you did for me after I got hurt. Except for my parents, no one (and I mean NO ONE) has ever taken care of me like that. You made me feel special, somehow…that a woman like you would go out of her way to spend that much time with me. For a long time I didn't feel like I was worth very much unless I was doing something that impressed or entertained people. But even in those quiet days and nights in my room when we talked about nothing important, you stayed.

It's been four weeks since I've seen you. Don't worry—your hair, eyes, and smile will be burned into my brain forever. But only seeing you in my memories and not in person is a certain kind of hell, and one I never thought I'd be in.

I don't know where I'm going with this, but (1) I got in the habit of writing things down (thanks to you), (2) I wanted to tell you how badly I want to hate you for how this turned out, but (3) I don't hate you. I love you.

Fuck. Now I'm crying.

Graham

★ ★ ★

Graham slammed the laptop closed without sending the email. He'd known the second he started typing he wouldn't send it to Claire, but he wanted to write it, anyway.

Angrily swiping at his cheeks and relieved Chris wasn't in the apartment to witness his breakdown, he leaned forward and put the computer on the coffee table. Using that sixth sense dogs had, Gertrude snuggled her way into his lap. He fell back onto the couch, aka his makeshift bed, and held his tiny dog, accepting her offer of comfort.

He let himself wallow for a few more minutes before pushing to his feet. He'd been cast-free for weeks now, and was pretty fucking motivated to bust through physical therapy with flying colors. He'd been religious about doing the recommended daily exercises, and continued his upper body regimen and riding the stationary bike set up in Chris's living room. He'd lost a lot of muscle tone in his legs, which was expected but frustrating nonetheless.

It would be another month before he could climb again, and even then, he'd need to stick to easy routes for a while. He'd take what he could get, and planned to head to the mountains the very day his doctor cleared him.

Staying with Chris had been great for the most part. They got along well, and Chris didn't mind that Graham came with a dog. But it was hard watching Chris leave for the mountains every few days, knowing if it weren't for his accident, Graham would have been with him. But he didn't want to wear out his welcome, so he'd started looking for other places.

Nothing was as good a deal as what he'd had living with Claire and Reagan, which only pissed him off. He tried to direct his anger to a third party, like the drug company who'd priced his mom's medication so high and effectively reduced his monthly income by several hundred bucks.

She'd had fewer flares since starting the new drug, though, so it was worth every penny.

Speaking of his mom, she presented another issue entirely. She'd asked about Claire several times in the last few weeks.

His dad even joined in, and when Graham asked why they were suddenly so interested in her specifically when they'd never been with past girlfriends, his mom had gone and wrecked him.

*You were different when she was around,* she'd said. *It wasn't the first time I've seen a woman look at you with interest, but it was the first time you seemed to realize you were worth looking at.*

He'd ended that phone call pretty damn quick.

So far, he'd been able to avoid telling them he and Claire weren't on speaking terms and had effectively terminated their relationship, if he could even call it that. But it wouldn't be long before they figured it out.

A knock sounded at the door and Graham frowned as he stood. The only entrance to the apartment was directly from the store below, so Chris must have let someone up.

Graham opened the door to find Noah.

"Hey, man," Noah greeted.

Graham stepped aside to let his friend in. "Hey. What are you doing here?"

"Had to drop my bike off for a tune-up and thought I'd say hi. You haven't taken me up on any of my offers to grab a beer, and Chris says you haven't gone much of anywhere other than work and physical therapy."

Graham looked away and sat at the small kitchen table. "Just trying to focus on getting my strength back."

"Are you sure that's all it is?"

Glancing up to see Noah leaning against the counter, arms crossed, Graham lifted an eyebrow. "What do you want me to say?"

"Nothing in particular. I just want you to know I'm here if you want to talk."

"I appreciate it," Graham said. And he did. "I've actually been, um, journaling. It sort of feels like I'm talking it through, even if it's not with another person."

Not that Graham would have ever expected it out of Noah, but it was still a relief that his buddy didn't bust up laughing.

"That's cool. I've never thought about doing that before," Noah said. "Might have come in handy ten years ago."

Graham had thought about that, too. He was surprised how much he'd taken to it and wished he'd had an outlet like it after Nathan died. "Claire suggested it, actually. I've been doing it since a few days after I got out of the hospital."

"Well, I'm glad you have something that's helping. As long as you know I'm always happy to listen, okay?"

"Thanks."

"How's the physical therapy going? What are you allowed to do now?"

Graham stretched his legs under the table. "It's good. I go three times a week and they're happy with my progress. I can walk on it without restriction, but can't do high impact things like running. Mountain biking's still too rough, too."

"Could you go on a hike? If it was an easier route?"

"I think so." He'd thought about heading up to the mountains for something just like that, but kept finding reasons not to go. Going alone and taking an easy route didn't hold the same appeal, and he didn't want to bring his friends down with him.

His lack of enthusiasm probably had something to do with depression, too, which was hopefully temporary. He'd seemed to find a lot of reasons to stay in instead of hanging out with Noah or going out to eat with Chris.

"Wanna go hiking at Waterton Canyon tomorrow?"

Graham sighed. "You don't have to do that."

"Do what?"

"Offer a pity trip. I know you'd rather climb or hike a more challenging trail."

Noah shook his head. "Nah. I love that stuff, sure. But it's a lot less fun without you."

Graham scratched at his jaw, ignoring the warmth settling in his chest. "Really?"

"Yeah. It's been two months since we've done anything outside together, that pit stop at the tourist spot excluded. Turns out I miss hanging out with you. Who knew?"

"I don't know why you seem so surprised. I'm a fucking delight."

"Sunshine personified," Noah deadpanned. "So put me out of my misery and come hiking with me tomorrow, okay?"

Graham rolled his eyes. "Fine."

"Good. I'll come by to pick you up at nine."

"Fine," Graham said again.

Noah cracked a smile.

"Good."

# 27

*One month later*

It had been one of those days.

The ER was packed from the second Claire walked in to the moment she made her way back to her car. She'd officially transitioned and her responsibilities as an NP were different than they used to be as a nurse, but it definitely wasn't easier.

She didn't mind being busy, but it just so happened several things had reminded her of Graham today, which threw her off-kilter.

She'd spent the past month thinking, healing, and giving a relationship with Matt the dentist a fair shot.

He was as hot in person as his picture portrayed. Even better, he was as kind and funny in person as he'd been through messaging. He'd also been very up front about his divorce, which had been finalized a year ago, and no current girlfriends showed up to interrupt their first date. It was going surprisingly well.

As far as getting over Graham, some days were easier than others. But this past week in particular Claire had actually felt the possibility that she might be moving past what happened.

Which was why everything that happened today was so irritating. Could the universe not let her move on?

First, she saw Marvin, which sent her back to the night Graham had witnessed their good-night kiss. Which then shifted her memory to her first kiss with Graham, which had been incredible. Her traitorous heart compared it to her first kiss with Matt, which, while it had been sweet and surprisingly pleasant, had no hope of toppling Graham from first place on her list of Best First Kisses.

She saw Dr. Mackey, the orthopedic surgeon who'd done Graham's surgery the day of the accident, and he stopped to ask her how Graham was doing. Too embarrassed to say she didn't know, she lied and said he was doing great.

She didn't know if he was great or not. She hadn't even let herself ask Mia if she'd seen or talked to him. The one time she had, the week he'd moved out, it had been too painful. He should have been out of his cast for two months by now. Was he walking normally? Going into the mountains with that breathtaking smile on his face, using the fresh air and adventure to forget about her and what happened?

Then, a firefighter came in. Turned out to be a sprained ankle from playing volleyball at the station, but anytime she saw someone brought back in that navy uniform her heart temporarily ceased beating.

*Have you considered you'll have the same reaction for the rest of your life, whether you're with Graham or not? You let yourself get in too deep, and you'll never go back.*

She frowned at the thought as she walked to her car, telling her subconscious to shut the hell up. Her phone rang just as she tossed her purse onto the passenger seat and she dug it out before starting the ignition.

She glanced at the screen and winced, knowing she couldn't keep avoiding her best friend.

"Hey, Mia."

"Whoa, sorry," came Mia's voice. "I wasn't prepared to interact with a live person. I had my standard *Hey, it's Mia, remember me? Call me back* ready to go."

"I'm sorry I haven't." Claire stopped short of giving excuses like, *Work's been busy* or *I wasn't feeling well for a few days*, because they were bullshit and they both knew it.

She wasn't even sure she could fully explain why she'd put off talking to Mia. She missed her friend's company and always felt better after spending time with her.

But Mia knew Claire better than anyone. She'd see too much and might ask questions Claire wasn't ready to answer. For once, she was trying to sort through things on her own.

The emotional roller coaster she'd gone through at work today indicated it wasn't quite working out as planned. It was probably time to hash things out with Mia, something they'd done countless times throughout their friendship.

She'd been a coward to put it off in the first place.

"No problem." Another thing Claire loved about Mia—she didn't hold grudges. "But I'm seeing you tonight and I won't accept no for an answer. If you don't want to go anywhere I'll just come over."

Even if Claire hadn't come to her senses in the last two minutes, it was nice to know Mia would have forced the issue. Sometimes good friends had to barge in uninvited to get shit done.

"We can go somewhere," Claire said. "I have some questionable stains on my scrubs, though, and based on the caliber of patients I saw I'd like to go home and change first."

Mia emitted a grossed-out sound. "Please do."

They decided to meet at a casual café halfway between their places, and half an hour later they were seated across from one another on the patio. They kept the conversation light while they ate and Claire's ravenous stomach appreciated that. Being hangry wouldn't encourage a calm, reasonable mindset.

But when the server took their plates and their orders for postdinner lattes and dessert, Mia leveled Claire with a look. "Okay. Spill."

Claire made a completely pathetic, half-assed attempt to deflect. "About what?"

"The last time we talked, you and Graham had admitted to being in love, had a huge fight, and you started talking to the hot dentist. Then you basically dropped off the face of the earth and started avoiding me."

"Because I knew you'd ask me how I was. Like, how I *really* was."

"Yeah, I've been known to do that." Mia twirled long, dark hair around her finger. "So tell me how you are. *Really.*"

"I don't know!"

Mia just looked at her across the table with the patience of a saint.

"I mean it. I really don't." Claire twisted her palm against her forehead. "That's the problem. Some days I feel great. Positive, happy, and super stoked about how things are going with Matt. Other days I sort of fall into this valley where I think about Graham and wonder if I made a mistake. Rinse and repeat. Is this gonna go on forever?"

Mia, ever the reasonable one, suggested they break it down. "Let's start with Matt. Tell me how that's going. You seemed excited about him several weeks ago, so I guess it's a good sign you're still talking. Do you like him? Do you look forward to seeing him? How do you feel when you're with him?"

"Yes, yes, and happy."

"That's great, Claire," Mia said, genuinely smiling. "What do you like most about him?"

"He's the whole package. Seriously. I don't even care that he's divorced—they grew up in super religious households and got married really young before they really knew who they were or what they wanted out of life. It sounds as if ending it was a mutual decision that benefited both of them." Claire balanced her elbows on the table. "He's so nice. Thoughtful. Funny, but in an unassuming way...like he doesn't mean to be. Super smart. It's nice he's in the medical field, because he understands some of the stuff I deal with at work. It sounds so cliché but the only fault I can find in him is he almost seems too perfect. I keep wondering when he's gonna realize I'm the kind of girl who speaks before thinking and shows every emotion on her face, even when it's inappropriate."

"You don't think he knows that already?"

Claire shrugged. "I've been myself around him. It's just... nice guys like him usually don't stick around for long. But he seems pretty damn interested. It feels too good to be true, you know?"

"No. You're a great catch, and the things you seem to think are faults are my favorite things about you."

Claire smiled. "Thanks, friend."

"Some of those nice guys want a woman like you, you know."

"Maybe."

"Can I ask a personal question?"

"No, we haven't slept together yet."

Mia laughed. "How'd you know that's what I was gonna ask?"

"You blushed." Claire shook her head. "Which is hilarious, knowing how you and Noah are. You're no innocent."

Mia's flush deepened. "We're talking about you, not me. And I think that's great that you haven't. I was just curious."

Matt was definitely interested in taking their relationship there, but so far Claire had held off. While she wasn't super conservative about it, sex was something that meant something to her. The arrangement with Graham had been completely out of character, but even if it had been based on a weird spur-of-the-moment understanding, he was still a man she'd known for years, liked (most of the time), and trusted. The chemistry between them, once tapped, had been off the charts.

Maybe some unconscious part of her had known all along it would be like that. She'd be lying if she said she was all that surprised about how good it had been.

It didn't feel right to sleep with Matt when she was still unsure where her heart stood with Graham, even if the rational part of her had moved on and was impatiently waiting for the rest of her to catch up.

Sweet guy that he was, he didn't seem to mind waiting for her.

"Have you talked to Graham?" Mia asked.

"Not once."

Her friend's brow was marred. "How's that been? Going from living together for over a year, close friends, then lovers to nothing at all?"

"It's not great," Claire admitted. "Lovers part aside, I miss his friendship. I miss watching trash TV with him and going out for beers when we have hard days. I miss his sarcasm. I even miss his stupid dog."

"He misses you, too."

"How do you know?"

"For a while he avoided Noah like you were with me. I assume for the same reasons."

It wouldn't surprise her. The four of them were well versed in each other's defense mechanisms.

"I'm the one who hurt him," Claire said. "And I don't think there's anything I can do to fix it. So I've just been avoiding."

The server dropped off their lattes. Mia curled her hands around the cup. "You're not hurting, too?"

"Of course I am. I hate it here. But he's the one who put everything out there—a massive step for Graham, as you probably know—and I'm the one who said no. That puts us in different corners of the ring and I don't think I should be the one to come out first. If our roles were reversed, I'd want to be left alone. If he tried to talk to me after rejecting me, it would just piss me off."

"He probably just needs time. You both do."

Claire scraped a spoonful of foam from the top of her latte and put it in her mouth. That bitch in her chest thought it was a good time to toss up a memory of how good Graham's dad's coffee had been the weekend they'd stayed there. *Better than Starbucks*, she'd told him.

"I have one more question," Mia said. Her tone was hesitant, which both piqued Claire's interest and put her on edge. "I promise I'll only ask it once, but I gotta. I get your reasons for breaking things off with Graham. As much as I can, anyway. No one can truly be in your shoes and know how it felt to go through what you did. But now, after months of being apart and still missing him like you do, are you sure it's the right choice? Like, without a doubt, one hundred percent, you'll-never-regret-this-choice sure?"

Tears welled up in Claire's eyes and she blinked away the burning sensation. "What the fuck kind of question is that?"

Sympathy shone in Mia's eyes. "I'm sorry. It's just… I thought I knew what I was doing when I kept away from Noah for so long. I thought it was for the best, too. I was so very wrong, and I've never been happier since realizing it. As your best friend, I just want to make sure you don't miss your chance to do the same."

Frustration built along Claire's spine. "Do we ever know with absolute certainty if the decisions we make are the right ones in the long run? All I know to do is look at what I've gone through and where I am now and decide based on that information. I'm not psychic. I don't know what I'll feel next week, next month, or next year."

If only that were possible.

"You make a great point, but I'm not sure you realize it actually cancels out your argument for cutting things off with Graham."

"How?"

"You just said you couldn't base your decision off future feelings, but that's exactly what you did."

Claire frowned, shaking her head. "No, I…"

"When you think about the past with Graham, what's the first word that comes to mind?"

"Irritation."

Mia snorted. "Any others?"

"Fun. Loyalty. Friendship."

"Now, think about the last time you were with him, before the fight. When things were good. Do you remember how you felt in that moment?"

Claire squeezed her eyelids shut, once again trying to keep from crying in a public place. A display like that wasn't her style.

She didn't say any of the words out loud. *Tender. Loved. Connected.*

She could only nod.

"Yes, I remember how I felt." Her voice trembled and she hated it.

"If your answer to this next one is yes, that's it. You know what's right for you. But I don't think you can move forward until you address this with yourself. You know how you feel about him, and how you felt when you were with him. Anything beyond that is pure speculation. Are you willing to discard all of those things based on assumptions for how you might feel down the road?"

Claire's heart raced, torn between defending her decision and accepting the good points Mia was making. "It's not complete speculation," she argued weakly. "I was so freaked out that day I thought he was injured at a fire that I went home and kissed the hell out of him."

Mia tucked her lips between her teeth as if trying not to smile. "Is that supposed to sound like a bad thing?"

"The fear was. It's debilitating."

Mia sobered. "I know. I worry about Noah, too, you know."

"You do?"

"Of course. He goes on almost every climbing trip Graham does."

"That's true." Mia seemed so matter-of-fact about it. Claire envied her for it. "How do you do it?"

Mia shrugged. "I guess I just try to focus on the time I have with him instead of obsessing over when our end date might be. His brother died in a car accident, which could happen to any of us. People have sudden heart attacks, aneurysms, get cancer. They fall down stairs or are in the wrong place at the wrong time when someone walks in with a gun. Terrible things happen all the time and they can happen to anyone. If I let myself think about every little thing that could take Noah away from me I'd be a walking basket case every minute of every day." Her voice was near a whisper. "What a horrible way to live and miss out on the best thing in my life."

Claire swiped at her cheeks. "Shit, Mia."

Mia didn't apologize. Rather, she looked down at her phone resting on the table and tapped it. The lock screen illuminated with an image of her and Noah, faces pressed together, ridiculous smiles on their faces. She took in a shaky breath and smiled. "They say love drives out fear. That it brings light into darkness. As long as I have a choice, I'll choose love and light and hope the power of that choice, and the person that comes with it, does the rest."

★ ★ ★

Claire left the café even more confused than when she arrived. She couldn't remember the last time she'd walked away from a tough conversation with Mia without a firm idea in her mind of where she'd go from here.

It was after ten by the time they said goodbye and walked to their cars. She'd put her phone on silent during dinner and now checked the screen before turning on the ignition.

Matt had called, then followed up with a text.

Matt: Hey beautiful. Just wanted to say I hope you had a good day at work today. If you're free on Friday I'd love to cook you dinner. Call me later.

Claire didn't reply and slipped the phone back into her purse. Gripping the back of her neck in one hand, she leaned her head back and sighed.

She *really* hated it here.

A huge yawn caught her off guard. *Give yourself a break. You just worked a twelve-hour shift on your feet and had an emotionally draining conversation with Mia.*

All good points. She turned on the car and pulled onto the main road, allowing herself to put off thinking about men, relationships, or plane crashes until tomorrow.

The restaurant was only a few blocks from her house, and

she let her brain go on autopilot to get her home. She reached down to turn on the radio, and when she looked up again she was blinded by bright lights coming straight at her.

Disoriented, she grabbed the wheel with both hands and hit the brakes, hard. Something slammed into her from behind, forcing her body forward. Another crunch sounded from somewhere in front of her, and everything went black.

# 28

"I can't believe it's been four months since I've gone camping."

Noah glanced back from his spot a few feet up on the trail. "Have you ever gone that long?"

Graham returned his eyes to his feet, careful of his footing. How long would it take before he stopped being worried about reinjuring his leg? As impatient as he'd been to get the cast off and get back to his normal life, he didn't intend to mess things up and go back to square one.

"Honestly, I'm not sure if I have. Since my first trip when I was ten."

"I'm glad I suggested it, then."

"Me, too," Graham said.

He inhaled deeply, taking in lungfuls of the fresh mountain air. Only one thing smelled better, and she wasn't here.

After ten more minutes of an easy, fairly level hike, Noah slowed. "Almost there."

The comment was unnecessary. Graham knew exactly where they were. This was one of their favorite camping spots, close to a river for fishing and within hiking distance of a few lesser-known climbing spots. The best part: it was low traffic and devoid of loud, often inconsiderate tourists.

They reached a small clearing and a familiar voice stopped him in his tracks.

"Took you guys long enough."

Graham's gaze snapped up to find Claire, in hiking boots, shorts, and a tank top, standing in front of a partially erected tent. Her hair was messy and she stood with her arms crossed over her chest.

His heart ceased beating for several seconds and literally the only thing he wanted in this moment was to keep his composure. The odds of that happening were low, because she was so damn sexy standing there angry and proud for no apparent reason, and it was so very Claire and the embodiment of everything he'd fallen in love with in the first place.

Two months and one week since he'd laid eyes on her and somehow he'd told himself he'd be okay.

He was not okay.

"What's going on?" he managed to get out.

Noah dropped his pack by the tent and pointed. "Need help with that?" he asked Claire.

She glared at him, and he held his hands up.

"Never mind." Noah tossed a look at Graham as he headed toward the trail. "Good luck, man."

"What?" Graham looked between the two. Claire just stared at him, and he couldn't handle those eyes on him for long. He swung his gaze back to Noah, who had a smug grin on his face. "Where are you going?"

"Yeah. I, uh, lied. It was Claire's idea to go camping, not mine. You two have fun and I'll be back with the car on Sunday. I hope you get everything figured out by then."

Noah winked and picked up a jog down the trail, quickly disappearing between the thick trees.

Graham turned back to Claire and blinked. He expected her to say something. Explain herself and what this was all about, maybe?

But she didn't, and he couldn't stand to look at that gorgeous face he loved, knowing she wasn't his. And he wasn't hers.

He dropped his gaze several inches.

"Are you staring at my breasts?" she asked sharply.

"Seemed like the safer choice."

"Safer for what?"

He cleared his throat. "My sanity."

"I can't tell if that's a compliment or an insult."

"I'm not sure, either."

With a sigh, he stepped forward and swung his own pack from his back, letting it hit the ground beside Noah's. Or Claire's, apparently.

He resisted a smile when he saw what appeared to be Claire's attempt to set up the tent. After witnessing her response to Noah's offer to finish it, he decided to let it be for now.

He straightened, faced her, and slid his hands in his pockets. "You gonna tell me why I'm here?"

*Why* we're *here?*

He had a few thoughts, of course, most of them hopeful and dangerous to entertain.

Her eyes scrolled down his body slowly, lingering on his right leg. "Do you, um, need to sit down or anything?"

He shook his head. "Nope. Feels great."

She nodded, her brows relaxing. "That's good."

In a flash, the arrogant demeanor she'd reflected when they first arrived was gone, replaced by something softer.

"It's probably pretty obvious," she started, gripping her hands in front of her. "This is my attempt to win you back."

Graham's knees nearly gave out.

Maybe he should have sat down when he had the chance.

*Stay calm. Collected.* "Win me back?" His voice came out strong and steady. *Keep it up, man. You got this.*

"As you know, I'm not really the camping type. But you love it so much I thought it might be different to experience it through your eyes. Maybe you could show me what I've been missing."

He let himself focus on her eyes. Even from several feet away, he saw apprehension in those hazel depths.

"Also, I figured it wouldn't hurt to butter you up a little, and you'd be more likely to forgive me if you were in your happy place."

She was his happy place, but she didn't need to know it yet.

What she had to say was probably just as important for her as it was for him.

"I have no idea what you're thinking right now, but your silence is ideal and I'm just gonna go with it. I don't want to forget anything I wanted to say. Here goes." She breathed deeply, shaking her hands out. "Obviously I've had a lot of time these last two months to think. About us and what happened. There were days I felt justified in my decision and others where I just knew I'd ruined both our lives and I was officially the stupidest woman on the planet. But I wanted to take the time to really get ahold of myself and figure things out. I talked to my mom, I talked to Mia, and I even started dating a little."

Graham stiffened, hoping she wouldn't stay on that point for long.

"Through it all, one thing remained constant. I missed you. And not just the obvious stuff, like your smile that stops my heart or that thing you do with your tongue when we kiss. I missed your sarcasm and the way you're always up to go out.

I missed ordering takeout with you and pretending I can't do stuff around the house so you'll do it for me and I can watch your forearms work. I missed the way you look at me and feeling like I can be myself and you'll still like me.

"But even so, I was scared. I'm still scared. My decision to change my mind—and I'll get to that part in a second—doesn't mean I'm not going to worry about you all the fucking time. It's important you know up front that we'll probably fight about that. I'll yell if you do something reckless, or if you take hours to call me back when you're on shift at the fire station. I can't just turn it off and I won't be easy. But if there's one thing I know about you it's that you don't shy away from a challenge. You face it head-on, and I hope you'll do that with me."

Graham's chest was so tight he could hardly breathe. Just when he was about to ask what changed her mind, she kept going.

"I was in a car accident a few days ago, and—"

"What?" He lurched forward, canvassing her person, searching for sign of injury. "What happened?"

She held out her hand when he was three feet away. "I'm fine, Graham. Don't touch me. Please, not yet—I want to get through this. I can't if you put your hands on me."

Oof. Hard same.

"Some guy crossed the centerline, and instead of swerving I hit the brakes. It was a weird reaction, maybe, but I didn't even think about it. I got rear-ended because I stopped so quick and the guy that had been coming head-on clipped the front driver's side. The airbag knocked me out. I'm a little sore, but otherwise I'm completely fine. I promise, okay? Stop looking at me like that."

He tried to relax his jaw, but he had no control over the wild look she probably saw in his eyes. Thank God she was okay. He couldn't even think about what he'd have done if it had been worse...

"I bring that up to say this: even though the accident wasn't that bad, it still brought clarity. Earlier that night, Mia had pointed out how fragile life is and how things can happen to any one of us at any time. And then when my mom was camped out at my bedside in the ER while we waited for discharge, I finally told her everything. About us. And when I got to the part about how scared I was because of what she'd been through, she stopped me. Said my brain was focused only on the bad parts, because when she thought about the years she'd been with my dad, it wasn't the days he was gone. She'd worried about him, sure, but her memories were filled with times he was there and we were together, and how happy we all were. She promised me that even knowing how it would turn out, she'd do it all again, just to have that time with him. That was...eye-opening. And a relief, honestly, because I want that to be the case for us, but I've just been so afraid." She swallowed, brushing her palm across her collarbone. "Oh, and going back to therapy has helped, too. So yeah, you might give me heartburn, but I know the good times with you are worth it. They're everything."

Graham squeezed his eyes shut, his nails digging into his palms in his attempt to keep from pulling her into his arms. He sensed her move closer and her fingers slid into his hair with a featherlight touch.

"The last thing I wanted to say is I decided what I wanted to be remembered for. Loving and living with abandon and adventure and not letting the worst moment of my life define how I lived the rest of it. I want to live it with you."

He opened his eyes just as several tears slipped down her cheeks. Slowly, he reached up and brushed them away with his thumbs, cradling her face in his palm.

"A life with me won't be easy," he said softly. "I know I've made progress, but I'm still not used to talking about things. I'll keep working on it, but you'll have to be patient with me."

She blinked, sending another tear down the same path. "I don't want easy. Lord knows that's the last word anyone would use to describe me. I just know I want you. Before I freaked out, we figured things out pretty well, and I have faith we can keep doing that. As long as we do it together, that's all that matters."

He slid his fingers into her hair. "I want you, too. Turns out you're all I've ever wanted."

A soft sigh left her throat and she pressed her forehead against his.

"Fuck's sake, please say I can kiss you no—"

She cut him off with her lips, and he felt whole for the first time in months. He wrapped his arms around her waist and lifted her off her feet, smiling against her mouth.

"I'm sorry," she said, looking down at him. "I love you."

He couldn't quite wrap his mind around what just happened. Other than the "I love you, too," he rasped against her neck, he didn't know what else to say.

He kissed her again, then set her on her feet and tipped his head toward the tent. "Can I fix that?"

Like flipping a switch, her expression went from hazy and desire-filled to affronted. "I wasn't finished. I took a break, that's all."

Graham dropped his hands and stepped back, immediately missing her body and scent. He shrugged. "I was just thinking we could get in there and do stuff, and I can have it done in three minutes. But if you want to take care of it yourself, I'll just wait over here till you're done."

He'd taken two steps toward the folding chair set up near the firepit before she spoke.

"Graham." Her voice sounded a little breathless.

He glanced over his shoulder to where she balanced on one foot, untying her hiking boot.

"Fix the tent, will you?"

He grinned. "Gladly."

He'd never pitched a tent so fast in his life.

"Did you bring condoms?" she asked, digging through the pack Noah brought and pulling out a sleeping bag.

Graham stared at her from his perch near the corner of the tent. "I thought I was camping with Noah. So...no."

Her eyes went wide. "Shit. I didn't think this through."

If Noah hadn't come through on this, Graham would walk to the main road and flag down random motorists to get a ride to the nearest convenience store. He stood and gracelessly grabbed the pack out of her grasp, making quick work of searching each compartment. When his hand closed around the familiar square packages, he dropped his head back in relief. He owed his friend big-time.

"Get in there." His voice was rougher than intended, but the flash of heat in her eyes and the way she dived into the tent like her ass was on fire told him she was okay with it.

He pulled off his boots and ducked his head into the tent.

Claire spread out the sleeping bag and lay down with her arms stretched above her head, giving him a delicious come-hither look from under those long, curved lashes.

"Come here and lay on top of me. Hurry, please. I finally get to feel the weight of your body on mine."

He almost cried with joy as he zipped the tent from the inside and went down on his knees, then leaned forward to anchor his hands on either side of her head. He carefully lowered his torso, achingly slow, and as each new piece of their bodies connected, she released a sigh, a moan, a lick of her lips.

He kissed her thoroughly, trying to tell her through his touch how much he'd missed her. How much he wanted her.

"Oh, my, yes. That's…" She trailed off, her sexy voice thick with desire.

He didn't want to crush her, but she pulled his body down harder and kept releasing sweet breaths, humming her pleasure.

He dipped his head and dragged his lips along her neck, following with his tongue. "Good?"

"Mmm," she mumbled, arching up as her lips parted. "I love it. I love this. Please, can you just stay right there? On top of me? I want to lay like this forever."

He thrust his hips forward and she squeaked, followed by a throaty moan.

"*Exactly* like this?" he teased.

Her nails dug into his back and one leg sneaked out to curl around his waist. "Maybe with less clothes. And a few parts rearranged."

"Camping doesn't seem so bad now, does it?"

"I'll cast my final vote in a few minutes."

Graham lifted his head. "A few minutes? Give me a little credit, here."

"A few hours?"

He winked at her and slid his hand down her body, feeling his body heat rise as she trembled beneath him.

"That's more like it."

# 29

"I've decided camping's all right."

Graham paused on the step above her and looked over his shoulder. "Just all right?"

Claire refused to waste time fluffing his ego. The sex had been amazing and he damn well knew it. "I meant the actual camping part, Honey Grahams. How about we look into an RV next time?"

He snorted and continued his way up the stairs. Muted voices from Chris's store rose from below. "First, they're too expensive. Second, that's not camping."

Claire rolled her eyes at his back.

"Don't roll your eyes at me."

She stopped beside him at the landing and elbowed him in the ribs. "How'd you know?"

"I feel it when you look at me." He shrugged. "Always have."

"Really?"

He nodded. "At first you looked at me like you thought I was an arrogant asshole. As you got to know me I earned a few grudging looks of respect and admiration for my exceptional wit and deep insights about the world. Glances of exasperation have always been plentiful, and the occasional glimpse of happiness. Those used to be my favorite."

She bit her bottom lip to control her smile. "Used to be?"

He smiled softly and reached up to gently tug her lip free with his thumb. "Mmm-hmm. The way you look at me when you want me moved to the top pretty quick. But even that one got knocked down a notch. My favorite now, and I suspect forever, is when you look at me like you love me. I'll never get tired of it and I'll never get over it."

"Are you trying to make me cry?"

"Right there—that's the exasperation. Go back to the love one, please."

She laughed and threw her arms around his neck. She couldn't help it. "What am I going to do with you?"

He hugged her tight, burying his face in her hair. "Let me get my stuff and take me back to your place so I can take you against the wall like I've been dreaming about for three fucking months."

Oh.

She pushed him back and tapped the door. "Stop waxing poetic and get your things, then. Let's *go*."

Graham winked and opened the door, holding it for her to walk in first. A tiny bark of glee came from somewhere in the living room and before Claire knew what was happening, a brown ball of fur came barreling toward her and leaped into her arms.

Surprised, Claire fumbled to hold on to the dog as Gertrude wiggled in excitement, licking anywhere on Claire's face she could reach. "Whoa, Gertie. Hi. Yes, I see you! I've missed you, too."

When she finally got Gertrude settled and positioned where she could keep her steady and scratch her chin at the same time, Claire glanced at Graham, who had stopped in the middle of the doorway.

He was just staring at them, one hand covering his mouth.

Claire's heart clenched. "Are you crying?"

"No."

"Are you sure?"

"No."

Walking forward, she tucked herself and Gertrude up against his chest, feeling warm and happy all over. "Is this gonna become a thing now? You're in tune with your emotions and you'll walk around crying all the time?"

"No. Maybe."

Claire rested her head on his shoulder and sighed. "Look at us. You, me, and Gertrude. One big, happy family. Who woulda thought?"

"Not me."

"Me, either."

He dipped his head to meet her eyes. "Are you happy, Sugar Lips?"

"Yes to the happy, no to the pet name."

Graham let out a growl of exasperation. "You're making this so much harder than it needs to be. If I'm gonna be in a real relationship I want to call my girlfriend something special. When we're out and I have to get your attention, just saying *Claire* doesn't tell anyone we're together. You could just as easily be my sister or an old friend. But when I yell out, *C'mere, Snookums*, everyone will know you're mine."

She wouldn't have thought she'd be the type of girl to like a man being possessive about her, yet here she was. "Why would you be yelling?"

"It's us. We're loud."

He had a point. "Fine. I'm vetoing Snookums, though."

Graham released a long-suffering sigh and got to work packing his things. Half an hour later as they descended the stairs, he tossed over his shoulder, "Love Muffin?"

"No."

"Sparky?"

"No."

"Wonder Woman?"

Claire paused. "That's an improvement, but still no."

He continued without hesitation, "Wait, I've got it. Lambchop."

She snorted.

Graham kept going as they exited the store through the back and continued spouting off suggestions the entire drive to the condo, each one worse than the last.

Claire laughed and rolled her eyes the entire way.

When he pulled into her usual spot and put the car in Park Claire made no move to get out. She gently ran her hand along Gertrude's fur and looked over at Graham, admiring his large body situated in her driver's seat. His dark, sexy eyes assessed her curiously, his hair a mess from spending the weekend in a tent.

"What?" he asked.

She lifted her chin and met his gaze. "Is this our future? Your never-ending quest to find some perfect nickname for me, constantly hounding me, and driving me crazy?"

"Probably." He grinned. "Especially the drive-you-crazy part."

She shook her head, smiling.

"You okay with that?" he asked.

She put on a show of considering her options, scrunching

her nose and lifting her shoulders. They both knew the answer, though.

"Yeah," she said, because she was.

She so was.

# EPILOGUE

*One Year Later*

Something was off.

Ruthie had been shifty all day, avoiding eye contact and checking her watch. Claire might not have noticed, but the ER was unusually slow (she'd *never* say the word out loud lest she jinx it) and as she propped her feet up on the desk, careful not to knock over her coffee, she eyed her friend.

"What's with you?"

"What do you mean?"

"You're being weird."

"I'm not being weird."

Claire stared. Did a slow blink.

Ruthie sat down with a huff. "Fine. I have a date tonight and I'm nervous, okay?"

"You what?" Claire's feet dropped to the ground and she held up her hand. "About time you moved on from that bitch of an ex."

Ruthie eyed Claire's hand with distaste. "I don't do high-fives. And she wasn't a bit—" She paused. "Okay, she was. Anyway, I'm just a little out of sorts today."

Claire dropped her arm. "I used to get nervous before dates, too. But you're a catch, and if this woman knows anything about what's good and wonderful in this world, she'll see it right away. I have no doubt. And if it doesn't go well just call me and I'll meet you for booze and greasy burgers."

Ruthie laughed. "Deal." An alert sounded on her phone and she dug it out of her pocket. A strange look passed over her face and she tucked it away. "Hey, I've gotta check on this patient in 7, could you do me a huge favor and grab some small gloves from the back supply room? I didn't realize we were out up here."

Claire shrugged, not even glancing around to see if a tech or assistant could do the task instead. She had nothing else to do until the scan results were back for pod 3, anyway. "Sure."

The supply room was at the end of a short hallway, even more silent than usual on the quiet day. This spot was one of her places to escape for a breather when things were especially chaotic in the main space.

She swiped her badge and the lock clicked open. The overhead light was already on, and she eyed the glove boxes stacked like LEGOs along the left side for a moment before realizing she wasn't alone.

His delicious scent was the first thing she noticed—and a good thing, too, or else she might have screamed bloody murder—and turned to find Graham propped against the opposite shelf. His upper back rested against the metal, one foot crossed over the other. Tan, muscled arms crossed in front of his chest and one corner of his mouth tipped up in a cocky grin.

"The hell are you doing in here?"

He pushed off and took two slow steps forward. "I missed you."

Same, but she had a reputation to uphold in this relationship. She propped a hand on her hip. "So you came to accost me in a supply room at work?"

"I didn't accost you." His smile widened. "Yet."

A shiver ran through her at the thought of her number one fantasy coming true.

His eyes darkened and…yeah. He noticed.

One step closer and his large, warm hand slipped around her waist. "Think we'll be the first ones to make out in here?"

Heat skated across her skin as she lined her body up with his and buried her fingers in his soft, thick hair. "Hardly."

"Mmm," he murmured, dipping his head.

"We can't, like, *do it*," she said against his mouth. "I'm on the clock."

He muttered a "fine" before sealing his lips over hers. A soft groan left the back of his throat and settled deep inside her chest, reminding her it had become one of her favorite sounds over the past year.

Graham never hid how much he wanted her. And as the only man she'd ever been her true self around, that felt pretty damn wonderful.

After what he'd been through as a kid, she made sure he knew just how lucky she was to be his, too. Even if he laughed them off, he secretly loved her public displays of affection and possessiveness. She saw it in the light in his eyes and the way he pulled her close, and she could only hope there'd never again be a day where he wondered if he was enough.

His hips forced her back against the shelf and her arms wound around his back, urging him closer. She angled her head to the side for a deeper kiss, and just as she was about to announce she was calling out for the rest of the day, he was gone.

It took her brain a few seconds to catch up, her arms falling to her sides as she searched for him, finding him down.

Kneeling before her.

On one knee.

She froze.

"Claire."

She…squeaked?

His eyes searched hers, uncharacteristically serious.

"I'll never forget the day you came home all worked up after seeing a proposal in the emergency room. That might have been the best day of my life, because it's what started us on the path we're on now. I'd have convinced you to hold up our original marriage pact, sure—and don't even try to say it wasn't real because we both know it was. But doing it this way is so much better. Instead of defaulting into marriage because we didn't want to end up alone, I get to ask you to marry me because I can't imagine my life without you. I'll never want anyone else the way I want you, and according to you no other man could handle you. Which is fine by me, because I never want to take my hands off you."

He paused and swallowed. "I don't know what I did to deserve you, but being with you makes me happier than when I've hit the top of a half-day climb, and nothing else has ever topped that. I can only hope I make you that happy, too—but if I don't, I'm sure you'll let me know." He smiled wide then, that broad, unrestricted, magnificent smile that took her breath away, and held out a ring. "Claire Harper, will you marry me?"

"Oh, my gosh," she blurted. "Ruthie doesn't really have a date tonight, does she?" She was in on it and set this whole thing up!

Graham cocked his head, a frown descending on his brow. "Uh. I—"

A laugh bubbled up, joy expanding in her chest as tears burned beneath her lids. "Never mind." She grabbed his hand

and tugged him to his feet. "I just— I can't believe— I had no idea," she babbled, incoherent thoughts of shock and amazement bouncing around in her brain. "How long have you been planning this?"

He sighed, indulgent amusement etched across his features. "Claire. Could you answer my question, please?"

She framed his face and kissed him hard. "Yes. Yes, I'll marry you."

His arms came around her waist and he lifted her, smiling up at her grinning face. "Yeah?"

She kissed him again. And again. "Yeah."

"You'll be Claire, Graham's fiancée?"

She wrapped her legs around him and buried her face in his neck.

"Finally, a nickname I can get on board with."

★ ★ ★ ★ ★

# ACKNOWLEDGMENTS

My goodness, Claire and Graham were fun to write. They began as side characters in *Would You Rather* and quickly took on a life of their own. I'm so happy I was given the opportunity to tell their story because I had a blast doing it.

Thank you to Margot Mallinson for believing the premise of this book was worth it and Dina Davis for ultimately working on it with me and making it shine. Thanks to the MIRA and Harlequin teams for everything you do behind the scenes to get these books on the shelves. I still can't believe I can walk into a bookstore and see a book with my name on it sitting there. Which brings me to Kim Lionetti, my powerhouse agent—without you I'd have never known that reality. I appreciate your expertise, knowledge, and calm guidance as we navigate the publishing process.

While I'm in the medical field and have done a fair amount of rock climbing, I'm not a nurse or a trauma physician and I'm not a rock-climbing expert by any means. So thank you, Jessica Payne, for reading an early draft and being the first to tell me nurses aren't supposed to do stitches (oops) and for cleaning up the climbing scenes. As a fellow author, you also gave me an early confidence boost that maybe this book didn't completely suck. I'm sorry I'm too scared to read your thrillers (but everyone else should!).

Thanks to Scott Mackey, ER physician extraordinaire, for answering all my questions about intubation, trauma bays, and what injuries I could swing without being completely outside the realm of possibility. Yes, I named the surgeon after you. J.K. Feisal, I probably threw a couple of questions at you, too, so thank you for that and for being so supportive of my books (I'm still a little salty you didn't stay after fellowship, though). Nicole Carroll, best neighbor, mom friend, and ortho PA, thanks for reading an early draft and helping me with the logistics of everything a broken leg entails. Your IPA (ew) is on me next time we're out.

As always, thank you to my author friends who I couldn't do this without, because we all need someone who understands this process and can vent/celebrate/trudge through it with us. Especially Denise Williams, I'll always remember when you said this one was your favorite yet. Thank you to the readers out there who tell a friend when they love a book—I hope you never stop. Thank you to all the #bookstagrammers, bloggers, and reviewers who help share and promote my books, I'll never be able to describe how important that part is for my survival as an author. I hope the books I write keep bringing you laughs, tears, and most of all, joy.